THE
BROTHERHOOD
AND THE SHIELD
THE THREE THORNS

MICHAEL GIBNEY

Published by Tantrum Books for Month9Books
Cover by Adam McDaniel
Jacket design by Victoria Faye
Cover Copyright © 2014 Month9Books

This book is dedicated to two people. The first is my Grandfather, David Thompson, from whom I inherited this precious gift and love for the written word. Your imagination never ended with you...it lives on in me and I will carry it until it's my time to hand it over. I love you Grand-Dad.

To my dear friend and greatest advocate, Van Dyke Parks. You taught me what true courage and conviction really means. I will be forever grateful for your genuine love, humility and hand in friendship you've shown me over the years.

THE BROTHERHOOD AND THE SHIELD

THE THREE THORNS

MICHAEL GIBNEY

Prologue: New Born

They say all great legends start small. This one begins with three crimson-wrapped bundles on a rainy evening in London. The year was 1900, but not much had changed to make the turn of the century overly special. Not much, that is, except for the three abandoned babies found that night.

For they were royalty, bound to a destiny that would one day change the world. But on the night of their arrival, they were merely orphans, crying with misery and about to perish in the cold.

***

A minister and his maid opened the large door of an old church to distraught screams. It was late winter and the rain had been ongoing for days.

The frail baby had been wrapped in maroon silk that bore the image of a two-headed snake embroidered through a golden crown.

Without hesitating, the minister swaddled the infant in his knitted woolen sweater, enveloping it in the warmth of his body. Having made up his mind, the minister embraced the infant as if it were his own. He took the crying baby inside the towering church while the maid shook her head behind him, closing the massive doors to shut out the miserable weather.

"What are you doing, Minister Brannon?" she asked.

"A cry for help should never be ignored, Miss Illingworth," replied the minister, shooting a look of disappointment at the cold-hearted woman.

***

That same night, a second screaming baby appeared on a different doorstep that belonged to a wealthy couple who owned a multitude of opera houses along the city's prestigious West End. Some would say this child had landed on his feet, but not all was what it seemed, nor did everything glitter brightly with promise in the shallow world of show business.

Puffing heavily on her cigarette, the retired theater actress rolled her eyes at her husband after they had stopped bickering about who was to answer the door first. A look of disgust crossed the woman's face the moment she heard the whimpering sounds of an infant. Her husband stammered and gently shrugged his shoulders back at her the moment he opened the door.

"Well, you did want a baby."

"This is not exactly what I had in mind, Viktor," she snapped, taking another drag through her cigarette holder.

"What do you want me to do?" her husband snapped back as she walked away from the doorstep.

"You want it, you raise it." Her voice echoed through the large hallway of the theater without a care.

Wrestling with his sense of morality, the theater owner lit a cigar as he pondered whether to keep the baby or report it. Then he noticed the two-headed snake symbol through a golden crown on the silk robe, and the businessman suddenly saw the baby as a possible financial investment. Without much persuasion, he made the choice to bring the baby inside.

***

When the rain was at its heaviest, a third baby landed in the worst place of all...the gutter.

A common cook was dumping leftovers in the alleyway when his ears perked up to the light whimpering coming from an empty waste bin. Immediately the concerned cook ran back into the restaurant to fetch his manager along with several staff who came out to have a look at the startling discovery.

That afternoon the authorities came to take the infant to a place where it would be looked after and raised—an orphanage a little outside the main city of greater London—to become another statistic easily forgotten.

1

Mr. Jennings and the New Boy

Young Benjamin Brannon had just turned eleven when he stepped onto the grounds of Gatesville, Borstal Home for Boys. *What did I do to end up here?* he wondered, as he gazed upon the dark gray building towering over him like a castle of doom.

He squeezed the hand of his present guardian, Miss Illingworth, a cold, hard-looking woman from the Woodson County Orphanage, and hid behind her the moment she pulled her hand away. Until now, Benjamin had lived amongst the other orphans of Woodson County ever since the minister had opened his own orphanage in 1901, when Benjamin was almost a year old. The minister had fallen ill with an unexpected case of pneumonia at the beginning of autumn. Due to his sudden illness, Minister Brannon granted the cold-hearted maid a legal position to run the orphanage in his place. With Miss Illingworth in power, it hadn't taken long for her new legislations to be put into effect. The first statute she passed in Woodson County was a limitation on age. Anyone over ten years of age currently living at Woodson County Orphanage was immediately rehomed, and Benjamin Brannon was the first on Miss Illingworth's list to get the boot.

Benjamin hadn't been able to stand the sight of the vile woman and now here he was, willing to go anywhere with her as long as he wasn't left alone in this new and unfamiliar place.

Benjamin Brannon was a very short boy for his age, a few inches smaller than the average eleven-year-old and unusually portly for such an active spirit. He was just big boned that way. Would the other boys laugh at him for his size and shape like they did in Woodson County? Would they bully him because he was smaller than most of the children he could see running in the foregrounds? All of these fears ran through Benjamin like a heavy gust of wind.

Whilst brooding, Benjamin caught sight of a tall thin man walking toward Miss Illingworth, which made him forget his initial fear of the other boys. The man wore a creased old suit and looked just as ragged as his clothes.

"Pleased to meet you, Mr. Jennings," greeted Miss Illingworth, taking a tight hold of Benjamin's hand. As the man approached, the unsettled feeling Benjamin had became sheer dread, especially when he noticed the extensive burn marks on the man's hands. Benjamin stepped backwards, far enough to stay behind Miss Illingworth. She began to struggle with Benjamin, trying to bring him face to face with the old man.

"Eyes to me, boy!" Mr. Jennings snapped. His voice caused Benjamin to jump.

"He's very troublesome. I'd keep my eye on this one," Miss Illingworth warned.

Benjamin glared at the wicked woman. He had been well behaved on their travels from Woodson

County, and now this was her cruel way of repaying him.

Mr. Jennings smiled at Miss Illingworth through crooked gray teeth before sneering down at the orphan. "They're easily trained here," he replied. It sounded like a sinister threat.

Mr. Jennings took Benjamin's hand and squeezed it tightly, until Benjamin could no longer feel his own fingers. He eyed the other boys gawking at him.

Miss Illingworth gave Benjamin a patronising smile and handed him his personal belongings in a torn paper bag.

"Good luck."

Leaving him in the hands of Mr. Jennings, the hard woman made her way to the borstal's front gates.

Mr. Jennings led the way toward the front doors of Gatesville. The grim building looked more like a prison than a standard home for unwanted boys.

Benjamin studied the long corridors ahead. The ghostly place proved to be bleaker inside than out, and the musty smell was strong enough to make his stomach turn.

When they reached the first floor, a prefect in charge of reporting misbehavior greeted Mr. Jennings and took Benjamin's bag of belongings from him.

"Johnston, take this one to his room, then show him around," Mr. Jennings said quietly.

"Yes, Sir."

Once Mr. Jennings whistled his way down the stairs out of sight, Johnston tossed Benjamin's bag of belongings back to him. A toothbrush, a hat and a moth-eaten scarf scattered across the floor spilling out from a piece of maroon silk cloth when the wet paper bag tore apart. Dropping onto his hands and knees, Benjamin wrapped up the items in the cloth, and then scrambled onto his tired feet.

Johnston tilted his head once the strange golden crown and snake emblem on the cloth caught his eye.

"What's that?" he asked rudely, pointing at the emblem.

"It's mine, my minister gave it to me," Benjamin said, clutching the cloth tight to his chest. It was the only thing he could think to say. He was unclear as to what the emblem stood for, but he knew the maroon cloth was important, for it was all he had that held a clue to his beginning.

As they walked down another corridor, Benjamin's heart began beating in his throat. He felt sick and nervous. Butterflies had fluttered in his belly ever since he met the horrible Mr. Jennings, and the growing tension he felt refused to leave him. He felt like crying when he noticed the crammed bedrooms along the corridor. All he had ever wanted in life was for someone to love and care for him. He had truly believed that one day he would be placed with a loving family like the other children of Woodson County had been.

Now his dream was over. Benjamin was abandoned in Gatesville; alone and sad at eleven years of age.

"This is your room. Mr. Porter will be here shortly to show you the curriculum, he can show you around," Johnston said bluntly.

Benjamin tried to mutter the words 'thank you' but stumbled when all he could see was the back of the boy's head leaving him alone in his room.

Everybody within the old compounds of Gatesville seemed to be cold and uncaring like Miss Illingworth. It was a borstal, an orphanage for grown boys and funded by the government to keep orphans and teenage runaways off the dangerous streets. All the boys in Gatesville had either been abandoned at birth or taken into government care after their parents' death. But there were a few that found themselves placed in Gatesville by a court of law for misbehavior.

There was one boy in particular who caused Benjamin to be so fearful that he started to have reoccurring nightmares about him. The boy was the same age as Benjamin. His name was Tommy Joel.

The most frightening thing about Tommy was his eyes. His left eye was a natural sky blue and his right eye was hazel green. He used to tell the other children that he'd received his piercing blue eye from a gypsy's curse when he was little. Telling them the truth about being born with a genetic characteristic was all too boring for him (as well as embarrassing).

Tommy was forever telling stories, especially to get out of trouble. He loved making up fabrications to impress and frighten the others. Most of the boys believed his stories and followed him around like they were his apprentices. He was undoubtedly the leader of the pack.

The very first time Benjamin crossed Tommy Joel's path was in the playground a week after his arrival to Gatesville. Benjamin was sitting next to the rusted fences, which had become the usual spot he chose in order to be by himself and furthest away from the other children. And there he would sit, gazing out into the distance across the wet docks of London.

It was 1912, and London hadn't changed much in the eleven years since he had been abandoned. It remained a cold, filthy place. But even its grim appearance was a better view than the Gatesville building behind him.

As he nibbled at his last sandwich, a small stone unexpectedly grazed the side of his forehead. The sharp stinging pain woke him from his daydream and made him look over his shoulder. He knew right away the nature behind the fired attack and it didn't surprise him when he noticed three boys, much bigger than himself, walking toward the fences, including Tommy Joel, his friend Jimmy Donald, and the brash prefect George Johnston.

"Hey, you!" Tommy shouted.

Benjamin's heart raced as he froze on the spot.

"What's your name, pip-squeak?" Tommy asked in a broad, harsh, cockney accent.

Benjamin found it hard to utter a word and nervously dropped his sandwich. "Benjamin," he mumbled.

The other boys immediately mocked his name, but Tommy looked hard at Benjamin, examining the cut on his forehead. Tommy turned to the boys on either side of him who continued giggling.

"Shut it," he snapped. "So, you're the new boy?" he asked, turning his attention back to his victim.

Benjamin looked intensely at the bully.

"Are you gawking at me?" rasped Tommy. The bully's eyes appeared even more bizarre up close, which fascinated Benjamin, for he had never seen such an extraordinary feature in a person before. Not realising that he'd been staring, he swiftly looked away.

"Well, what are you staring at, oddball?" Jimmy interrupted.

"Nothing," Benjamin replied, avoiding eye contact.

"This is our spot now," said Tommy, pointing his finger at Benjamin.

Without hesitation, Benjamin picked up his sandwich from the grass and slowly walked past the three boys, keeping his head down and eyes to the ground.

George Johnston handed Tommy a field rat and using great stealth the odd-eyed bully placed the rodent inside Benjamin's lower coat pocket the moment Benjamin passed him. The other boys started to snigger while Benjamin walked off, ignorant of what he carried with him.

Benjamin disliked Tommy but he also envied him. Tommy Joel was everything that Benjamin Brannon wasn't and everything Benjamin Brannon wanted to be: bold, brave, popular and respected.

Even though Benjamin longed for the same adulation Tommy received, he never looked up to Tommy's bullying ways, nor did he seek Tommy's notoriety. Benjamin was confident in his own way. He was aware of his own strengths and weaknesses. Showing no weakness in the face of punishment was one of Benjamin's many strengths, but even that didn't make him feel more at ease at Gatesville, especially now that he had a notorious bully on his back, watching his every move.

After lunch, Benjamin made his way to the main classroom for the eleven to twelve year old groups in Gatesville. The government had recently offered jobs to unemployed teachers who were sent to work in struggling borstals, teaching two compulsory subjects of English and Mathematics to the underprivileged. Gatesville's staff had no objection, for the classes kept most of the boys out of trouble...somewhat.

Benjamin followed the long line of boys into the room and sat at the front of the class, far away from

Tommy and his gang who usually sat in the back row.

Class began, taught by Mr. Porter, the very odd-looking mathematics teacher. He was a large rounded fellow and spoke in a voice so low it could put the most energetic soul to sleep.

"Let's begin, shall we?" Mr. Porter yawned. "We are going to start with long division today."

Mr. Porter began to write numbers on the black board while everybody in the class copied his instructions onto their books, giving a long sigh. Everyone was putting pencil to paper except for Tommy Joel and his sidekicks, who were preoccupied making paper airplanes.

Benjamin was unsurprised to realize he had no pencil. Most of his stationary had been stolen from his room since he had arrived at Gatesville, and even if he had a sharpened pencil at the ready, he was already lost because he had never been taught mathematics. Panic set in, and his heart raced. If he told the truth to Mr. Porter, the rest of the class would surely laugh at him. Everyone in Gatesville would brand him stupid, a long-term taunting he could not afford to let happen, not this early in his stay.

Benjamin started to sweat. He looked around the room, which seemed to be getting smaller by the second. *Maybe I have a pencil in my coat pocket,* he thought to himself. When his fingers reached into his coat pocket, he could feel nothing but damp fluff that had gathered due to natural wear and tear, until his left hand tried the other side. Nothing but fluff again… at first…then something moved. Something alive!

As he dug deeper to find out what exactly it was that his fingers touched, he felt the sharp stinging pain of a bite.

"Get it off!"

The entire class, including Mr. Porter, stared in shock at the fat black rat that dangled from the tip of Benjamin's index finger—its tiny teeth locked deep into the skin.

"Good Lord," gasped Mr. Porter, fixing his spectacles onto his round face to get a better look. Benjamin gave his hand one mighty shake that flung the black rat across the room, to the top Mr. Porter's gray hair.

"Benjamin Brannon, you are in deep trouble, boy!" Mr. Porter shouted, trying to grab the rat. But the rodent was too quick and agile for the large man. It leaped onto the teacher's desk, startling another boy at the front of the class who shooed the rat off it. Mr. Porter scattered a stack of pages onto the floor in an effort to detain the rodent under a pile of paper.

At this point, all the boys in the classroom burst into hysterical laughter at Mr. Porter's feeble efforts. Benjamin looked around the room while the class pointed at the flustered teacher and a sudden relief came over him, which turned into excitement. He couldn't help but smile, for this was nothing short of a victory. Tommy and his pals couldn't have foreseen such an unexpected outcome in Benjamin's favor. They had hoped the rat would have terrified Benjamin or at least make a fool out of him. Instead, their planted rodent had turned Benjamin from the vulnerable weakling into a comical classroom hero.

Tommy Joel was the only boy in the class who refused to laugh. The bully glared at Benjamin, oozing hatred and jealousy.

Mr. Porter tried to shift the pile of papers he had scattered onto the floor using his foot to reveal the rat, but it bolted too fast for him to spot and headed for the door. The laughter and cheering for the rodent was suddenly broken by a loud and unexpected stamping sound. The class gasped.

Standing at the doorway was Mr. Jennings, and under his foot was what remained of the rat. At that moment Benjamin felt nothing but sorrow for the poor creature. Mr. Jennings shot his accusing eyes at him. Popularity contests didn't matter to Benjamin now. All he could do was stand still and take whatever punishment was coming to him.

"Go to the caretaker and get something to scoop that mess up!" Mr. Jennings shouted, pointing at the dead rat. "Five lashes for that boy when he comes back," he added, turning to Mr. Porter.

As Benjamin walked out of the room he noticed a small boy with white curly hair sitting in the middle of the class. The peculiar boy gave a pleasing smile and nodded his head at him respectfully. With one simple nod back, Benjamin had made his first friend at Gatesville Borstal Home for Boys.

Benjamin did not see the strange looking boy again until later that night. Stepping into the cold corridor beyond his living quarters, he caught a glimpse of the white haired boy near a window at the very end of the walkway. The moon glowing off his hair silhouetted him like a ghost.

The boy held something dead in his hands before raising it high above him to the moonlight. Benjamin noticed the lifeless tail of the motionless creature hang down between the strange boy's fingers. Moments later the furry creature stirred, awakening from its death before the boy let loose the rat in his hands. It was the same rat Mr. Jennings had killed, for the distinguished markings on the creature were identical.

The rat bolted up the long corridor toward Benjamin, sticking to the skirting at the bottom of the sidewall until it reached his feet and crawled over them.

It felt too real to be a dream. Benjamin gazed back toward the corridor to address the strange boy, but he was gone.

Staring back at the rat, Benjamin giggled nervously in amazement at the living miracle. "You're not going to bite me again are you?" he asked, slowly stepping back into his bedroom doorway, hoping the rat would not follow before successfully shutting the rodent out.

Time seemed to go by slowly after that incident. He had spent only a month at Gatesville, but it felt a lot longer. Unfortunately his new glory didn't last either. Eventually Benjamin became just another face in the hallways while he searched every day for the mysterious boy with the white hair, checking different classrooms and Gatesville's rota.

He longed for the day of his sixteenth birthday when he would be legally free from the guardianship of Mr. Jennings and Gatesville altogether. But Benjamin wasn't willing to wait five years for that day to come. He couldn't. With a zealous desire for freedom growing inside of him, Benjamin planned his escape.

2

Food Fighting

Benjamin sat alone in the dinner hall one day. The walls were painted the most morbid colors imaginable. The top half of every wall around the canteen was a light shade of gray, the bottom half a cracked layer of dark green. The dire colors suited the mood of every soul in the borstal.

Benjamin looked just as miserable, staring at the dark brown stew that filled half his bowl. Thoughts of his old orphanage, Woodson County, ran through his mind. He never thought that he would miss his old home so much, especially the kind minister who regularly visited him.

Suddenly, a splat of the dark brown stew exploded onto his front collar, severing his train of thought. Benjamin glanced up to see none other than Tommy Joel and his two sidekicks, Jimmy Donald and George Johnston, laughing at him from a table opposite his. At first Benjamin thought Tommy was responsible but soon realized that George was the culprit holding the dirty spoon in his hand.

Soon, the entire cafeteria was laughing. A room full of faces jeered at him and whispered to each other. Tommy simply shook his head and gave Benjamin a look of disappointment before gesturing to him to fight back.

Glaring back at his stew, Benjamin sensed something unfamiliar stir in him. His temper soared. He felt hot and flustered. His spoon rattled for a brief moment and at first glance, he thought it had just been the trick of his eyes. Slowly his unused spoon rose off the dinner table at a snail's pace, too slow as for anyone to notice. Benjamin trembled with fear and excitement but he didn't dare break his concentration, willing the spoon to scoop deep into the center of the bowl and fling a large lump of stew back at George. When the older boy noticed the dark brown mush coming at him he ducked fast, leaving Jimmy Donald to take the splat. The spoon bounced heavily off Jimmy's forehead and flung back across the two tables, landing directly back into Benjamin's bowl like magic. An uproar of laughter from the table next to the bullies boomed out of the dinner hall doors.

Jimmy, embarrassed that Tommy was laughing at him and surprised that the new boy had retaliated in such a bold move, rapidly hit back at Benjamin, throwing his entire bowl at him. Just then, Mr. Jennings strolled directly into the line of fire. Every set of eyes in the dinner hall widened as a half bowl of brown meat and mashed vegetables showered Mr. Jennings's ragged suit.

"You filthy brat!" yelled Mr. Jennings.

It was too late for Jimmy Donald to begin blaming others, for he was the only one out of his chair in the dinner hall and the only boy who was missing his bowl.

Jimmy pointed at Benjamin. "It was him, Sir, he made me do it."

"Poppycock!" yelled Mr. Jennings, eyeballing

George and Tommy. "You two will go without food today too. You're thick as thieves, the lot of you."

Two older prefects took each bowl of stew away from Tommy and George as part of their punishment as Mr. Jennings led Jimmy Donald out of the dinner hall by his ear.

Once the rest of the boys in the dinner hall continued eating, Tommy and George walked over to another table to steal a bowl of stew from two smaller boys who were too intimidated to ask for their lunch back.

After they had finished the bowls of stew, George whispered something into Tommy's ear before he showed him a cigarette. Both rebels immediately got up from the table and scrambled toward the exit doors of the dinner hall. Benjamin tried desperately to recreate what he had done with his spoon earlier when Tommy kicked his chair as he passed him. The sudden jolt broke Benjamin's focus.

A few minutes later, Mr. Porter arrived at the dinner hall and requested that everybody go outside for sports activities, Benjamin's most hated subject. Following in line from the dinner hall into the wide open space of the outside playground, Benjamin could feel his tormentors watching him from a distance, waiting for the right time to get him on his own again.

3

Inside the Library

It was a warm day for the end of autumn. Everyone was outside in the playground, including Mr. Jennings who walked around the grounds keeping a close watch for any signs of misbehavior.

Mr. Porter sat in the shade eating a piece of his strawberry jam covered crumpet when Benjamin snuck past to make his way to the library beyond the back doors of Gatesville.

Benjamin had been to the library hall earlier that morning and smuggled his belongings amongst a shelf of dusty books. He planned to escape Gatesville that evening and was prepared to bide his time in the library until night time when he could make a subtle departure through the library window.

Benjamin entered the library with a smile on his face, for his excitement at the thought of escaping couldn't be contained. There were cobwebs hanging everywhere, from the front doors, to the tables, to the shelves at the back of the room. The smell of mildew was enough to make him feel smothered. Still, Benjamin felt more at peace in this gloomy part of the building than anywhere else. The lofty library had the highest ceiling of any other room in Gatesville and had the tallest windows to light hundreds of old books on display. While reclaiming his hidden belongings from a shelf at the front row, Benjamin stumbled across a few suitable titles. He lifted out *The Complete works of William Shakespeare* from one shelf and a second book called *The Time Machine* from another. He then sat at one of the dusty tables to decide which he should read first.

Soon after he started reading *The Time Machine,* he felt extra warmth fill the room as if someone had entered the library. Putting it down to his imagination, he ignored his initial feeling and continued his reading.

Just then a loud sneeze came from the far corner of the room. Peering from behind the hardback book, he saw that it was the boy who caught his eye before in Mr. Porter's class, staring right at him. Benjamin set the book down and stared back at his odd-looking peer. The boy's hair was a blur of piercing white curls and his skin was very pale. His face was pointy and looked older than the other boys.

"You must be new," muttered Benjamin finally. "I'm quite new to this place, too.

I'm Benjamin Brannon, what's your name?"

"H. G. Welles," the boy replied.

"That's your name?"

"Whom you're reading. It's a great book," the boy added, pointing at the copy of *The Time Machine*. "You can call me Peter."

Benjamin placed the books back on the shelves and kept a watchful eye on the strange boy. "Why are you in here?"

"I saw you go in here, so I followed you," Peter replied, unaware that his honest answer made Benjamin a little cautious of him.

"I don't like to play outside," Benjamin said, smiling bashfully at his own portly frame, "as you can probably tell."

"Me neither," Peter said confidently.

"Why do you have white hair?"

Peter studied Benjamin's height and began to laugh. "Why are you so small?"

Benjamin was stuck for an answer and became distracted when he heard numerous footsteps approaching the library.

"Who is that?" asked Benjamin.

"Principal Jennings," Peter whispered.

Fear struck Benjamin's heart, causing his face to turn almost as white as Peter's hair. Dashing from the front shelf to the back of the library, Benjamin motioned to grab the boy's attention.

"Quick, hurry up."

Peter took his time, coolly walking to the back of the long room. "What are you so afraid of?" he asked placidly.

Benjamin sunk into the darkest corner in order to easily hide amongst the shadows.

"Do you know how much trouble we could get into if we're caught in here?" Benjamin mumbled nervously as he peeked between the books on the rear shelf.

"That didn't stop you from sneaking in," Peter said before Mr. Jennings walked into the library with two older boys.

"I would like you to clear out any dust or dirt you find," ordered Mr. Jennings, rudely keeping his back to the pair of prefects. "For once, I would like to have a clean and orderly library to walk into. Understood?"

The two older boys rolled their eyes at each other. "Yes, Sir," sighed one boy. The same moment, Benjamin accidentally lost his balance whilst crouching and fell against the back wall of books. A book fell to the ground with a loud thud, alerting the three orderlies. Benjamin cowered further into the shade of the bookcase when Mr. Jennings and the two boys peered directly at the back of the room where Benjamin and Peter were hiding.

"Who's there?" rasped Mr. Jennings. "Get out here now!"

Benjamin was frozen to the spot. Peter knelt down beside him.

"Sometimes it's better to face your enemy than to avoid confrontation," Peter whispered assuredly.

"Be my guest," Benjamin insisted.

Mr. Jennings strode up the aisle with his two trusty prefects at either side of him. "I only ask once. Now your life is going to be nothing short of hellish when I get through with you."

Benjamin shut his eyes, wishing he would disappear, when Peter grabbed ahold of his shoulder. "Don't be afraid of him, Benjamin. Face them," he urged.

"I...can't," Benjamin sobbed.

Peter shook his head in disappointment and let go of him. "I'll face them, then," he sighed, shrugging like it was no big deal. Peter got up and confidently stepped into the aisle, leaving his friend to hide.

Mr. Jennings and his two companions stopped dead in their tracks once they saw Peter step into view.

"Well...well. I don't think I've seen *you* before," Mr. Jennings snickered.

"I was studying, Sir," said Peter.

"Silence!" Mr. Jennings shouted. "Who do you think you are back talking me like that? You will speak only when spoken to."

Peter remained silent whilst smiling in a sardonic manner, which baffled the prefects.

"Wipe that smirk off your face! How dare you come in here without permission, especially when the library is closed?" Mr. Jennings rambled on until they were face to face. "I don't think I like the look of you, boy, which is going to make my choice of punishment rather delightful," he sneered.

"For your disobedient behavior, you'll get twenty lashes and extra duties for a week. And you will learn to respect my rules, or I will make your life not worth living."

Mr. Jennings gave Peter another evil grin before he grabbed him by the ear and marched him toward the library doors. Mr. Jennings stopped once he had reached the doorway. His eyes were filled with suspicion. "Was there anyone else in here with you?"

Peter glanced at the end of the library where Benjamin hid behind a shelf of books, watching anxiously through a gap. Benjamin's eyes remained fixed on Mr. Jennings while his fear turned into hatred for the man.

Mr. Jennings stared in anticipation, patiently awaiting Peter's response. "Well?"

Benjamin was sweating even more, anticipating Peter's answer. Hesitantly, Peter looked to the ground and lied, "No."

"You're lying!" he snapped, tugging Peter's ear even harder while he marched him back down the aisle toward Benjamin, followed by his two trusting prefects.

Something stirred in Benjamin. Anger began to rid him of fear and this sudden feeling of power drove him to stand up to Mr. Jennings for the first time. The creepy old principal was only a few feet away from him when Benjamin got a dangerous idea.

Mr. Jennings and Peter reached the last row of shelves where they peeked around the corner to the back row. The principal fell silent. He could see nothing but shelves and books. Benjamin was gone.

Mr. Jennings yanked Peter's ear again and handed him over to the two older boys. "Make that a month's worth of duties for you."

The prefects escorted Peter toward the library doors when a creaking sound caught the attention of the old man's ears. A few seconds of silence followed the second creak. After a third creak came a loud smashing sound of several books piling onto the wooden floor. Another bang of shelves and flutter of books followed another.

Peter was the first to notice the sudden mess on the floor. Row upon row of tall shelves came hurtling toward them like towering dominos spewing out heavy hardback books. Peter broke free, knocking the two boys to the ground to reach the library's exit.

Within a few seconds, the last standing shelf tilted directly above Mr. Jennings and his prefects.

Peter watched in amazement when the bookshelf finally collapsed on top of the three orderlies, burying them under a pile of dusty books. Mr. Jennings let out a high-pitched scream but was soon drowned out.

Peter stood in complete awe at the aftermath of destruction Benjamin had created. At the other side of the library Benjamin stood in shock. His spontaneous idea had worked.

"I didn't hurt him. I-I didn't mean to," Benjamin stammered.

Peter smiled and walked over to greet his new friend. "A villain like Jennings never stays down for long," Peter laughed.

"Get these books off me now!" screamed Mr. Jennings.

"See. I wouldn't worry about him."

Benjamin observed the mess of books and furniture around them. Luckily, he spotted the golden emblem on his birth blanket shining between two scattered books on the floor before carefully salvaging it.

"Wow. Did I do all this?" Benjamin asked timidly, stumbling back through the heap.

Peter quickly led the way toward the ground staircase beyond the library doors and ran up it with ease, taking three steps at a time. For a pale boy, Peter was noticeably agile and energetic. Meanwhile, Benjamin's short and stocky legs struggled to keep up, his feet tripping on certain crooked steps.

Below, a large group of boys had approached the library to investigate the sudden racket.

"There's little time left," warned Peter.

"Time left for what? There's nowhere we can hide now," Benjamin whispered.

Peter hurriedly lifted Benjamin up after he had sat down to rest. "We won't have to hide," Peter smiled. "We're leaving this place."

4

Running From a Mob

The last flight of stairs led to a small, crammed tower space that had been kept locked for years. Peter gently opened the boxy door and invited Benjamin inside.

"What are we doing here?"

Peter didn't answer him. Instead, he walked over to the far end of the roof and opened a set of wooden shutters. Light immediately filled the room.

"Who's there?" a voice whispered.

At first Benjamin couldn't make the figures out through the cloud of smoke that surrounded them, until Peter opened one last shutter.

With the room fully lit, Benjamin realized who the figures in the smoke were. By the edge of the window sat Tommy Joel along with his sidekicks George Johnston and Jimmy Donald.

"Why did you bring *him?*" snapped Tommy, glaring hard at Benjamin.

"You know each other?" Benjamin asked Peter.

"I'm not as new to this place as you thought, Benjamin," Peter replied.

As Tommy offered his cigarette to Peter, the odd boy casually stubbed it out with his foot.

"Hey, what did you do that for?" Tommy sighed.

Peter knelt down to show the boys a rusted silver key in his hand.

"Benjamin's coming with us," Peter said firmly, staring directly into Tommy's piercing blue eye. "We can trust him," he added, then carefully placed the silver key into Benjamin's hand to secure his inclusion. "Take this, Benjamin. It is the key to the back gate."

"How did you get this?" Benjamin gasped.

"Swiped it from Jennings's desk a few days ago. He's been searching for it ever since," Peter sniggered along with the other boys.

"So, where are we going?" asked Benjamin.

"We're getting out of this dump. We're going to live and work on a farm," George explained excitably as Peter nodded in agreement.

"I know a friend in the country. He'll give you work and a better life, if you want to go." Peter added.

"You bet I do." Benjamin smiled. "I was just thinking of leaving, myself, actually."

Tommy pointed to Benjamin. "Dare slow us up, and you'll be left behind. Understood?"

Jimmy extinguished another newly lit cigarette and lifted out a small torn travel bag that was hidden behind a few dusty boxes. George grabbed his tatty coat and hat while Peter climbed out onto the balcony space of the rooftop's window. Benjamin tucked the key safely in his maroon blanket.

Peter coolly turned around to look at all four of them through the window. "I'm going to climb down and check that the back gate area is safe. Everyone is inside so far as I can tell. They won't be able to see me from here."

George rushed down a few steps to open the attic

door. He nodded back to the rest of the group after he had checked that the top floor was clear.

"Like we planned, remember? Make your way to the back kitchen in the dinner hall and climb through the top window," Peter whispered. "Trust me," he added, before vanishing from sight to inspect the back gate.

Tommy grabbed a jar of pennies and emptied them onto the dusty floor. He separated them into three piles, scraping the first pile off the old wooden floorboards and sticking the pennies in his trouser pocket. He handed one pile of pennies to George and another to Jimmy.

Benjamin was the last in line, of course, carefully following the group on the unstable steps of Gatesville's tower space.

Mr. Jennings' screams still echoed through the library from the mound of books he was buried under.

"Sounds like that old crab Jennings," George whispered.

Tommy motioned for Benjamin to come closer. "What happened?" Tommy asked.

Benjamin took a deep breath. He proudly explained how Mr. Jennings had caught Peter in the library and how he had pushed a giant bookshelf on top of the nasty principal and his prefects. George and Jimmy laughed in amusement at Benjamin's daring act, but Tommy sniggered at him.

"You're not telling us fibs, are you?"

Benjamin earnestly shook his head before the bully gave him a respectful nod.

"Not bad, for someone so small," Tommy reluctantly admitted.

"Anyone who pulls a stunt like that on Jennings is

all right in my book," George said, much to Benjamin's pleasure.

Tommy padded down the top staircase silently toward the second floor. He searched around for a brief moment then whispered up to them. "It's all clear."

Angry cries from Mr. Jennings boomed up at them from the library and across the corridors.

Mr. Jennings and the older boys were pulled up from under the rubble of books by Mr. Porter and several prefects. "Give us some help over here!" yelled Mr. Porter.

The bruised and shaken principal finally stood up straight in front of the crowd that had gathered around the library's entrance.

"I'm going to kill those boys," he growled. "Porter, you come with me. I need volunteers to search for the two brats who did this to me."

Mr. Jennings's face grew red with anger. "Whoever helps me find the culprits will be off cleaning duties and mathematics study for the remainder of the year," he announced.

The math teacher sighed when every boy in the room shot their arm into the air to volunteer.

Mr. Jennings grinned as he picked out thirty boys from the crowd.

"Bring me Benjamin Brannon!" he shouted. "You have one hour. Happy hunting, scrappers!"

Meanwhile, Benjamin and the boys could hear every word loud and clear. When Mr. Jennings shouted out Benjamin's name, Tommy and his friends looked at the boy, now trembling.

"I knew you would be a problem," whispered Tommy.

George tapped Tommy on the shoulder. "Peter says we should take him with us, remember?"

"I don't care what Peter says. He's not *my* leader," Tommy snapped back.

"Then chase me, one of you. It's the perfect distraction you need." Benjamin replied.

Tommy stood up and pulled Jimmy up onto his feet. "Go with him and pretend to chase him into the kitchen. George and I will meet you at the back gate."

Jimmy nodded and ran down the stairs after Benjamin, heading toward the kitchen at the same time Mr. Jennings and Mr. Porter stepped out of the library.

Benjamin flew in between them like the wind, missing a head-on collision by an inch. Spinning around in a full circle, both teachers gasped in surprise.

Mr. Jennings screamed hysterically. "I don't believe it, there he goes! Get that brat! Over here, you fools. That way! That way!"

As Jennings stepped into the corridor to shout to the crowd of boys, Jimmy couldn't slow himself, and charged into his principal. Mr. Jennings screamed like a girl when he was shoved to the floor again. He pulled Mr. Porter down with him while Jimmy stumbled over them.

"Okay, that didn't go as planned," Jimmy puffed.

Crowds of boys spotted Benjamin making his way toward the kitchen. When he reached a double turn, he realized he had forgotten whether to take a right or a left turn in order to reach the dinner hall. Feeling rushed, he took a hesitated guess and headed right.

Jimmy came to the same double turn Benjamin had, but took a left instead.

Benjamin reached a dead end. Two black exit

doors lay in front of him, which had been padlocked. He remembered the rusty key and tried to unlock the locks with it.

"Oh no," he whispered. The key and padlocks were incompatible.

As the crowd and orderlies continued their pursuit of Benjamin and Jimmy, George and Tommy coolly slipped by everyone and paced toward the front doors of the Gatesville building. Mr. Jennings and Mr. Porter were so caught up in the pandemonium that the boys were able to exit the building undetected.

Both boys instantly ran to the back gate, fearful they would be spotted cutting through the main playground if they lingered too long.

Peter stood behind the locked gate, waiting for the group to arrive.

"How did you get behind the gate?" George asked.

"I climbed it. Where is Benjamin?" Peter asked, crossing his long skinny arms over his chest.

"The whole place is rootling for him," George answered, breathing heavily.

"You left him behind?" Peter gasped.

Tommy smirked at Peter without answering his question. "What do you care? We've made it, haven't we?" he panted, bending down to catch his breath. Tommy then grabbed the handle of the gate only to discover it was still locked.

"Open it," he ordered.

"I can't," Peter replied calmly.

Tommy grabbed the rusty bars of the gate door and began to violently shake it in frustration. "You'll pay for this," he threatened. Time was of the essence and all Tommy and George could do was wait and hope.

"Well, we had to wait on Jimmy anyway, Tommy," George muttered.

"Shut up!"

Jimmy rammed the kitchen doors wide open and searched for the exit. He hastily barricaded the doors when he noticed Mr. Jennings leading a mob down the hallway after him. The crowd of thirty boys reached the double doors and started shoving their way through the weak blockade of tables and chairs.

"Hurry up, you weaklings. Put your back into it!" yelled Mr. Jennings.

With a mighty force of ten boys pushing together, the kitchen doors flung open. Jimmy was already halfway out of the window when the first boy in the crowd grabbed his leg.

"I've caught one, Sir!" the boy cried.

Jimmy called out to his friends for help.

When Tommy and George heard him, they ran cautiously around the corner of the building. Tommy was the first to rush toward him. He frantically attempted to tug the rest of his body out of the open window.

Inside, Mr. Porter pushed a group of boys out of his way to grab a hold of Jimmy's legs.

Tommy and George were almost pulled inside the window along with Jimmy by a huge tugging force. Jimmy kicked violently to break free until his large foot struck Mr. Porter's chest, sending the man slamming to the ground. With one last heave, Jimmy flew out of the window and landed on top of his friends. The three boys quickly dusted themselves off and ran back to the gate.

Each looked around for ways to climb the gate, but they couldn't find anything to cling onto, for it was a solid rusted gate with singular poles running from its top to its bottom.

"I'm afraid we cannot leave until Benjamin comes with us," Peter said.

"Why is that pip-squeak so important?" Tommy asked with a long sigh of frustration.

"Because I told him we would leave together. I will not go back on my word."

Tommy reached between the bars and grabbed Peter by his collar. "What about the rest of us?" he rasped.

Peter stood fearless in the face of Tommy's sudden outburst.

"I'm afraid your fate is in Benjamin's hands now," Peter replied bluntly. "He has the key, remember?"

5

Escaping the Barrier

Mr. Jennings and Mr. Porter led the hunt for Benjamin. A heavyset boy from the crowd had briefly taken a pit stop near the double turn due to a stitch in his side. When he'd reached the double turn by himself, he was unaware of what direction the other boys and orderlies had taken. His group had outpaced him and was no longer in his view. This sudden dilemma proved too great a puzzle for one so dim-witted.

The boy lifted a penny from his pocket and tossed it into the air.

"Heads for left, tails for right," he breathlessly muttered to himself. He glanced at the sweaty palm of his left hand, awaiting the coin, and then slapped it onto the top of his right.

When he lifted his left hand off the coin, it was facing tails. The boy proceeded to slowly jog down the right corridor, rubbing the side of his torso to sooth the stitch. Right then Benjamin dodged him, running the opposite direction.

The startled boy screamed. "Mr. Porter! Mr. Jennings! Come quick! I've found one! It's him!"

Upon hearing the boy's scream, Mr. Jennings

and Mr. Porter marched into view at the end of the corridor, leading the crowd toward Benjamin.

"You, there!" yelled Mr. Porter, pointing his fat finger at Benjamin.

Benjamin pulled at the side door at the dead end—just when Gatesville's custodian pushed it open from the inside. The custodian carried a tall pile of fresh bed sheets that towered over his face. He didn't notice Benjamin until the panicked boy ran into him, knocking him onto the floor.

"Don't let him pass you!" shouted Mr. Jennings at the custodian, but it was too late. Benjamin was already inside.

Mr. Jennings stopped for a brief second to glare at the custodian who had unknowingly given Benjamin his last chance to escape.

"You idiot," Mr. Jennings scolded. "I'll deal with you later."

Benjamin found another exit door inside the laundry room just when a crowd of prefects appeared behind it and blocked his path. Thinking fast, he jumped onto a row of wooden washing benches above them and struggled to avoid the multiple hands that reached up to grab him.

He raced across the unstable benches, heading for the nearest window. It seemed utterly hopeless until a foot booted through the windowpane ahead of him.

Speckles of glass splashed over the crowd. Just two more benches were all it would take to reach the helping hand that presented itself through the window's frame. He plucked up enough strength to make the space in one giant leap, extending his right arm to grab hold of his rescuer.

The hand swiftly pulled him up to the window

within a split second, revealing the identity of his hero.

It was Tommy.

He's going to let me go just to be wicked, Benjamin thought.

But to his surprise, Tommy used all his strength and effort to pull him out and away from the mob below them, just in time.

"Leg it!" Tommy cried, sprinting away from the hands that grasped for their feet through the window frame.

Once they'd reached the gate, Tommy shook it again. "I got him. I got him out," he cried as each boy threw his bag of belongings over the gate.

"Come on, open it up," George shouted nervously, peeping over his shoulder.

Jimmy jumped up and down in anticipation. Everyone seemed tense except for Peter. Benjamin looked to Peter and then to Tommy and shrugged his small shoulders.

"The key, where's the key you little–," Tommy rambled, grabbing Benjamin by the scruff.

"Oh, right," Benjamin laughed nervously. "It's here, I have it somewhere," he said. Benjamin reached deep into his trouser pockets and pulled out...nothing.

The three boys on the inside of the gate gasped in horror. "Hurry up, unlock it!" George cried. Benjamin searched his pockets, then his coat. Still he found nothing.

"I-I've lost it." Benjamin stammered in a panic as he vigorously searched his pockets. Tommy and George scolded Benjamin while Jimmy started to sob.

Peering over Tommy and George's shoulder, Benjamin saw Mr. Jennings, Mr. Porter, and thirty or more boys, all stomping toward them from the front of the building.

Jimmy stared down at the ground with a miserable look on his face. He'd already given up.

Benjamin was trying desperately to find the key, searching inside his pockets and upon the ground while Tommy pointed at Peter through the gate.

"This is all your fault!" he shouted. "I shouldn't have trusted you."

Shaking in fear, Jimmy tried to climb the gate. After several failed attempts, he managed to jump high enough and grab a firm hold of the rusty bars. The rest followed his lead.

Benjamin's skill at climbing showed when he passed the others, reaching the top of the gates first. Missing a footing, Tommy slid back down following after George. Both boys stood staring up at Jimmy and Benjamin.

Benjamin's arms burned in agony when he swung them over the top of the gate. A shimmer of silver light crossed his face the moment he tried to climb down the other side. Dangling right there on top of one of the gate's spikes was the silver key. It had fallen out from somewhere inside his maroon silk blanket. With a free arm, Benjamin carefully stretched to grab hold of the key before he threw it down to Tommy.

Tommy caught the key in one swift grasp and unlocked the large gate. Mr. Jennings and the mob were a few feet away when Tommy swung the gate open and ran out, followed closely by George, who tripped over himself. Jimmy still held on to the bars but Tommy couldn't wait for him to let go. He slammed the gate tightly shut and reached round the keyhole to lock the gate from the inside when Mr. Jennings grabbed his arm. With a stroke of luck, Tommy swiftly locked it and broke the key trying to pull away from the principal's grasp.

"Give me back my master key, you thief," Mr. Jennings growled, giving him an evil glare.

"Let go!" Tommy demanded.

Peter peered up at Jimmy who was losing his grip fast. "Sorry, old chap," Peter muttered.

Jimmy watched in horror as Peter charged toward the gate to kick it. The heavy vibration of Peter's kick caused Jimmy to lose his grip and fall on top of the group below him. Benjamin managed to balance and hold onto the gate at the top.

The mob of boys stumbled and banged into one another, which crushed Mr. Jennings. The old man remained standing but was shoved so hard by the group of youngsters that he lost his own grasp on Tommy.

"Can we leave now?" yelled George.

"We have to help Benjamin," Peter replied.

From the high view, Benjamin could see Jimmy being escorted away by Mr. Porter along with a group of four prefects.

"No. I don't want to go," Jimmy called out, crying loudly across the playground.

Mr. Jennings ordered the remaining mob to shake Benjamin from the gate's top.

"I'll catch you, Benjamin!" shouted Tommy.

Even though his arms were exhausted, Benjamin somehow found the strength to drop down the other side of the gate, but not without giving Mr. Jennings a cheeky wave goodbye. As promised, Tommy caught him, falling back onto the gravel.

Holding onto his bruised back, Tommy shoved Benjamin off him. The successful landing was over and the four boys looked back at the crowd to laugh at them, especially at Mr. Jennings.

"This isn't over! You will not get far, you little hoodlums!" the man screamed back with contempt.

Peter turned to the three boys with a huge smile across his face. "The easy part is over," he said calmly.

Benjamin giggled to himself. "You thought that was easy?"

"We must keep moving, they'll soon be after us," Peter said seriously as he led the way forward, down the hill that Gatesville was built upon. Tommy paused to turn back and slowly lifted the other half of the broken key out of his pocket to tease the furious principal.

"Mr. Jennings...catch!"

6

Enduring the Mush of the Moors

The farmlands between Gatesville and the great city of London lay just a few miles down a path of wet mud and dead grass. The late afternoon's weather had changed for the worse. Rain poured heavily down on the four boys as they began their lengthy journey toward the great city. Benjamin had passed through London with Miss Illingworth on his way to Gatesville a little over two months prior, but he had never stepped foot there since he was an infant. From the moors, the city looked fascinating and tempting. But the closer they got, the darker the gray clouds became.

Several hours had passed since they had made their great escape. They ran fast at first and had great bursts of energy that put distance and time between them and the authorities. But their journey through the sludge and mud made them weary. The miserable, bleak weather matched their mood. Everyone was feeling tired and miserable by the time they'd trekked half way across the moors, except for Peter.

George took his hat off and handed it to Benjamin.

"For me?" asked Benjamin with a sparkling look of gratitude lighting up his face.

George frowned at the sight of the poor lad, for

Benjamin looked like a drenched dog.

"I have another one," George replied.

Benjamin took the large hat and covered his ears and forehead with it. It felt nice and warm.

Mud and sludge coated their legs as they continued crossing the soaking moors. Tommy struggled to carry Jimmy's personal belongings. Finally, he dumped the extra baggage onto the muddy grass.

George swiped the bag from the mud and handed it to Benjamin. "Here, if you can carry it, it's yours," he whispered.

Another hour went by until the boys stopped for a rest under an old tree. The tree was rotted away at the roots and provided little cover from the rain. Their pit stop proved to be very uncomfortable.

"Here, you better take this, just in case we lose anyone," Peter whispered to the group, lifting three exact maps of England out of his bag and handing one to each boy.

"This is where we're going," Peter explained, pointing at a name beside the destination. His optimism was encouraging.

"Who's Jacob?" Benjamin asked, curious and suspicious of Peter's somewhat classified plan.

"He is the one who can give us all a job on the farm," Peter replied.

Tommy rudely knocked Jimmy's bag out of Benjamin's hands. "Who said you could have that?" he barked. A large envelope and a case of cigars spilled out onto the muddy grass.

"What are these?"

Both Benjamin and George shrugged their shoulders at him before Tommy grabbed the envelope and started to open it. Benjamin, George and Tommy stared in disbelief when money fell out. "Money! I'm rich," laughed Tommy. George tittered along with him until Peter grabbed all the notes off of the ground and snatched the envelope out of Tommy's hand.

"Hey, give it back!" yelled Tommy.

"Benjamin will hold on to the money from now on," Peter said, handing Benjamin the bills. "This money has to last the four of us. It can get us to where we need to go, unless you want to take your cut now and leave," he continued.

Silence fell upon the group once again. "What's it going to be?" Peter asked.

Tommy nodded his head slowly. It was surprising for him to back down so easily, especially from a smaller person. Either he was following orders from Peter now, or he'd become too exhausted to argue with anyone.

***

It was getting darker and colder when Peter led them into the city.

Gatesville could still be seen past the mist that covered the moors. When Benjamin took his last look at the old haggard building, it looked very small and desolate. The bare trees of autumn's end surrounded its outer walls, making it look like an abandoned asylum. Benjamin shuddered at the haunting sight. The entire group shuddered with him when two policemen came into view from a bend in the road.

"Patrolmen?" whispered George.

"What now?" Tommy asked Peter. "You said this

was the road to the city."

"It is. But it looks like Jennings has already alerted the police," Peter said, leading the three boys to hide in a ditch. Choosing the smallest, the three of them lifted Benjamin up to peek at the policemen's feet that stood only a meter away from the ditch. "What do you see?" Peter asked.

"Two of them, there's only two of them," Benjamin whispered loudly.

"Only two on patrol?" Tommy grunted sardonically.

"*Bicycles!*" Benjamin gasped.

On Benjamin's count, Tommy and George snuck out of the field's ditch and rose up to ground level once the bobbies patrolled the area at a safe distance. Tommy tiptoed toward one of the parked bicycles and climbed onto its seat.

"Quick, jump on," Tommy insisted, handing George a bicycle.

Benjamin signalled in panic when the bobbies returned from scouring the area and spotted both runaways trying to steal their bicycles.

Peter grabbed hold of Benjamin's arm and helped him onto the seat of the bicycle George was steering.

"Ride!" shouted Peter after he rode on the back of the other bicycle with Tommy.

Both bicycles raced down the uneven road toward the city, when each bobby made an effort to cut through their path at a sly angle.

George let out a loud yell, nearly crashing into one of the men who made a lunge for him.

"Turn right! Right!" screamed Benjamin as they shot past him at great speed.

With a tight swing one bobby took hold of Peter's coat in a desperate attempt to upset their balance. But

Tommy remained undeterred from peddling forward.

"Gotcha!" rasped the policeman with a gloating grin seconds before Peter knocked the helmet off his head. The bobby let go of his grip to reach for it before tripping up.

Tommy and George peddled faster until they were all safe and out of reach of the police.

It didn't take long for the tall buildings and back alleyways of London to conceal them as they entered the city.

George and Tommy climbed off their bicycles to stretch their legs while Peter studied his map. After the group had enough rest, the excitement and wonder of the city life slowly built up inside them. Travelling through the city was the beginning of Peter's plan to reach the northern countryside.

London was not a fit place for children to roam about freely, but nobody seemed to care.

Pushing the stolen bicycles through the marketplace attracted several stall owners, shouting words at them in city slang they didn't understand.

To his relief, Benjamin soon found himself onto another street with engine driven cars and old carriages. Long dressed ladies walked their groomed fluffy pets along cleaner pavement, shielding their heads with matching umbrellas.

Peter had lost his direction through the madness of the market place and consulted his map. Instead of moving further along the posh area, Peter re-directed the group through a shortcut down a remote lane.

The air was fresher here than the odd smells of the markets, but unfortunately, the city alleyways proved to be just as dark, even in daylight, as anywhere else.

Benjamin was the first to spot three young

hoodlums loitering at the end of the alleyway, blocking the exit.

George stopped in his tracks, gripping the handlebars to the bicycle with all his might.

"L-let's go back," he stuttered. Peter calmly motioned for Benjamin to follow him toward the new faces at the bottom of the alleyway's exit.

One boy appeared to be the same age as Benjamin and Tommy. The other two were much older and somewhat fierce looking.

"What 'ave we 'ere lads?" asked the eldest gang member in a very harsh cockney accent. "Looks like a bunch of silver spoon babies."

"What is your name?" Peter asked the leader confidently.

"Duncan," he muttered. "Just because you know my name, doesn't mean we'll let ya pass. This is our patch."

Benjamin glanced behind his shoulder when he heard the clicking sounds of bicycle spokes approaching.

"Two more, this is going to be a fun fight," mumbled Duncan to his fellow hooligans, before raising his fists to the four of them. Tommy threw his bicycle to the ground.

Duncan seemed unsure of Tommy for he looked more menacing than either of his friends. "I 'ate you borstal boys, always coming round our turf."

"Out of my way," commanded Tommy.

Duncan laughed unexpectedly with his friends then lifted a large piece of broken wood behind a rusty bin and tapped it in his hand.

Tommy's eyes widened in alarm.

"We're not from here," Peter said hastily.

"Clearly," Duncan snickered.

"If you lead us to the central train station, we will give you these bicycles in return."

Duncan looked to his friends who both raised an eyebrow to the offer, and a sudden smile spread across the tough boy's face.

"Very well, Guvnor," he replied. "This way!"

***

After a five-mile stretch across the city by foot, the Gatesville runaways overheard the mighty whistles and horns of a real train station for the first time.

"We're almost there," Duncan shouted back.

London's central station had large queues at every platform. Tommy was fascinated by the beautiful black steam trains in front of them. One train in particular filled his multi-colored eyes with wonder. George wasn't impressed by anything, except the food stalls nearby.

"I believe you owe us something," Duncan demanded.

Peter motioned to Tommy and George and without hesitation the boys handed over the bicycles.

"Maybe we'll bump into each other again someday," Duncan said. "We could do with another bicycle."

Tommy watched from the corner of his green eye as the three street thugs walked out of sight. Steam filled the air around them.

Peter took a single bob note out of the envelope from Benjamin before handing it back. He then purchased four tickets for the northbound line to Warwickshire at the ticket office.

Through the crowds and the steam, Benjamin spotted the smallest member of Duncan's street gang look back to get a sneak peek at the envelope as he walked away.

"Our train will be leaving soon," said Peter, leading the way through the small entrance to the platform.

Peter handed the train inspector four tickets. After punching a hole in each ticket, the train inspector permitted them to walk through to the northern line platform, mistaking them as part of a family traveling in a group, a common occurrence for a busy place such as London.

The four boys stood waiting for a few minutes before one loud train conductor began to shout. "Warwickshire train, all aboard. All aboard North Line to Warwickshire."

Peter swiftly handed each boy his ticket. "Keep this safe," he reminded them.

Benjamin placed his ticket deep inside his left pocket. He let out a nervous laugh when his fingers frantically searched his inner coat. It only took him a few seconds to realize that he had been pickpocketed.

Without making it too noticeable, he stepped away from the group to double check all of his pockets, but it didn't make any difference. The envelope was gone.

Fear of being disowned from the group prompted Benjamin to keep his silence about it until he was on the train, for at least he couldn't be parted from them then.

A sudden commotion erupted ahead of the platform. Loud shouting and stomping feet echoed across the station.

"We have to get on the train. I think we're in trouble," Tommy said nervously once he saw Duncan trip over his bicycle to flee from several policemen.

Notes flew out of Duncan's pockets as he made his way through the gathering crowd.

"You little weasels," Benjamin said out loud to himself, realizing that Duncan and his friends had lingered around the station to pickpocket travelling passengers.

Peter pulled Benjamin out of the passenger line and led him to an unoccupied area behind the crowd.

"It's about to get very busy," he warned.

Other passengers whispered and gawked at the commotion as a large crowd gathered to get a better glimpse of the chase while unintentionally blocking George's only path of escape.

"Push your way through," Tommy called out to George as he tried maneuvering through passengers from the opposite side to reach his friend. Seconds after Tommy got within reaching distance of George, he accidentally bumped into a frail elderly lady. The old lady let out a gasp of shock and lost her balance, falling onto her hip. Just as Tommy turned back to apologize, a man and his wife pulled him away from the old lady.

"What the blazes are you playing at, Sonny?" yelled the man, tightening his grip.

"Let me go!" Tommy cried. The man and his wife looked down their nose at the young boy, curiously, before a cross expression spread over their faces. Tommy's worst fears arose when the couple called to the policemen running toward them.

"Officers! We've got one! Hurry!"

7

Panic on the Platform

Thinking on his feet, Tommy slammed his foot down upon the man's toe as hard as he could. The businessman gave out a loud moan but remained holding fast to the boy.

Tommy was about to give up until Duncan desperately tried to run through the couple to evade the policemen. Tommy wriggled out of his coat to free himself from the distracted man's clutch. It was the stroke of luck he had needed to make his daring break, leaving the nosey couple to capture Duncan instead.

Tommy crouched down and crawled through a row of legs to get behind the crowd.

When he finally broke through to stand up, he saw one policeman pulling at Duncan's ear and leading him off the platform while George followed behind in handcuffs, escorted by another policeman.

"That's four of them, Sir. We caught two more culprits pocketing wallets at the station's entrance. Must be the Gatesville boys," one policeman called out to his superior. Tommy silently backed away from the crowd.

"Time to go," Peter whispered, appearing with Benjamin behind the boy as if by magic.

"What about George?" Benjamin muttered.

"He's not coming this time," Peter answered for Tommy as the boisterous bully looked to the ground to hide his sadness.

"There's another way to get on the train without being spotted," Peter informed, sneaking Tommy and Benjamin near the unoccupied area beside the back of the train. Peter climbed his way through the small black doorway at the end carriage followed by Benjamin.

Deafening sounds of the steam blasting into the air made Tommy jump. The train's piercing horns alerted everyone on the platform of the boarding call.

Peter snuck to the front of the train, carefully crossing through the carriages to inspect the engine room ahead of him. Tommy took a seat next to Benjamin who nervously fiddled with his torn ticket between his fingers.

"Where is he off to, now?" Tommy tugged Benjamin to follow him as he led the way through several carriages toward the middle of the train. Both darted in opposite directions to hide behind seats when the fireman of the train forcefully rushed past them toward the engine room.

Slowly peering over the carriage seats, Benjamin and Tommy spotted Peter up ahead of them, inside the engine room.

"He's not supposed to be in there. He's going to get us caught," whispered Benjamin.

"Shut up, pipsqueak, or you'll get us caught," Tommy threatened.

Tommy peeked through the divider door to the next carriage and saw a long row of empty seats ahead. Just then, the train driver burst through a divider door behind them.

"Make sure you've checked the regulator," the driver yelled up to the fireman when Tommy and Benjamin froze directly in his path. The sweating man looked so anxious and troubled that his manners were very blunt.

"What are *you* doing here?" snapped the driver. Tommy raised his ticket in front of the driver's face for inspection hoping the ticket would somehow shield him from any questioning. By a quick and rather rude snatch, the train driver read the date on the new stub and handed it back to him.

"Well, sit down lad. I need to get past, this train ain't going to drive itself," he insisted. Tommy nervously stepped aside to let the older man pass.

Benjamin and Tommy were too distracted to see Peter slip out of the engine room amidst the crowd of boarding passengers, leaving his two friends to journey unknowingly alone.

Unfolding his original copy of the map, Peter used his index finger to follow the trail from London's central station to another 'X' mark that highlighted the name 'Viktor' placed on the west end of the city.

"We're ready for departure," called the driver to the train conductor.

"Good, we're already behind schedule," the train conductor hollered back while he ushered more passengers onto the train.

Most of the passengers took to their seats in a hurry to rest their feet when the mammoth train eased its way out of London's central station.

Both boys leaned out of the window to wave a fond farewell to the city. That was when they spotted Peter waving back to them.

"What in the name of King Henry are you doing

down there?" Tommy yelled in panic.

"No time to explain boys. Just follow that map!" Peter called back, just enough time before the train took Benjamin and Tommy from sight.

***

Silence filled the train when the passengers settled. The hypnotic rocking of the carriages had sent Benjamin off to sleep as the train sped through the countryside at a great pace.

Thoughts of Peter stranded back in London worried Tommy. He bore the guilt for leaving George. Now with Peter gone too, Tommy felt alone with the added pressure of Benjamin to look after.

"At least we have the map," Benjamin mumbled in his sleep, as if he had read Tommy's anxious thoughts.

Outside, trees and bushes flew past the train window, showing beautiful scenery and many fields in the distance. But Tommy's troubled mind refused to give him any peace, making the entire train journey a strenuous one.

Another hour had gone past when he surrendered to his tiredness and drifted off, resting his head on Benjamin's shoulder.

It felt like he'd just closed his eyes when the train conductor shook both of them out of their sleep.

"Your stop, young Sirs," he chuckled lightly.

Yawning loudly, the boys jumped off the steps of the train and landed on a hoary platform overgrown with moss. They looked around, smelling the fresh air and enjoying their first taste of true freedom in the middle of the countryside. The woodland area ahead was calm and completely desolate, which suited both runaways fine.

Tommy exited Warwickshire Station first, shuffling inside his pockets for the map.

"Check your pockets Benjamin, do you have the map?" His voice sounded desperate.

Benjamin eagerly unfolded his own map, relieved that Tommy hadn't mentioned the money yet. No one really knew where the money came from or whom it belonged to, but Benjamin suspected it had something to do with the shifty-eyed Mr. Jennings, an idea he didn't like to entertain.

Tommy quickly snatched the map and studied its directions to the black 'X' mark with the name 'Jacob' on it. The instructions were surprisingly simple to follow, leading them to a narrow path at the bottom of a tall muddy hillside.

"Well, that was easy," mentioned Tommy after he lined the map up with the hill in front of them.

"I wonder what's up there?" muttered Benjamin.

8

The Winter's Stranger

"Follow me and don't slip," Tommy instructed as he led the way up the dark hillside. The road was bare and the hillsides lay empty, devoid of human life.

Poor Tommy felt just as scared as Benjamin but he had to ignore his fear and become the leader, since their group had been torn in half.

The night's cold air settled over them unexpectedly, biting Benjamin's ears and numbing his hands and toes. From a distance, the dark hill hadn't looked steep, but now it seemed to tower above them menacingly. Benjamin kept slipping in the icy mud until he reached the top.

Tommy fuddled around the map and struggled to read the further they were from the station's lamps. "This Jacob fellow shouldn't be that hard to find. There's only a stretch of countryside to get across before we reach our destination. How hard can it be?" Tommy chattered on to keep himself warm.

The woods around them were spooky. Howling winds brushed through the massive branches and blew against their frigid faces as the pair made their way toward the opposite side of the hill. A huge frost-covered field lay ahead of them.

"I-I think we should go back," Benjamin suggested, raising his voice over the wind.

"Don't chicken out now, Brannon," snapped Tommy. "We stick with Peter's plan until we find this farm."

A second howl came from the woods ahead, only this time it didn't sound like a gust of wind. It was more animal sounding.

Maybe it was a fox? thought Benjamin. He could only hope.

"I'm going back to the station," Benjamin said, turning around and running face-first into something sturdy and large. Benjamin bounced back to the ground before he gazed up at a large figure standing over him. The strange character firmly clutched a few dead rabbits in one hand and raised a lamp to his face with the other. The light of his lamp revealed a deep scar on the left side of his face, accompanied by a few smaller scars on his right ear and forehead.

Benjamin screamed in fear while Tommy ran to the nearest tree to break off a branch. Hurrying back to Benjamin's aid, Tommy held the broken bough like a weapon and pointed it at the stranger's chest.

"Keep away from us, or I'll stick you and your rabbits, old man," Tommy threatened.

The rabbit hunter hooted loudly. "You won't do much damage with that thing, lad," the man said smugly. The rabbit hunter fell silent shortly afterwards when he heard the same howling noise echo through the dark woods ahead.

"We'd best be on our way, gentlemen," he whispered in his thick country accent. "Hold this for me," he ordered, throwing Tommy a large bag of dead pheasants and rabbits. The rabbit hunter then helped Benjamin to his feet with a mighty tug.

The man was large but quite short for an adult.

"I don't travel with adults," snapped Tommy after he threw the bag back at the man's feet.

"Neither do I," the man replied, smiling back. "My name is O'Malley. I am a hunter of these fields and I have a permit, so you know...and you are?" he asked, eyeing both boys.

"Oh...my name is Benjamin, Benjamin B-Brannon, Mr. O'Malley."

"O'Malley! What kind of a name is that for a hunter?" whispered Tommy to Benjamin, who was trying desperately to ignore his friend's rudeness.

The countryman leaned in toward Tommy. "And what do they call you then, boy?" O'Malley asked with a mischievous grin.

Tommy looked up at the sturdy man and jerked when he heard another howl from the woods behind him. "T-Tommy's the name, Tommy Joel."

The large man took another step forward bending down slightly to look young Tommy in his fear-filled green eye.

"Indeed...do *you* have *your* permit, Thomas?" he whispered.

The boy could only muster a silent 'no' in reply, whilst shaking his head. O'Malley took another glance into the woods behind them and picked his bag of dead animals from the frosty grass.

"The look on yer face. I'm just joking with ya, lad," he chuckled, as he began to walk away from the pair.

The two boys stood in the frost watching the stranger walk down the other side of the dark hill toward the massive open fields. O'Malley stopped a few feet ahead of them. "Well come on then," he called back.

"We don't *walk* with strangers neither," Tommy shouted back stubbornly.

"Suit yourselves, I'll walk home by myself then. I can't wait to put my feet up by a nice warm fire and eat some of my homemade rabbit stew. Hmm, or maybe I'll have some tomato and basil soup. It goes well with pheasant. Anyway, good luck with the storm, boys. Tomorrow's the first day of winter." He chuckled again and continued walking, whistling, without a care in the world. The beautiful glow of the full moon gleamed down on him, lighting up the rows of the fields in the distance.

O'Malley seemed a very odd character, which made Tommy extra cautious of him. The toughened orphan had never had any good experiences with adults or guardians before, much less a wild hunter from the country.

Benjamin also had little, if any, trust for adults, especially strangers. But O'Malley appeared a bit too jolly to fit into either category. It was a risk between joining this stranger or trekking through the bitter cold and possibly freezing to death.

"I think we should go with him," suggested Benjamin.

Tommy rolled his eyes and pushed his smaller friend forward. "You go with him if you want to get yourself caught or worse...kidnapped. I'm following the map."

Benjamin kicked at the frosted grass in frustration at Tommy's stubbornness.

"Well, I'm not going to freeze to death trying to find my way in the dark," Benjamin sighed as he followed the rabbit hunter's footsteps.

Tommy slumped next to a tree to memorize the

map. Hypnotic sounds of branches rustling inside the woods sent him into a restless sleep until a loud howl woke him. He peered over the hill's edge to see a large stretch of land close below, but Benjamin and O'Malley were no longer in sight.

Winds blew fierce across the fields as Tommy made a late start toward his destination.

Adrenaline kept his body going while he ran down the opposite side of the hill. A stone embedded in the ground instantly caught his shoe and flung him forward. Rolling the rest of the way down the steep hillside, Tommy roughly landed flat on his face in the frost.

The winds had grown stronger and he could feel the frost bite at his bare knees where his trousers had been ripped. His legs were cut and bruised from the tumble, which made him feel wretched. Picking himself up from the frosty ground, he limped his way across the first patch of field.

Meanwhile, in another open field a few miles ahead, Benjamin wasn't having too well a time himself. Having abandoned his only companion to follow the prodigious stranger caused him to panic. After all, anything could happen to him now, and Benjamin's imagination usually thought the worst. His sudden anxiety exhausted his body, and the blistering cold had made his feet twice as heavy. He couldn't go on. Feeling sick, chilly and downright miserable, Benjamin's body finally gave up.

The rabbit hunter immediately took off his large animal coat made out of wolf's skin and wrapped it around the fainting boy. Lifting Benjamin in one arm over his free shoulder, O'Malley started to slog through the rest of the field while he listened to the sounds from the forest.

The cold was like nothing Tommy had ever felt. His mind couldn't concentrate on anything. He lost all sense of hope and briefly forgot about Benjamin and Peter. He even forgot about Gatesville and how he came to be in this serious situation.

The only thing he had the strength to think about now was a warm bed. Thoughts of comfort became more vivid the icier the weather became. He longed for rest.

After he reached a patch of forest, his hazel green right eye detected a small light in the distance. A torch? A flashlight?

The moonlight danced off a pearly set of teeth that shone back at him through the shadows. Bright snow under its body reflected a fierce glow in its piercing eyes as the boy moved inches away from the beautiful face of a lethal wolf.

Unwittingly, the boy's eyes locked onto the beast's dazzling electric ice blues and caused him to faint with fear.

Tommy could sense another light behind his closed eyelids but was too weak to show any sign that he was still semi-conscious. The light exposed an unusual sight of wolves still lingering near the seemingly dead boy. The ravenous wolf pack stood still, curiously watching the man rescue what was supposed to be their long-deserved meal.

O'Malley shouted at the wolves that stood several yards away from the boy while he covered Tommy in more wolf skin. The wolves stood as still as stone statues, beautifully silhouetted by the light. None howled nor made a sound. Tommy slipped into a comfortable deep sleep when the heavy fur shawl coated his upper body.

Heavy snow swept across the open field. With the aid of one large stick and a newly lit beacon in the other hand, O'Malley continued his heroic journey toward the sanctuary of his house, carrying the unconscious boy the rest of the way he had carried Benjamin.

9

The Unforeseen Visitor

Rain pelted down over Gatesville that night. There was a new wrath to be endured for the children, especially the captured runaways. No one had seen hide nor hair of George Johnston since he was ushered back to the dreaded borstal, and even Jimmy Donald had begun to think the worst. Double shifts and extra duties for failing to capture Benjamin Brannon was just the start of a year-long punishment set in motion by the prideful principal of Gatesville.

It was past midnight when a noisy car pulled up to the front gates. Nearly every boy from the east side of the building block took to their bedroom windows for a careful glimpse at the unforeseen visitor. Two policemen and a peculiar, overly dressed man entered through the main gates. The rain and wind became so severe it almost blew all three hats off of the figures, causing the boys in the east block to laugh aloud before they hushed each other. A man in a trench coat followed Mr. Porter after greeting him, and within minutes the police were escorted into Gatesville's main corridor.

"We've come a long way Mr. Jennings. You said this was urgent?" The tall, rugged man asked, making himself comfortable as he sat in the principal's guest chair in his office.

"You don't think stolen police property is an urgent matter, Inspector?" Mr. Jennings asked smugly, pouring himself a cup of freshly brewed tea.

"Two bicycles and a satchel are hardly urgent matters. That case is now closed. We caught the perpetrators and recovered the stolen property, including your money." The Inspector smiled proudly, seeming victorious in front of his police guards. He then took off his black hat and shook the raindrops onto Jennings' luxurious carpet.

"It most certainly is not closed. I am still missing three of my boys," Mr. Jennings snapped after he gulped down his cup of black tea. "One of whom never registered with us here at Gatesville. He's totally off the books, no trace...like a ghost. Explain that."

"Mr. Jennings," the Inspector said calmly, "whomever you allow to slip under your nose is ultimately your responsibility by law. What we can do for you is draw up a missing children's report and–."

"Those reports don't amount to a hill of beans," Mr. Jennings interrupted, jumping upright from his chair.

"Nevertheless...it's standard procedure, Mr. Jennings," sighed the Inspector as he fixed his black hat back onto his head.

"Once we have a legitimate lead, we'll let you know," said one of the policemen whilst the three headed for the exit door.

"Don't bother...I've saved you the trouble," Mr. Jennings sniggered, throwing a crumpled piece of paper across his desk at the Inspector who grappled to catch it in one attempt.

"What's this?" asked the Inspector, unfolding it.

"One of my runaways you brought back had this in his possession. It's a map. I think that's lead enough for you, don't you think?" Mr. Jennings boasted.

"We'll take this to the station for review," the Inspector concluded.

Mr. Jennings' expression suddenly changed from a boastful grin to an angry disgruntled frown. "What? That's it? That's all you're going to do?"

"I would mind my tone if I were you, Mr. Jennings," the Inspector said coolly. "There are hundreds of runaway cases to be dealt with every day. We have to first run a check on these areas to know for sure they exist. For all we know they could be meeting points that have elapsed by now," he continued.

"Or *they* could be at any one of these spots," Mr. Jennings interrupted.

"Let us check it before we use up any manpower and the people's taxes on a widespread manhunt. We're just making sure this will not turn out to be a wild goose chase. Then we can proceed. I've had more experience in these matters than you have, Mr. Jennings, and many cases like this prove unsuccessful... however, if I find these areas to be habited by the boys, I will certainly contact you in due course, when and only when I have the available staff to do so," the Inspector added bluntly, turning his back on the old man to exit the office.

"Ridiculous," Mr. Jennings hissed. "Lucky for me I have made an extra copy; get to the bottom of this myself, I will," he rambled, muttering under his breath.

"I strongly advise against taking police matters into your own hands...or you'll be the one we'll come back for," one policeman threatened. Mr. Jennings screwed up his face in disgust when the Inspector motioned for his men to leave.

"Good night, Mr. Jennings," the Inspector sighed.

"Oh forget it, you good for nothings!" Mr. Jennings yelled back once his office door slammed heavily behind them.

The flickering of the Victorian lamps at the front gate dimmed for a few seconds, then glowed brighter. Neither bobby seemed to notice it at first until the Inspector pointed out the random change in the flame's color. The normal ember radiance suddenly turned ice blue then changed rapidly to an earthly green and back again. The flame eventually faded to a light gray as if it had been drained of all its color before burning out.

"That was strange, don't you think?" one policeman tittered at the Inspector.

"It has stopped raining too," the other policeman added, staring at his colleagues who were both bewildered.

"I'll meet you back at the station," the Inspector muttered in suspicion after noticing the orphans peering through the window at him. Taking the piece of paper from his chest pocket, the Inspector hurriedly unfolded the map and took another glance at it.

"Inspector?" the second bobby asked, waiting on an explanation for the Inspector's delay.

"I need to speak with this Jennings character one more time. I'll send for someone to collect me," the Inspector replied with a reassuring nod. "Go on."

"Very well, Sir," said both policemen together.

Once the police wagon left Gatesville's premises, heavy wind picked up around the grounds. The Inspector was only a step away from entering the building when an enormous blast of wind picked him off his feet and flung him into the darkness of the playground. Wet autumn leaves violently swirled around the man, blowing his hat off as they encircled him.

"Get off me. What is this?" the Inspector yelled punching at the thick wall of leaves that entrapped him.

Lightning struck through the clouds seconds before it stood in front of him. The darkness shielded the monstrosity from his sight. Its terrible presence was felt yards away the instant it parted the swirling leaves. Its rancid stench swept across the entire playground, reaching the windows of the east block and causing every boy to cough and splutter and cover their noses.

Dazzling light shone out through the leaves and briefly lit up the playground long enough for everyone watching to see the nine-foot creature's scary form. The Inspector screamed for help prior to his whole body evaporating into a vanishing light that left behind his hat. The children gasped in horror as they observed the giant monster morph into a human man to mimic the Inspector. Changing from the feet up, the creature's frame magically imploded. Its heavy chained armor rapidly transformed into the form and frame of the Inspector's dark cotton suit and pocket watch. Its steel armored feet followed next, converting into shiny black shoes. The final stage was the beast's face. It stepped out of the playground and into the lit entrance of Gatesville, still transforming into the Inspector's facial features until its conversion was complete a few seconds later.

A calm breeze carried the Inspector's hat across

the playground, rolling to the feet of his imitator.

Now mimicking his victim, the monstrous imposter knelt down gently to pick up the black hat before giving a bow to his audience of children who stood aghast behind their bedroom windows. After shutting their curtains tight, every boy ran from their windows in fright. They weren't to get a wink of sleep after they heard the imposter enter the building with thunderous steps that echoed through the corridors, all the way to the principal's office.

"Did you forget something?" Mr. Jennings grumbled, briefly glancing up from his desk with a raised eyebrow as he put down his calligraphy pen and dramatically crumpled up a letter he had been writing.

"I think I am mistaken, Mr. Jennings. This map seems quite genuine. If we hurry, it should lead us straight to them," the false Inspector said sharply.

"My, my. You've changed your tune," Mr. Jennings sniggered, fixing his glasses on his beaky nose. "Why, a second ago, you couldn't have cared less."

"Like I said, I was mistaken." The false Inspector's eyes shot back a cold, emotionless gaze that unnerved and shook the old principal out of his comfort zone.

"No harm done. I-I'll arrange a meeting with you to discuss further action. I don't want my runaways getting too comfortable. The sooner the better," Mr. Jennings spluttered.

"I was thinking sooner," the dark-eyed Inspector hissed, approaching Mr. Jennings's desk.

"Blimey, you are keen," Mr. Jennings tittered. "Alright, I'll be at the station first thing tomorrow morning." Mr. Jennings let out an impatient sigh, while he rudely continued to write. In one speedy move, the Inspector lifted the calligraphy pen out of the principal's scarred fingers. It took Mr. Jennings a few seconds to take in the sudden odd behavior of the Inspector before he felt a little unnerved.

"Much sooner than that, Mr. Jennings," the Inspector replied.

"How soon?" Mr. Jennings asked in a faint whisper, followed by a gulp.

"Now," the Inspector whispered eerily, slowly handing the pen back to him, revealing a silver glint in his eyes and an eager smile that was filled with bad intent.

10

Sebastian Cain

The show was about to begin. The prop boy could tell from the thundering roar of the orchestra that the first set of curtains had been opened. He couldn't see much ahead of the opera house floor. The heavy lights that stretched across the circular ceiling above the audience began to dim, setting the right atmosphere for the play to commence. Coughs and conversations from the audience died down and their attention turned toward the stage, addressed by the prop boy's charming and charismatic father.

"Greetings Ladies and Gentlemen," the sharp-suited aristocrat bellowed, dramatically pacing up and down the stage platform. "What you are about to witness is the wonder and excitement of our fiftieth theatrical presentation. I assure that none of you will be disappointed, but rather enlightened, entranced, and above all else, inspired by this very unique portrayal of one civilization's quest for absolute survival. Let me remind you that nowhere else in London, or England, or even the whole world and beyond will you find a play that entertains as much as this one does," he rambled, building up the audience's expectation. Viktor Cain was a great showman who knew his trade well.

"So without further ado, it is my great pleasure to announce to you, the Royal Opera House's newest attraction, *The Reigning Masks*."

Elsewhere, backstage, another worker the same age as the prop boy turned to him behind the curtain.

"Wasn't that your idea, Sebastian?" he asked, cupping one hand in a loud whisper across the stage.

The prop boy looked embarrassed and bobbed his head.

"That's another one ol' Viktor's stolen from ya. When are ya gonna learn, eh?" With a mop in hand, the worker continued his leftover duties, leaving Sebastian his words to ponder over.

The stage lights faded until the entire auditorium was pitch black. Squeaking noises from the apparatus that lifted the main dark velvet drapes caused many audience members to shudder at the uncomfortable sound. Viktor swiftly marched to the backside of the stage and pushed his son out of the way to roll back the heavy wheel himself. Music erupted from the orchestra in sync with the moving curtains until the stage set came into view. Sebastian was on the floor nursing a cut on his dusty knee when Viktor's large hands grabbed hold of him.

"Can't you do anything right, you little pest?" he rasped. Viktor's face was grubby and rugged, sprouting a pier styled moustache that accompanied his cropped black hair.

As the play continued through its first act, Viktor and his son Sebastian walked past several prop assistants and workers along the backstage hallway. The man pushed staff members to the wall and slapped a few on the head with his hat for blocking the way.

Charging through one of the dressing rooms, the

large man threw the skinny boy into a couple of barrels that were rusting in the dampness of the corner. "I've told you time and time again, boy, to oil that blasted curtain lever," Viktor yelled, loosening a horsewhip prop from his side belt.

Raising the horsewhip high above his shoulder, the despicable man was about to strike his son across his back when an old coarse voice ordered him to stop.

"You do realize we have the company of the Mayor after the show, Viktor. What would he say about us if he were to see our son all black and blue?" she asked, after taking a long drag from her cigarette holder. Smoke surrounded the wrinkly and bony woman like a veil.

"My grand opening was almost ruined because of this incompetent little weakling, Greta," snarled Viktor, spluttering from the stale smoke that irritated his nostrils.

"Punish him later, we have enough work to do and more money to make tonight."

Viktor grunted at his acquisitive wife who kept puffing at her cigarette holder by the doorway. The woman wore heavy makeup and a lot of expensive jewelry on top of a feathered animal skin coat that covered her tall body in an attempt to disguise how unattractive she really was.

Giving another grunt, Viktor stormed out of the dressing room. Sebastian turned to his mother, hoping for some sign of empathy.

"Don't look at me like that. You're in enough trouble, Sebastian," Greta snapped after inhaling another mouthful of smoke. Gripping his chin between her bony fingers, she pulled his head up from staring at the ground.

"Look at me! I don't need you ruining your Father's

big night," she said scornfully.

Sebastian concurred, hoping his cruel mother would leave him alone in the dressing room without any further scolding.

"Clean this mess up and then wait for me until after the show," she instructed as her smoke trail followed her out the doorway.

***

Sounds of huge applause filled the theater several hours later at the massive crescendo of a heroic soldier boy defeating an evil king and liberating all the creatures from the king's wicked spells.

Viktor and Greta had not expected such a positive and successful response. Photographers gathered around both theater directors to take pictures of the actors and stage crew.

Sebastian stood behind the scenes and watched miserably at his cruel parents taking the credit and adulation for his play. As they soaked up the attention, posing for the press and boasting to their admirers, Sebastian picked up his broom and duster and faded into the background, pushing through the stage curtains.

The congested air cleared up, as did the crowds, until the grand theater was nothing more than rows of empty seats again. Their new stage hit had sent Viktor and Greta into a celebratory mood, which relieved Sebastian, for his punishment had been forgotten.

After a loud pop, Viktor showered his actors and crew with fresh bubbly champagne, followed by a victorious toast to a job well done.

"Here's to theater, and to us, the real showmen... and women, of course," he said, adding a glorious "Hear, hear."

They all drank and laughed in celebration of their success while Sebastian watched angrily from behind the stage curtain. Viktor went on to make another boastful toast when it was abruptly interrupted by loud bangs on the theater's side doors.

"What in blazes is that racket?" Viktor yelled, in love with the sound of his own voice. "Where's the boy?" he snapped at Greta, who showed no sign of being in any way intimidated by the Russian's threatening demeanor.

"Where he should be," she replied casually, lighting herself another cigarette.

Hearing his name called just the once, the obedient prop boy arrived at his father's side in seconds.

"Get the door," Viktor ordered in the softest tone Sebastian had heard his father speak.

The scruffy weakling pushed the large rusted bars down to unlock the double iron doors at the side of the theater. The left door was pulled open hard from the other side, almost tripping Sebastian to the ground. A dark figure loomed over him, casting the boy in his shadow.

"I say, what the devil is going on here?" roared Viktor.

Gazing up at the dark-eyed man, Sebastian appreciated the strong sound of his father's voice more than ever before.

"Away from me, brat," Mr. Jennings snapped, motioning with his gloves for Sebastian to get out of his way.

Sebastian followed the blunt order of the elderly stranger and hurriedly took a step to the side, behind a row of theater seats.

Mr. Jennings and Mr. Porter arrived accompanied by several police officers, including a mysterious Inspector who entered the theater's side door at the same time.

Viktor was clearly outraged at the sudden intrusion on his celebration. "Who in blazes do you think you are? I demand an explanation for this unlawful trespassing," he rambled, carrying his weight toward the wide-eyed principal and the Inspector who stood side by side.

"Quiet, Mr. Cain. We are not intending to cause you or your family any problems," replied the Inspector, raising a glove covered hand to silence Viktor's ranting.

"Not yet anyway," Mr. Jennings threatened.

"We are investigating several runaways belonging to this gentleman," the Inspector said. Clicking his fingers, the Inspector ordered a constable to stand behind him, ready to take handwritten notes.

"What makes you think I know anything about missing runaways?" Viktor sniggered, puffing at his lit cigar and crudely blowing smoke rings in the Inspector's face.

The Inspector smiled, taking off his spectacles to wipe them clean. "Because you recruit them, Mr. Cain. They are your actors, your cleaners and your workers. We have turned a blind eye to your cheap labor for far too long," the Inspector explained, stepping closer to the large man.

"Surely a man of your copious wealth and status wouldn't want to have an unexpected visit from the taxman, let alone the press. You know how reporters are, always itching for a scandal," the Inspector teased.

"What do you want from me?" Viktor replied, unable to take his eyes off of Mr. Jennings' glare.

"Just some simple co-operation. These runaways managed to slip past my men...*twice,*" the Inspector informed, slowly walking back and forth to gaze upon the grandness of the theater's interior. "They're of great importance to this gentleman."

"And this is?" Viktor sighed.

"Mr. Jennings, he runs the borstal home for boys at Gatesville," the Inspector replied, fixing the wire-rimmed legs of his spectacles around his ears.

This time, a large smoke ring fell across Mr. Jennings' face, from Greta, who walked slowly over to her husband's side to involve herself in the conversation.

"Tell me...what is so special about a bunch of runaway strays, Mr. Jennings?" asked Greta, raising her cigarette holder up to her lips once more, her eyes filled with morbid curiosity. "Surely this isn't the first time a child has escaped that prison you call an orphanage."

Mr. Jennings' smirk flumped when he fixed his sight upon an equal set of dark cold eyes. "Gatesville is not a prison, Madam," he replied, forcing a smile.

"There must be hundreds, if not thousands, of runaways in this city alone. Why on earth would you expect to find any answers here, Mister...?" asked Viktor impatiently.

"Inspector will do fine."

The Inspector silently passed a piece of neatly folded paper to Mr. Porter who persisted to unfold it at a snail's pace and then held it in front of his own face for the Cains to see. It was a carefully sketched map of routes from Gatesville to London's city center and beyond, which included three distinctly marked destinations. One of the locations marked with the 'X' mark had the name 'Gatesville' written beside it. The other was a particular area in the north countryside that bore the name 'Jacob' beside the mark. In between the two marked areas was the biggest 'X' of all three and outlined by a circle around the name 'Viktor' written over the Royal Opera House.

"My men found this in the coat pocket of one of the runaways when they caught him at the central train station, half a mile from here," the Inspector uttered. "Do you have any idea why *your* name would be marked on this map, Mr. Cain?"

Viktor snatched the map and held it up to the stage light so he and Greta could get a clearer look. "Of course I don't," he sneered, tossing the piece of paper back at Mr. Porter.

"It looks to me your runaways are headed to the countryside, Mr. Jennings," added Greta.

Victor began to nervously titter under his breath.

"Be quiet, you great oaf," Mr. Jennings snapped as he took one step closer to the stubborn entrepreneur. "Make no mistake, they're coming here for a reason, and we're going to be here to catch them this time."

Greta ordered the rest of the cast and crew to leave the auditorium, including Sebastian, while the policemen searched the theater. Sebastian kept his head down passing his parents, but then looked around himself when he reached the safety of the stage curtains. Sebastian always liked to look at the grand architecture of the auditorium before going to bed, especially as this was the newest theater on this side of London that his parents had recently purchased.

The Cain family never stayed in one place for too long. But Sebastian was rather fond of this building in particular. It didn't seem cold like his previous residencies. The building's interior design and the artwork on its ceilings were often the last things Sebastian gazed upon every night.

But something suddenly appeared out of place this time. Something lurked in one of the top balconies. The troubling sight caught Sebastian so off guard that it demanded a second glance. An odd face lit up and peered out of the front row of the right balcony. It was the face of a boy his age. The face suddenly faded into the shadowy background as quickly as it had appeared.

Sebastian had a creepy feeling that someone had been watching that evening's events unfold.

11

New Friends of Warwickshire

A wake! Finally awake.

"Where am I?" Benjamin whispered to himself. The muffled sounds vibrating along the thin walls had stirred him from his deep slumber. A chesty cough echoed through the hall ahead of him. Maybe he had coughed without realizing it.

He pondered for a while, rubbing his burning eyes to rid himself of blurred vision. Another husky cough came from the hall, louder this time.

Benjamin sat up on the hardened suede sofa and felt the room begin to spin. Aches and pains ran across his winter-beaten body. He must have been asleep a long while for he was fully dry, and his wet coat and damp shoes were nowhere to be found.

He stood up in an attempt to shake his dizziness off. The warmth of the prickly carpet tips brushing through his toes contributed discomfort to his soaring temperature.

Still dazed and confused, Benjamin slowly gravitated toward the sounds along the hall.

The hallway looked warm and cosy with a varnished wooden ceiling overhead. Peach wallpaper with patterns of gilded flowers covered the walls around him. It was obvious that a person of great wealth and taste lived here.

When Benjamin drew nearer to the coughing noise, he thought of Peter and Tommy.

Following the strange rabbit hunter across the cold countryside was the last thing he could remember. Or did he follow a kidnapper? Was the rabbit hunter the owner of that coarse smoker's cough? *There's only one way to find out,* Benjamin thought.

Bravely, the sick boy walked along the last stretch of hallway, nearing a small dip in front of him. Three carpet-covered steps led to a short landing that joined another three identical steps leading upward toward a door, slightly ajar. A beam of light shone through the gap in the doorway and widened as the door began to creak open.

The rabbit hunter stepped into the smaller landing below, blocking the glow from the doorway that silhouetted him. He looked up at the terrified boy standing three steps above him, then walked closer to reveal his face half covered in the shade. His face was round and colorful and welcoming in the clear light, which made Benjamin feel less afraid of him.

"How are you feeling, son?" O'Malley asked in a deep voice as coarse as his cough.

Benjamin noticed the man's large red scar along his right cheek again, but this time he could see it in all of its grotesque detail. The scar started on the side of his forehead and ran all the way down his cheek and ended next to his chin. It was a very severe and wide scar, which was unfitting on such a handsome and kind face.

"I-I feel sick," Benjamin muttered honestly. O'Malley immediately turned and opened the door behind him fully to reveal a brightly lit kitchen.

"Well then," replied O'Malley, "you'd best come in and have some food."

Benjamin slowly took a step down until he peered behind O'Malley's shoulder and saw Tommy Joel. Tommy sat comfortably at the large oak table in the kitchen, sipping steaming tomato soup from a big bowl. An older boy sat near Tommy, shoving big chunks of bread into his mouth using one hand.

"He's like a pig," Benjamin accidentally said aloud.

O'Malley chuckled. "Please, have a seat," he said, attending to a small burning pot under a stone fireplace. "You boys are a long way from home, huh?"

"Oh, we don't have—." Benjamin began to speak when he was interrupted by a clout across his scalp by Tommy.

"Yes...you could say that, we're here to visit a relative...of sorts," Tommy tittered nervously as he forced a smile at O'Malley.

"I can't remember how I got here?" asked Benjamin curiously, keeping a suspicious eye on the rabbit hunter.

"You fainted due to the cold. You both did," muttered O'Malley, pouring thick, steaming tomato soup from the boiling pot into a spare bowl.

The kitchen was even richer than the hallway and a lot cosier. Dried flowers and herbs hung from the wooden ceiling. A small fireplace built into the wall warmed the room. A black teapot hung directly over the glowing coal and slowly began to boil and whistle.

"Mind your plate, son. It's rather hot," O'Malley warned, setting the steaming bowl of soup in front of Benjamin. He then rushed to lift the whistling pot of tea away from the fire.

"Thanks for the, you know, shelter and everything," Benjamin mumbled awkwardly.

"You mean for saving your life? You're welcome. You boys would've frozen out there if I hadn't found you."

"Well, we don't want to take up any more of your time, Sir," Tommy added, motioning to Benjamin to eat quickly.

Benjamin tried one full mouthful of soup, which was so hot that he spat it out.

"Look who's eating like a pig now," Tommy teased.

Shaking his head at Benjamin, the rabbit hunter gave a long sigh. "I told you the soup was hot."

"We need to get moving, Brannon. I've checked the map, this Jacob fellow can't be far from here," Tommy whispered, unaware that the older boy was eavesdropping beside them. "And I don't trust this guy."

"Eat up, son, you need to keep up your strength," O'Malley interrupted as he took to his seat at the end of the table. After O'Malley sipped his cup of tea he put on his reading glasses then rustled through pages of a recent newspaper. Benjamin noticed the front-page headlines:

"TITANIC INQUIRY:
HUNDREDS PERISHED."

"That's a big ship," Benjamin slurred with a mouthful of bread.

O'Malley slowly peeked from behind the newspaper, revealing only his eyes and the tip of his scar.

"She was," he sighed.

Benjamin was about to finish his last spoonful of soup the second he noticed the stamp mark on the front of the newspaper.

His eyes widened as he read the name *Jacob O'Malley*.

"Jacob?" Benjamin gasped the same time Tommy did.

"I was wondering how long it would take for you both to notice that," Jacob said softly, lowering the newspaper.

"*You?* You're Peter's friend?" Tommy asked, crumpling the map in his hands before Jacob motioned to take it from him.

"Forgive me, young Masters. I was supposed to meet with you when you arrived at Warwickshire Station. I've been travelling to that platform every day for over a month just to make sure I wouldn't miss your arrival. My carriage was frozen the evening you both arrived...so I went by foot," he continued. "I was expecting three of you."

"Peter stayed behind," Tommy said, handing Jacob the crumpled map.

Jacob gently unfolded the map on top of his newspaper.

"Peter is not the third. He was supposed to bring *three* of you here, for safety."

"We lost George at the train station," Tommy explained anxiously.

"Is George the boy from the theater?" Jacob asked intently, pointing to the Royal Opera House on the map.

Tommy and Benjamin looked bemused to one another and hesitantly shook their heads. "Theater?" asked Tommy.

"George was from the orphanage too I'm guessing, right?" Jacob asked patiently. "Never mind."

Benjamin and Tommy quickly shrugged their shoulders at one another.

"A boy who was brought into great wealth will complete The Three That Are One," Jacob whispered, returning a glance to the older boy across the table. Jacob didn't need to say anything; Benjamin and Tommy realized that the older boy knew exactly what the rabbit hunter was talking about.

"Three what?" Tommy demanded.

"You'll know...in time," Jacob replied, leaning back on his chair.

"So, does this mean we can stay here?" Benjamin asked.

"If you work, yes. I am in need of extra hands to run this farm. You can start tonight by helping Luther chop logs for the fire. As long as you work, you can stay." Yawning, Jacob lifted the newspaper and unfolded it in front of his face again, blocking his eager houseguests who looked to him for more answers.

"What about Peter?" Benjamin asked suspiciously.

"He'll be back," Jacob said confidently. "First thing is first, Masters; we need to get your living arrangements sorted. Benjamin's the smallest, so he can take the attic space. Don't worry boys, Peter will return."

***

When evening drew to a close, Jacob sat among the boys inside the large living room and lit a fire. Benjamin got to know all about Jacob and the massive farm he owned. He learned a lot about the older boy named Luther too. Years ago, Jacob discovered the frail and frightened boy sleeping beside his animals to keep warm. Luther was a mute since the day Jacob met him and welcomed him into his home. No one knew where he came from or how he had found Jacob...apart from Jacob.

When O'Malley's family died, they had left him all their wealth, including the farmland his father and grandfather had in their family for generations. Once his family passed away, Jacob took care of Luther and had him work on the farm in return for food and shelter.

Without much persuasion, Jacob told Benjamin and Tommy more about life on the farm.

In return, the boys shared their stories of Gatesville and, of course, the horrible and frightening Mr. Jennings.

After they had settled down near the toasty fire, loud neighing resounded through an open window in the hallway.

"What on earth was that?" Benjamin demanded while cautiously shifting closer to the fireplace.

"There are some scarves and long jackets on the hanger in the hall. Get your shoes on. I want to show you something," Jacob said quietly.

Handing the keys to Jacob while the man re-lit his portable lamp, Luther opened the main door to the farmhouse.

Outside, the massive top door of one stable had been blown open by the brisk winds of the harsh winter's night. Benjamin felt nervous once he heard the loud distressing neighing of a young steed up close. Jacob chuckled at Benjamin's fearful reaction and, with a reassuring hand, patted the boy on his shoulder.

"It's okay Benjamin...she won't hurt you," assured Jacob as he unlocked the bottom hatch of the stable door. "See for yourself."

Benjamin clapped his eyes upon the most sorrowful sight lying in the corner of the stable after Jacob's lamp reflected off the fresh, golden stacks of hay.

Other horses peered down at her from their stable dividers. Her deep auburn color was instantaneously eye-catching, along with her thick lengthy tail and heavy white hooves. Her beautiful eyes were full of fear that gripped Benjamin with compassion. Neighing louder in fright, the young horse tried to stand upon her feet to no avail. Stumbling down on the haystacks, the poor beast breathed heavily from exhaustion.

"Not so fast," Jacob whispered, reaching a hand out to slow Benjamin down, who was by her side in seconds. Soaking the moment in, Benjamin gently lifted his right hand to stroke her matted mane of hair.

"What's wrong with her?" Tommy asked curiously.

"She's caught a bad fever this winter...it hasn't shifted. It started a few weeks ago and just recently she's lost her appetite."

Jacob sighed, pausing for a moment to stare back down into the horse's glazed eyes. "But given the right amount of attention and care...I'd say she'll be right as rain," he added assuredly. "Any of you lads up for the job?"

It only took a second until Benjamin spoke up fervently. "I am."

"I thought as much," Jacob said, showing a proud

smile. "What do you think of her?"

"She's the greatest thing I've ever seen," Benjamin gasped, revealing a huge smile of joy he could no longer contain. "What does she need?"

"A friend," Jacob said finally.

"What's her name?" Tommy asked.

"I haven't gotten round to naming her yet. Maybe Benjamin could give her a name, since he's her caretaker now," Jacob smiled.

"Alright," Benjamin said happily.

"Good, you can start tomorrow. She needs company...and could do with a good groom. Who knows, maybe a little bit of extra attention is all she needs to get her appetite back."

Jacob and Tommy made their way toward the entrance of the stable door while Benjamin rested his head gently on the horse's body to hear her large heart beat.

"I'll get you on your feet again girl...I promise," Benjamin whispered.

The horse turned her head round to look at him face to face as if thanking him. Jacob dimmed the lamp.

"Time to show you how to lock these stable doors properly then, Benjamin," Jacob said.

***

Winter passed into a glorious spring. Benjamin assisted Jacob and taught Tommy how to read the great works of William Shakespeare and Oliver Cromwell by day. In the evenings, after working on the farm digging crops and planting seeds, Jacob would take the three boys horse riding to explore the countryside.

That was one of Benjamin's favorite activities. He took charge of cleaning the stables and tended to the horses, which gave Luther a break from his everyday duties. Horses rapidly became Benjamin's beloved type of animal, especially his very own horse he named Poppy after she had recovered in time for the poppy season. Jacob gave Poppy to Benjamin as a reward for the months of care and hard grafting he'd put into helping her and for the great job he did fixing up the stables.

Benjamin mostly helped Luther with indoor work while Tommy assisted Jacob in the open fields.

Jacob often taught the boys the old English sport of cricket, but Tommy's much-loved day was always a Saturday, for this was soccer day. With a group of only four, the games would last all afternoon, sometimes having to exclude goalkeepers so they could split into proper teams of two. Once summer had approached, activities such as fishing, hiking and camping were introduced to the boys for the first time.

They didn't want it to end, especially every time the thought of capture by Mr. Jennings crossed their worried minds.

12

The Disappearing Act

After Sebastian's methodical nightly search of the opera house balcony, he went back to bed. For months he had routinely checked the same spot where he had first seen the ghostly face of the white haired boy. But now Sebastian was beginning to believe he had imagined the whole thing. His eyes felt heavy once he moved his worn fingers over the golden embroidery on the maroon blanket he'd had since he was a baby. Before he could put the cloth back in his pocket he slipped into a deep sleep.

It didn't take long for Sebastian to dream. He quickly found himself standing on a luxuriously warm carpet upon a marble balcony. Judging from the height of the marble balcony and the architecture decorated with gargoyles before him, he was on the top level of some enormous castle. The timid whistling of soft wind was soon drowned out by an arrival of several screeching monsters that flew onto the balcony a few meters ahead of him.

Sebastian tried to back away the moment he saw the leader of the pack adorned in a tall white cloak. As the white hooded figure approached him through the gathering of monsters, a steel hand suddenly grabbed at Sebastian's neck from behind him. The touch was ice cold and began pushing him toward the monsters. Sebastian then saw two unfamiliar boys his age being forced to kneel in front of the hooded figure, whose face was concealed by a bronze mask.

In a split second, Sebastian witnessed the white-cloaked man strike at the necks of the two boys from a mighty and large needle-like sword. The two victims reached toward Sebastian for help until their bodies abruptly turned to burnt charcoal. Sebastian was forced to stand in front of the boys as their faces disintegrated into ash.

At that moment, the white-cloaked villain appeared through the ashy residue of the dead children, raising his deathly sword high over his shoulders as he prepared to strike Sebastian down.

"Sebastian!"

Greta's voice pierced through his little eardrums and echoed through the grounds of his nightmare. Fumbling out of his springy bed as he woke, Sebastian reached the sink in his quarters to splash a few handfuls of cold water over his sweaty face.

"Only a dream. Not real," he whispered to himself, staring at his reflection.

Greta's shrieks sent tension across his shoulders. Preparations for the early summer show remained unfinished, putting the Cain family under pressure. The props department and costume designers had been working night and day for the better part of two months now and the signs of exhaustion were beginning to show.

Viktor was grouchier than ever, intimidating his employees when given the opportunity. Sebastian knew the one thing that made his father even madder than a taunted bull was anyone who caused upset to his wife. And Sebastian was about to do just that.

"Sebastian Cain, you get here this instant!" Greta screeched.

Her relentless requests that afternoon irritated Sebastian as much as they exhausted him. Mop this mess! Clean those windows! Dust these rows! Wash these clothes! Paint these props!

The scrawny woman stood at the entrance to the theater's backstage door, tapping her long fingernails on each side of the doorframe.

"One of the main lights blew out near the top balcony. The props department needs someone small enough to climb up there and fix it," she said casually with a sarcastic smirk, knowing that Sebastian had a phobia of heights.

"B-but I'm supposed to help Father tighten up the loose seats in the auditorium," he pleaded to her. Greta raised one finger to silence him and headed back toward her dressing room, leaving a trail of smoke behind her.

"You heard her, boy," his father bellowed.

The familiar foreign voice always spoke after Greta's chastising. It was like a chain re-action. Viktor had a bad habit of sneaking up behind folk without making the slightest sound. His stealth baffled Sebastian and many of the other workers in the theater as to how such a large and loud person could be as quiet and indiscernible as a house mouse.

"Yes, Sir," Sebastian mumbled. Viktor handed him the new light bulb.

The heavy light proved very awkward for the puny boy to carry. Walking with the equipment was hard enough without having to climb scaffolding in the process. But Sebastian had no choice. It was either conquer his fear of heights on the spot or face a vicious thrashing from Viktor.

The props men and costume designers watched in anticipation. Even the orchestra stopped their rehearsal to look on when Sebastian started to climb. The conductor's jaw dropped in shock after he gazed up from his rehearsed notes.

The unstable scaffolding swerved a few inches back and forth. At one point, it swerved so far to one side it looked ready to topple. Carrying the ceiling bulb over his shoulder, Sebastian clung on tightly to the last bar above him. One last pull helped him reach the top.

But the weight of the bulb wires proved too heavy, dragging him backward until his body tilted over the side of the scaffolding. He flapped out his arms in all directions, trying to grab a hold of anything. The floor staff gasped in horror at the sight of Sebastian's near fall.

Viktor swiftly cried out for somebody to get his son away from the ceiling lights. Greta stood helplessly in shock.

No matter what Sebastian tried, he couldn't balance himself, until something caught hold of his arm just when he was about to fall. Sebastian looked down and yelped when he saw how high he dangled from the theater floor.

"Take hold," said the voice above his head. Sebastian instantly glanced above him to see the face he'd recognized before. It was the phantom of his parent's opera house.

"*You!*" Sebastian exclaimed, tightening his own grasp onto his rescuer's hand that lifted him up through a lighting hole in the ceiling.

Sebastian's disappearance from the scaffolding had attracted the attention of the entire staff of the opera house that crowded around the stage set to get a closer look.

"He's gone!" gasped a fellow worker, pointing to the ceiling above them.

"Where did he go?" asked another.

"Shut up, the lot of you!" Viktor shouted over the auditorium. He randomly led a lanky worker by the ear to the bottom of the scaffolding. "Get up there and see what's going on."

The worker was a bundle of nerves when he put one foot in front of the other at the base of the rusted metal joints. Viktor's chastising didn't seem to change the worker's velocity either, until he shook the scaffolding with his boot.

"Come on you monkey, climb. Faster! Faster!"

The panicky worker tried to hang on but the added pressure of Viktor's taunting caused him to lose his balance. At the same time the worker fell toward the ground, a man stepped next to the scaffolding from the theater's side entrance doors. To Viktor's horror, a stunned and furious Mr. Jennings broke the fall of the boy.

"Get this scrapper off of me," Mr. Jennings yelled, too weak and helpless to help himself. "If I had a penny for every time—."

"Just what is going on here then?" asked a familiar voice half hidden by the gloom of the stage corner.

Viktor kicked the lanky worker off Mr. Jennings, offering a helping hand to the old man. Lifting Mr. Jennings to his feet, Viktor almost jumped out of his skin when he noticed the Inspector emerge from the shadows.

"Well?" the Inspector continued.

Viktor couldn't think of a word to say in response to the Inspector's question, until another ceiling light blew out, followed by the entire row. Each light blew after the other from the far right of the ceiling to the left.

The Inspector smiled with a victorious sparkle in his beady eyes. "Care to *shine* some *light* on the situation, Mr. Cain?"

Viktor was unable to contain his temper. "Sebastian!" he screamed at the top of the auditorium. His booming voice travelled through the holes in the ceiling and strangled Sebastian's eardrums.

Sebastian crawled behind his new rescuer and watched his parents from inside the dome shaped ceiling.

"Something fishy is going on here," Mr. Jennings said with a scowl, pointing his bony finger in Viktor's face.

Sebastian looked on as the Inspector kept his calm, walking over to the scaffolding while studying the ceiling above. He thought for certain the Inspector had spotted them hiding behind the dome ceiling somehow, even though it would have been impossible.

"What is that peculiar noise?" the Inspector asked.

The reflective stage-lights below pierced through the ceiling's holes. Sebastian's eyes adjusted inside the dimness when his rescuer signalled at him to halt and not a moment too soon.

"What is it now?" asked Viktor, stepping closer to the Inspector. "I have a show to put together in less than an hour."

"Whom, may I ask, are you calling to, Mr. Cain?" asked the Inspector, in a suspicious tone.

"My son," Viktor snapped impatiently.

The Inspector slowly took off his spectacles and revealed a wide-eyed stare that chilled Viktor and Greta to the bone.

"You have a son? You never mentioned having a child of your own, Mr. Cain. How old is he?"

The man's questions came rapidly, unnerving the theater owner in front of his wife and staff, as well as the boys hiding above them.

"Our boy has nothing to do with your runaways, Inspector," Greta interrupted, nervously fiddling a match between her fingers until she successfully struck it and lit her cigarette.

The Inspector sneered and tilted his head to look back up at the ceiling. "Oh, I wouldn't be so sure about that," he smiled. "This boy of yours Mr. Cain...he is, in fact, yours?" he continued, staring back at both guardians. His eyes were scrutinising. The frightened couple swiftly looked to one another for a reasonable answer.

"My s-show—." Viktor stammered, noticeably changing the subject.

"Are you hard of hearing, Inspector? We have a show to put on here, so if you don't mind discussing this at a more convenient time," Greta scolded, clearly startled by the Inspector's probing manner.

"Well, it's just as well I purchased my ticket," the Inspector whispered, raising his hand to show the Cains a single ticket he held between two fingers. "I'm looking forward to the show. I reserved a balcony seat."

Sebastian kept perfectly still as he watched Mr. Jennings and the Inspector leave with the policemen. "You must follow me, Sebastian," the boy whispered back in a very faint tone.

"How do you know my—," Sebastian began, but he didn't have time to finish his question, for his rescuer was already at the other side of the inner dome ceiling. More calls echoed up to him from the stage floor as both boys slid a few feet down a steep horizontal drop, exiting the ceiling and entering the opera house's overly-large constructed loft space.

"I'm not going any further until you tell me who you are," Sebastian insisted, trying to balance himself on the bouncy insulation on the attic floor.

"You can call me Peter."

"You were here before, weren't you? I recognize your face. You hid at the top balcony when that Inspector visited here a few months ago," Sebastian said.

"He is a very dangerous and evil man. We need to leave," Peter said bluntly.

"Why?"

"If he finds out who you really are, he will spare no thought of killing you."

Peter's words sent an instant tingle up Sebastian's spine.

"Why would a policeman want to do that?"

"Because he isn't a policeman. We have to travel to meet an old friend of mine. We have to make it up to Warwickshire, so please, get a move on," pleaded Peter.

"Warwickshire?" asked Sebastian, standing still in disbelief. "You're one of those runaways they've been looking for, aren't you? You're one of the Gatesville boys." Sebastian stepped away from Peter in shock and awe.

"Don't be alarmed, I'm not going to harm you,"

Peter whispered. "I've come to help."

"I don't need any help. I don't even know you," Sebastian said.

"Just listen for a moment. There are others like you."

"Like me?"

"They're orphans too, only they're more than that," Peter insisted.

"I-I don't understand," Sebastian stuttered.

"Your parents are not your real parents, Sebastian," Peter said honestly.

"I know...they already told me a few years ago, so what does it matter?"

"When you were born, you were left outside one of their opera houses so that you would be taken into their care and looked after," Peter explained.

"You're not telling me something I don't already know," Sebastian said...until he realized something important.

"Wait a minute here...but how...how do *you* know all this?" he asked, staring curiously at Peter's honest eyes.

"Because I was there from the beginning," Peter said, showing the boy a piece of maroon cloth adorned with the same two-headed snake symbol Sebastian had been wrapped in when he was born. Sebastian's eyes lit up the moment he saw the golden pattern. "You've seen this before in your dreams, haven't you?" Peter asked confidently.

"Not in my dreams," Sebastian whispered in shock as he lifted out his own ragged cloth he'd always kept inside his pocket. "What is it?"

"It is the symbol of my King and his kingdom. I'm a soldier of that kingdom. That is why you have one just like it. You were covered in it when you were born…by your real Father."

"This can't be," Sebastian gasped. "You're just a boy yourself."

"Only to you. You're part of something much bigger than what this life has to offer."

"Part of what?"

"A Brotherhood."

"Wait…what?" Sebastian asked. He theatrically struck a pose of confusion that made Peter smile.

"The Brotherhood of Warlocks. Mighty sorcerers. There are two more like you, with gifts similar to yours. They were banished from their home when they were born, as were you," Peter explained.

"The boys from my dreams," Sebastian whispered to himself.

"Yes. They're real. I'm the one responsible for planning their getaway from Gatesville," Peter admitted before Sebastian pointed a warning finger at him.

"You stay away from me."

"I was sent here to bring you back too, Sebastian," Peter said. "You have to believe me."

"Back where?"

"Back home…to Abasin. The world you've seen in your dreams. It's real. I can show you I'm telling the truth. Please come with me," Peter implored with conviction.

"What good are dreams? They mean nothing. What have dreams ever done for me? Viktor and Greta just use my ideas I write down, it's all I'm good for," Sebastian said modestly.

Peter sighed. "And they take all of the credit."

Sebastian shot him a look of astonishment. "You

have been spying on me, haven't you?" he asked, shuffling away from the trespassing boy to put several dusty boxes between them.

"I've been protecting you, whether you knew it or not," Peter admitted, chasing the boy around the attic's stash of clutter.

"From who, exactly? Viktor and Greta?" Sebastian asked.

"The man in your dreams. You know who I mean, don't you? The one dressed in white," Peter said softly.

Sebastian stopped dead in his tracks at the mention of the white-cloaked man.

"How do you know about *him?*" Sebastian whispered faintly.

"Because he's not just a nightmare, Sebastian," Peter murmured up close. "He's real too."

"Get lost, or I will turn you in myself."

"Listen to me. Dreams don't haunt you like this unless they are real," replied Peter, peering back into the passageway toward the ceiling.

"And I should just trust everything you've said, right?" Sebastian asked, leaning against several unpacked boxes near the far corner of the attic. "No, it's my imagination, just my stupid imagination."

"If that were true then how could I know these things?" Peter asked challengingly.

"Then tell me, this white-cloaked masked man, who is he?" Sebastian asked hesitantly, his voice shaking.

"He is known to many as *the False One* but to his people he is King Sa—," Peter whispered when he was abruptly silenced.

"Stop! I already know his name. It's mentioned every time I dream. I don't want to hear it again...not if I don't have to."

Sebastian groaned, rubbing his neck to keep himself from shuddering. "So, how do I stop having these visions?"

"Come with me," Peter urged, nodding his head gently as he reached out a hand to the disturbed boy.

"Warwickshire sure is a long way north of here."

"Longer if you don't have a map to get you there," Peter said, unfolding his original copy in front of Sebastian.

"Oh no. The police already have a copy of that map, I saw them with it," Sebastian moaned.

"Then we'll have to be quicker on our feet than they are," Peter replied excitably.

Sebastian crept out from behind the boxes gawking at Peter through his overly large and dusty spectacles. "I'm not sure about this," he said hastily.

"I'm offering you a chance to know the real truth about yourself Sebastian, to know where you really come from, to know who your real parents were. This is your chance to do something great. You'll meet new friends like you and explore your abilities. You can use your gifts to help others and advance the Brotherhood," Peter said honestly. "Or you can stay here and look forward to washing Viktor's laundry, if you're not mopping the toilets for Greta after the show."

Sebastian looked around the cold attic. Staring down at the holes in his rags, he noticed his true poverty compared to his rich foster parents and realised there was nothing keeping him there. Sebastian smiled, a sparkle for adventure filling in his eyes.

"This better be worth it."

"I'm not going to lie to you Sebastian, if you come with me, you'll never be able to come back," Peter warned.

"That's a crying shame. Not even for Christmas?" Sebastian said in a sardonic tone to his bemused guest. "That was a joke, Peter."

"There isn't much time left, Sebastian. The False One has sent assassins. They'll be catching up to us if we linger. I fear they may have already tracked me down."

"Who? The Inspector?" Sebastian gasped, dumbfounded.

"He's one of them, I'm sure of it. I don't know how he got here but I know it's an assassin, even in that clever disguise. He's here for us and I've led him straight to you."

Sebastian took a deep breath again and looked hard at Peter.

"We must go now," Peter warned.

Compared to the usual neediness of Benjamin or the rude childish temperament of Tommy, Sebastian was an island unto himself. The prop boy was different. He had wisdom.

"Then let's leg it," Sebastian insisted, kneeling down to look through a hole in the wall light. "It won't be long now until the crowds pour in."

"But I can hear them already," Peter whispered back. "How will we slip past when it's so busy?"

"We'll have to become a part of the show," Sebastian gloated, scrambling to his feet to search the back of the enormous attic for old props and costumes.

"Go on stage? That sounds too risky. The Inspector will be in the audience," Peter reminded, cautious of the deadly assassin.

"It's the only way," Sebastian said courageously. "The stage will be the last place they'll expect to look."

"Then take this map, in case we lose each other,"

Peter said, calmly handing the boy the map.

"We won't lose each other, and we won't get caught," he smiled, stopping his large crooked spectacles from sliding off his nose with his free hand. "Besides, my encore is long overdue."

"Let's find some costumes then," Peter said encouragingly.

Both tore the large attic apart as quietly as they could in search of the perfect disguise to fit in with the show.

"I hope you don't get stage fright," Sebastian teased, tossing a costume on the floor to Peter.

"Hey, this is some form of beast." Peter stared warily at the grotesque donkey suit that was worn and torn.

"We used it for *A Midsummer Night's Dream* a few months ago, but it's okay because tonight they're doing another Shakespearean play called *Macbeth*."

"Macbeth?" asked Peter, his face undoubtedly honest by his lack of knowledge of the arts. "Well, the important thing is the play has horses in one scene as I recall," Sebastian jittered with excitement in his voice.

Peter lifted the dusty worn out donkey mask by his index finger and sneezed before studying it.

"It's perfect. Let's get ready."

13

Roaring and Curtains

Outside the auditorium an overflowing crowd of judges, politicians, barristers, doctors, and Shakespeare fans waited in line.

"What is taking so long?" one voice yelled amidst a muster of complaints.

A group of workers rapidly climbed to the top of the scaffolding to fix the ceiling lights as fast as their hands would allow them.

Peter and Sebastian could even hear one worker puttering around the inside of the ceiling space.

"Do you see him?" Viktor called up to the workers. His voice was troubled. "What's happened to my lights?" he demanded. "Can you see anything?"

"Of course they can't, you great brute, the lights are still out," Greta chastised, walking up the side steps of the stage. She steadied her cigarette holder to her lips and took a long puff. "We will deal with that indolent brat later; just get the lights working. The bouncers are ready to open the main doors. Hurry up and get that hideous thing out of here," she added, tapping the side of the scaffolding.

"I'm gonna kill him!" Viktor grumbled back to his wife, marching backstage to ensure his workers were performing their jobs properly.

It was hard to tackle the task, for the group had hardly managed to fix the lights until half of them went out again. Viktor was left no choice but to solve the slight setback later and go on with the show without them.

As the boys waited in the large attic space of the opera house, a trembling noise of feet echoed through the airshafts like a stampede of sound. The doors had finally opened.

Sebastian wore an old crumply archer costume covered in tin foil.

"Look at me, I'm Sir Lancelot," Sebastian laughed, swinging a piece of tinfoil and cardboard that had been shaped to resemble a sword. Its visible glue spots made the costume look cheap and shabby.

"What is Lancelot?" Peter asked. Peter's naive expression made him appear more alien to Sebastian than anyone he had ever met.

"You really haven't heard of any of these people, have you?" Sebastian asked, staring widely into the slits of Peter's donkey mask.

"We should go now," Peter replied.

"One moment. I have to make sure," Sebastian pleaded, scrambling toward the crack in the dusty floor to spy on the unsuspecting crowd below them. Audience members kept coming by the dozen to take their seats.

Sebastian spotted the prop boy who had taken over his job, ushering in the guests that evening using a flashlight. A feeling of relief swept over him at the prospect of a new life where he would never have to show some ill-mannered aristocrat to their favorite seat again.

The loud chatter from the crowd created the very advantage they were waiting for.

"Shortcut," Sebastian said, opening an old airshaft that led to Greta's changing rooms backstage. Both climbed into the airshaft dropping feet first down the chute.

A group of extras in the pantomime didn't seem to take notice of Peter and Sebastian's raucous entrance into the changing rooms when they shot out the bottom end of the airshaft and stumbled over each other. One extra gave out a sarcastic laugh at Peter's donkey mask that fell off his head and slid across the floor. Struggling to pick it up, Peter and Sebastian slid on the polished wet floor, appearing almost like a comedic duo act.

Luckily for him, Sebastian's knight helmet remained securely fastened on his head and was large enough to hide his face.

"I want you all behind the curtain, now." Greta belched from behind the changing room door. She was ready to head back out the door when she caught sight of Peter's donkey costume from the corner of her eye. Sebastian's heart almost stopped.

"Well, don't you two look adorable?" she cackled back at the camouflaged fugitives. Each boy awkwardly nodded back to her at the same time. It was obvious that the woman was too drunk to talk to them further. Dropping her keys at the doorway, Greta pulled the door behind her and slammed it shut. Both boys turned their heads slowly to one another and comically shrugged.

Sebastian swiped Greta's keys off the ground. "Now we can lock them in after we sneak out," Sebastian said excitably. "It'll better our chances."

The curtains rolled and the orchestra stirred until it roared wildly. To the audience's delight, the show started off strong. Everyone remained glued to their seats, apart from one member who sat in the upper balcony.

The Inspector's eyes kept searching around the auditorium for any signs of Sebastian. He had ordered his policing staff to search certain back parts and out of bounds areas of the opera house. Preoccupied giving out his orders, the lethal assassin in disguise hadn't checked an unlikely blind spot—the main stage, where Sebastian and Peter joined the rest of the extras in one of the crowded battle scenes. It was the last place anyone would think to look.

But as soon as Peter grabbed Sebastian to make a hasty run for the side exit, an extra unintentionally danced her way in front of his path and accidentally slammed into him. The unforeseen accident caused an immediate domino effect amongst the other extras on stage.

Just when Sebastian thought their situation couldn't get much worse, Peter's unstable donkey mask loosened again and rolled across the stage's edge, landing directly on top of the musical conductor's head, fitting his noggin perfectly. The audience burst into fits of roaring laughter at the unexpected and clumsy catastrophe. Even members of the orchestra laughed behind their instruments at the sudden shambles. Viktor stood at the opposite side of the curtain, cursing and shouting in Russian.

"I think it's time to run," Peter yelled, the moment Viktor came hurdling across the stage after him.

"He hasn't spotted me. I've got the keys to lock them all in. Distract him and I'll sneak out the side entrance," Sebastian said.

Peter nodded and untied the rope that held the large velvet curtains in place. In one fell swoosh the left curtain came crashing down on set pieces, which fell on top of the cast, covering Viktor last. Laughter from the audience gradually changed to loud booing. The sudden disruption of the evening's entertainment caused many in the audience to leave.

The Inspector had been too late to notice Sebastian sneak his way through the gang of extras on stage to the side exit of the auditorium. Just as his hands clamped down upon the large handle of the exit doors, Sebastian spotted his dinner suit stuffed into one of the hangers that sat behind the side of the stage. It was a snappy suit complete with newly polished shoes that he was to wear that night after the show. The Cains would usually show him off to exhibit the illusion of a perfect family to those in high society such as the Mayor of London, the press, and other aristocratic and political figures of Parliament or anyone who attended their after-celebration parties on a regular basis, before putting him to work the moment they were home. *Not this time*, Sebastian thought.

"Not ever again," he whispered aloud to himself.

Folding up his dinner suit around his new shoes that Viktor had purchased for him, Sebastian tucked the light bundle under his arm and headed back toward the exit door.

As soon as he stepped foot outside the side entrance, Mr. Jennings and Mr. Porter stood in front of him, each with a cigar hanging out of their mouth. Two other policemen kept watch for any signs of suspicious activity from the side of the theater, without realizing they had just found it.

Mr. Jennings sputtered out some leftover chewing tobacco onto the wet cobblestones. "That's a really shabby costume. Don't they pay you actors enough to buy something a little bit more believable?"

Mr. Porter hooted when Mr. Jennings added another negative critique.

"For goodness sake, you look like an old dustbin. What cheap toot."

Sebastian simply pointed inside to the stage through the side doors. The two policemen poked their noses through the door, curious about the loud booing and yelling from the audience. The heavy stomping and clapping from the crowd inside was enough to entice Mr. Jennings and Mr. Porter inside for a nosey look.

Once the policemen and orderlies were inside the building, Sebastian promptly pushed the side door shut behind them and locked it with the key he had picked out by touch. Sebastian had grown so accustomed to locking the theater doors and helping out with waste and rubbish that he'd learnt the shape and size of every key. Just by the sense of touch Sebastian could figure out blue prints, doors, locks and keys without giving it a single thought. It was a natural instinct, like magic.

Complaints echoed from the rowdy commoners who had paid for cheap seats at the back of the auditorium. The event had stirred an angry mob, all venting their anger at the cast and crew, but mostly at their larger-than-life Russian host.

Peter had secretly climbed to the top part of the main stage lights to reach the emergency balcony that was used as a fire exit. He was almost at the exit when the Inspector stepped in front of him on the stage rafters.

"Your disguise almost fooled me, traitor," the Inspector growled. "What do you think about mine? How do I look?"

The assassin turned around in its human form like it was admiring itself through a mirror. Peter silently took a few steps back.

"I have felt your eyes on me the whole time," it hissed, disgustingly. "Did I fool you...while you were spying on me?"

"Almost—you need to work on that stench." Peter smiled, holding his own nose.

"So, you're a protector? How pitiful. I can see this rescue isn't as organized as His Majesty predicted. Very good."

The false Inspector sneered at him as it took a step closer upon the rafter. Peter instantly armed himself, taking out his hidden blade from its pouch.

The assassin put its hands over its head, mimicking a surrendering stance. "You want to run little rabbit... so run. *We* will catch up," the false Inspector said, confidently motioning its hand for Peter to leave.

Peter stood his ground, baffled by the villain's gesture and irritated by the noisy crowd's ruckus below. Luckily, the audience's uproar distracted the assassin enough to lean over the rafter and watch the rowing multitude beneath him.

Peter took this opportunity gladly, throwing his dagger-like blade at the assassin as fast as he could. But the weapon proved feeble in its impact, bouncing back off the Inspector's guise and flying steadily back into Peter's open hand.

"Much too eager, little cheater," the false Inspector

teased. "It's never that easy."

Peter leapt off the balcony and slid down the theater's remaining side curtain. Dashing halfway toward the front lobby amidst the crammed crowd, the daring boy squeezed through several journalists and theater goers who had spilled out onto the London streets.

"They're just as powerful here," Peter said out loud to a little flickering of light that had suddenly appeared from under his sweater. The light was as big as a firefly and rapidly circled the boy a few times then disappeared back into his shirt pocket.

Sebastian didn't notice the running boy at first until Peter passed the side of the grand building.

"Peter, we made it," Sebastian called out to the panting boy, holding the keys up high over his head.

Carrying his dinner suit under his other arm, Sebastian led the way through the back alleys and nearby side streets. Running in the middle of the moonlit night, the boys jumped for joy in victory as they crossed the London Bridge.

When they had made their way to the outskirts of the city, Peter told Sebastian of his close encounter and more about who the Inspector was; frightening information that Sebastian felt he was better off not knowing.

"Why did the Inspector let you go?" Sebastian asked.

"It's not me he wants," Peter panted. "He's testing me...to see if the map is a decoy. He mustn't be sure, or they'd have tracked down the others by now. He wants to know where I'll lead him next. Now that he's found you, he'll follow us to find the others."

"Then we shouldn't lead him there, right?"

Sebastian asked, jumping onto the first set of closed train tracks that led out of London.

"We've no choice. Even if we lead the assassin elsewhere, the police have the map, and so does that orderly from Gatesville. We have to get the others out of Warwickshire as soon as we can," insisted Peter, keeping a watchful eye on their surroundings.

The journey to Warwickshire wasn't as fast or easy for them as it had been for Benjamin and Tommy. They frequently sought refuge in different villages, resting in barns and inns where it was safest. The time each dawn approached, they found themselves further away from the city and closer to Jacob O'Malley's farm. In the morning they would wander through different towns, stealing food from the market place and then later sneaking a ride upon the back of gypsy carriages and farmer trolleys, using the giant haystacks for cover and warmth. The pair journeyed through the great hillsides of England until they reached a train station in the country, one where its tracks led directly north.

***

"Is this Warwickshire?" Sebastian asked. The train station attendant looked hard and curious at the haggard boy.

"Near enough. One stop ahead of you, young Sirs."

"Thank you." Sebastian smiled nervously at the gawking attendant and scurried over to Peter on the platform.

"We have to use these tracks. It's the only way we'll be sure to stay on course. I can't afford to get us lost now," Peter spoke faintly, so that the attendant wouldn't hear, but it didn't work.

"You're not supposed to travel on those tracks by foot, lads. It's against the law," the attendant warned, calling back to them. Peter and Sebastian bided their time and sneaked onto the tracks anyway, when the train attendant helped an inquiring elderly lady.

After they had run for almost an hour, Peter and Sebastian inhaled deeply, taking in the beautiful summer scent of the countryside's nature around them. Sebastian's blistered feet needed a rest but he wouldn't show his discomfort.

Peter's eyes dashed in all directions, feeling a presence of something heading their way; assassins, a mob or a singleton, he couldn't tell. All they could do now was hope that their own route was enough of a diversion to make it to Benjamin and Tommy before the Inspector or Mr. Jennings would.

Another hour passed before they approached the platform for Warwickshire where Benjamin and Tommy had arrived six months prior. The moss on the tracks had grown over since then and weeds had sprouted through the cobblestone cracks on the platform. It looked like a neglected pit stop. Not much of a platform existed, for most of it had worn away due to bad weather during the winter. The station even lacked an information booth or post, and it appeared that no train station attendant patrolled the area.

"There's no one here," muttered Sebastian. His voice sounded coarse and groggy, for the air had grown a few degrees cooler now, affecting the boy's stamina.

Peter hopped a few feet up from the track onto the unstable platform. Sebastian took the privacy of the derelict area to his full advantage and used the nearby gentlemen's room.

"What are you doing?" Peter demanded.

"I was keeping this good suit for a special occasion. But now that we've made it here...I'm going to change out of these horrible rags. Besides, I need to change my shoes most of all. My feet are pounding."

The moment Sebastian changed, he appeared as though he could pass for a rich child from Oxford. Peter pointed toward the daunting hill. "My friend has a farm only a few miles beyond that hill."

"You mean we have to climb all the way up there?" Sebastian yawned. His tiredness made him grumpy and unwilling. "You could have told me *before* I changed."

"It's not so tough, I've done it before," Peter said encouragingly, tapping the boy forward.

Sebastian made a puppy-dog look with his big sad eyes behind his massive spectacle frames and said pleadingly, "But these shoes are new."

Onward they climbed for what seemed to be only a few gruelling minutes to the top. To Sebastian's surprise, the fields behind the hill's top proved dry and didn't ruin or stain much of his new attire that he wore proudly. The sumptuous sun-kissed countryside lay before them almost all too opulent to be true. It was a sight Sebastian had only dreamt about when he lived in London's West End. The scenery even astounded Peter for a brief moment, and then his sight caught something in the near distance.

A lustrous light glistened in the far secluded part of the forest opposite them. Sebastian was first to look up, but he wasn't the first to detect the sky. Clouds started to thicken and metamorphose into something that appeared quite unnatural, unnaturally fast. A look of fear crawled over Sebastian's face as they instinctively took off running down the hill and into the open fields.

Peter could still see the radiance of what emerged to be firelight a few miles away from them as he led the way to Jacob's farmhouse. Mr. Jennings and the police had made their own route toward the farmland from the city.

It was now a matter of which group would reach Jacob first.

14

Benjamin's Twelfth Birthday

It was massive! The luxurious dessert was covered in thick white cream that oozed from the sides of it. Rows of chocolate layers separated each part of the light flaky sponge and candy sprinkles decorated the icing on top with rainbow colors. It was indeed Benjamin's first ever birthday cake.

Jacob had cooked all day in the kitchen using fresh eggs from the chicken coop, goat milk, and a spare packet of flour.

The evening was bright. Purple clouds covered the skies and dim orange light from the sunset filtered its way through the tall windows in the living room, shining directly onto the birthday cake. Jacob initiated the birthday ritual by lighting the only candle they had on top of the cake.

And then, right at the moment as Benjamin blew out his only candle, a loud banging came upon Jacob's wooden farmhouse door.

Bang! Bang! BANG!

The sounds of thunderous thumping chilled the boys to the bone. In a few seconds the memories of those Gatesville days came flooding back to Tommy. A rush of blood and adrenaline pumped ceaselessly through Benjamin's heart.

Jacob let out a long sigh, as if the expectation of this visit had come to pass.

"It's all right," he said in his reassuring voice, before he calmly walked down the hallway to open the door and greet whoever was making such a racket. Luther was too busy eating his slice of Benjamin's birthday cake to notice much of what was going on.

Tommy and Benjamin grew anxious about who it could be loitering outside. Was it someone coming to take them back to Gatesville? Was it the horrible Mr. Jennings? Both worried that they might have been tricked as Jacob's calm attitude only fuelled their suspicion.

At the same time Jacob opened the door, another boy dashed through the doorway and into Benjamin's path.

Benjamin braced himself for the head-on collision. Before they knew what had happened, both boys fell to the ground in opposite directions.

"I didn't expect you to be this keen to meet each other." Jacob chuckled loudly, offering both boys a hand.

The frail, thin boy wiped the carpet hairs from his suit. Fixing his thick, crooked spectacles onto his nose again, he took Jacob's offered hand to lift him to his feet. Benjamin took a helping hand from Tommy.

"Watch where you're running, four eyes," Tommy scorned.

"Look who's talking," Sebastian replied, after staring at Tommy's odd set of pupils.

"Someone else is here to see you, boys," Jacob interrupted.

As Jacob slowly took a step aside from the front

doorway a figure stood in front of Tommy, casting a shadow over his already startled face.

"Better late than never," Tommy snapped.

"Tommy Joel and Benjamin Brannon, meet Sebastian Cain," Peter announced.

Without hesitation Benjamin put out his hand to greet Sebastian and was met with the same enthusiasm. Tommy wasn't as friendly to Sebastian, or as willing to make a new friend as Benjamin.

"Boys, *this* is the third person I was talking about," Jacob smiled.

"So, *he* is why you left us on the train," Benjamin muttered to Peter.

A sudden roar of thunder outside interrupted their brief reunion. The sky had darkened and the feeling of an undeniable evil presence quickly swept over the farmland, causing Benjamin to shudder.

"They're coming," Peter gasped.

"Who, Jennings?" Benjamin cried.

"Something much worse," Peter replied.

Tommy sniggered. "What could be worse than that old crab?"

"Jacob, I need the gate key," Peter insisted as Jacob nodded back.

"Benjamin, help me," Jacob called as he led the way into the living room and hurried past the window. With one mighty boot, he kicked open a large oak chest that lay beside the fireplace and took heavy weapons out of it.

"Keep close, can you do that?" Jacob asked anxiously, handing Benjamin some equipment to carry.

"Yes," Benjamin squeaked fearfully.

Tugging Benjamin by the other arm, they ran

back across the living room to the hallway when the window unexpectedly smashed inwardly toward them, accompanied by a huge gust of wind that blew Benjamin's cake into numerous bits.

Benjamin closed his eyes and held onto Jacob, digging his small fingernails into the back of the man's hand in fear for his life.

"Hurry, here they come," Peter called.

"Here, take the gate key and get them home," Jacob said, handing Peter a small pouch of seed and a crystal ball ornament as the group raced out of the doorway.

"They've tracked us down, already?" Sebastian added, terrified at the thought of his guardians appearing at any moment.

"What are you talking about, four eyes?" Tommy retorted, poking Sebastian's shoulder in an attempt to derive answers from him.

Instead of backing down, Sebastian bravely pushed Tommy back a few steps ignoring the sinister storm brewing above them.

Benjamin gave Jacob a look of dread once they heard the animal cries reach the stable fences. The neighing sounds of distress sent Benjamin running toward several stable doors.

"You hear that? It's Poppy! I have to get her," Benjamin cried, dodging Peter and Jacob's grasp for him while he bolted past them.

"No! Benjamin, wait!" Jacob commanded.

In anxious precision, Benjamin shot over the fence the moment several horses came charging out from their stable doors. He tried to grab hold of the reigns of his horse, but Poppy was too fast and too frightened to yield. She continued racing behind her herd and galloped into the dark countryside.

"Poppy!" Benjamin called, cupping his hands in one last attempt to retrieve his friend.

Thunder roared across the entire farmland. The beautiful summer's evening sky had turned as black as coal and brought with it a deathly smell. Tommy thought he was about to faint with nausea. Evil approached.

Sebastian covered his nose while he and Peter fought hard against the forceful winds that blew ruthlessly against them. Luckily, Sebastian was light enough for Peter to help pull into the barnyard. Jacob struggled to carry the heavy equipment on his shoulder while he helped pull Benjamin against the wind and away from the fleeing team of horses.

When Tommy regained his senses, he gazed over at Jacob and Benjamin struggling against the winds and noticed Jacob observing the skies, toward dark clouds that revealed horrible shapes.

Tommy watched the clouds appear to change into shapes more horrifying than mere objects. Leaves and dust kicked up from the ground beneath him. His eyes widened in horror the moment he realized what he had set his sight upon.

15

Meeting with Assassins

Faces! Dark, disfigured, distorted, evil-looking faces stared down from the black heavens. Clouds grinned at Tommy and Jacob. Their mouths twisted and their eyes squinted. In the far distance, deep inside the orifices of the cloud storms, two black figures slowly emerged, as if dispatched from the jaws of hell.

Jacob's feet started to sink into the thick mud. He was stuck.

"Peter, get them out of here," Jacob ordered, directing Peter, Sebastian and Benjamin toward the forests. The howling wind ceased unexpectedly and brought the entire farmland to a silent standstill. It was deathly quiet.

"What about you?" Peter whispered anxiously, watching the sky as he waited for the figures to reveal themselves. "You cannot fight them alone."

"Go!" Jacob shouted.

Peter reluctantly urged both boys to run to the woods. All three sprinted across the field until Benjamin remembered something, someone they had left behind. "Tommy!" he cried, calling Peter back. "I can't leave him."

"It's too dangerous," Peter yelled, hauling them

onwards, past the open field and into the dark forests that lay ahead. "Jacob will look after him."

Two giant creatures suddenly ripped through a hole in the dark sky and landed close by the stables. Jacob had managed to wriggle his legs out of the mud holes in time and made his way toward Tommy, who stood a few feet away, frozen with fear. Jacob shielded the boy from the monsters' sight as they came into view. The nine-foot figures of muscle and steel towered over Jacob.

The dreadful smell grew stronger the closer the monstrous assassins got.

Black steel made their shoulders look three times the size of Jacob's large frame. An armored mask guard covered the lower face of one of the assassins; only the white scars and burnt skin on the upper half of its face were revealed. Black, square pupils in its red goat-shaped eyes gazed piercingly out at Jacob, sending a shiver shooting up Tommy's spine.

The other monstrous assassin looked even more vicious. Its steel mask covered the top part of its face but revealed the lower jaw and mouth. Its skin was pale gray and bore graver scars than its companion. Its long gums and razor-sharp teeth appeared almost as black as the bushy, straw-like hair that puffed over its broad shoulders. Stinging bugs and cockroaches crawled and scattered around its huge black cloak. The cloaked assassin growled and snarled while the heavily armored assassin remained eerily silent. Thuds toward Jacob and Tommy shuddered through the pair. Jacob pulled a large ball and chain weapon from the bag on his left shoulder and held it in his hands.

"Get back to the house. Hide!"

Tommy speedily crept back until he was near the

front door of the house.

A few seconds was all it took for the assassins to tower over Jacob, one glaring down at him and the other smiling. Simultaneously, the assassins took out their long, shining metal weapons, which were too thin in shape to resemble that of any sword. These weapons were distinct otherworldly objects, so thin and razor sharp that they resembled gigantic needles made of fine silver. The heavily armored figure reached back with his other arm and lifted an enormous double bladed axe from a massive holder on his back. The axe alone was almost the same height as Jacob.

Even so, Jacob refused to back down at this terrifying display of dominance and superiority.

"Right this way," Jacob spoke calmly, swinging his own weapon round in circles in the air preparing to strike.

But his attempt to intimidate either assassin didn't work. The cloaked assassin cackled at Jacob's threatening demeanour. A gust of wind picked up again and howled once the two beasts prepared to do battle.

"I will leave you more than a scar this time," growled the heavily armored assassin as the first clash of metals met. The force of the creature's blow was far too powerful for Jacob to withstand, throwing the large man onto his back against the ground a few feet away from them. Jacob struggled in the mud but eventually got up. Moving quickly, the brave man avoided contact with weapons that swiped at him from both directions. Two giants against one man was cowardly and unfair, but the monstrosities didn't seem to intimidate Jacob either, like they had hoped.

After Jacob dodged several swipes, he leapt toward

his heavily armored nemesis to strike, but collided with the side of its gigantic axe. The force of the blow lifted him off his feet and tossed him high into the air. Jacob landed heavily in the mud only a few feet away from Tommy.

Tommy watched breathlessly, hoping for a glimmer of life in his guardian, but Jacob didn't get up this time. He didn't move at all. Tommy stood still outside the large front door. Vulnerable. Alone. He was abandoned now, facing each horrid monster that stomped toward him. Tommy had never felt such trepidation and alarm for his life. This wasn't a case of getting into a lot of trouble with the law or some minor orderlies. This was serious danger; a threat to his very safety.

Another stomping vibration through the earth shook his stance. One more followed after that, until the massive assassins stood in front of him, raising their enormous weapons, ready to strike. But still, Tommy could not move an inch. His mind went blank and his body went stiff through tension and shock. *This is it,* he thought to himself. And with no hope left in him, he shut his eyes tight to rid himself of the horrific vision.

At precisely the same moment the merciless assassins struck at their target, a cold bony hand grabbed Tommy's collar and yanked him back through the doorway. Each weapon bounced off the concrete slab. Tommy was gone. The thick oak door was now closed, locked and bolted. A beastly roar of rage from the two assassins echoed across the stables and farmland. Inside, the house had grown dim. Tommy found himself desperately reaching out into the blackness to grab ahold of anything that would keep his shaking legs from buckling beneath him. How did he escape? And how did he end up inside the house? There was only one explanation...Luther. The mute boy hadn't ventured out of the house since Peter's arrival, and everyone had forgotten him. "Luther?" whispered Tommy, as he nervously tiptoed across the carpet, feeling around the area for a door to cling onto.

Finally, after a few seconds of searching in the dark, Tommy came to a wall of photo frames. He could sense by the texture and imprint of the wallpaper that he was now in the hallway.

"Luther!" he whispered, louder this time, worried that Luther wouldn't be able to hear him and he'd be left alone again. A loud banging at the front door almost made the terrified boy jump out of his skin, but there was still no sign of life within the house. No reply could come from Luther anyway, and Tommy's eyes still had trouble adjusting to the darkness around him.

The second bang was followed by the crackling sound of wood breaking. Shattering through a little more wood at a time, the villains slowly but effectively tore the main doors apart. Tommy felt their desire to reach him. Pure hatred filled the air. He could almost taste their hunger for his blood. They would not stop until they had torn their way through the entire house to get to his fearful, pounding heart.

One small, dim beam of light outside pierced the hallway and made it slightly easier for Tommy to make his way toward several hiding spots. The thought of capture was unbearable. He knew that the hallway had small dipping steps that led straight into the kitchen, but the kitchen itself was already a dead end. *There must be some other way out of here*, he thought, scrambling his brain for an idea that would save him from the jaws of such lethal menaces. Maybe the rooms upstairs could offer a perfect hiding spot.

Luck had it that the lanterns on the upstairs landing remained lit alongside the walls. Benjamin had forgotten to blow them out that evening and this gave Tommy a better chance to find a hiding spot swiftly.

The thud of the intruders' footsteps downstairs made Tommy quiver. Loud noises of swinging doors squeaked through the rooms below him. Feeling faint, Tommy clutched the curtains at the end of the hall to steady himself. He knew if he fainted or froze in fear again, it would cost him his life.

"Time to hide." Tommy ordered himself in a breathy whisper, frantically searching for the perfect spot.

It's just like the games of hide and seek you used to play at the orphanage, Tommy kept reminding himself, trying to rid himself of his dread, for if the seekers found his hiding spot in this game, there would be no chance to play again.

Up the stairs they came; he could hear them breaking a hole through each step with their heavy feet. Tommy knew they drew close for the stench grew stronger.

Do something, hide somewhere, anywhere, just do it and do it fast, he yelled to himself, forcing his solid frame into a small side closet near the end of the hall. The scent of soap-washed towels inside the closet blocked out some of the rotten smell polluting the top floor. Tommy took a massive deep breath and held it for as long as he could. A sturdy thud followed by another vibrated throughout the landing so strongly that it made the rusted hinges on the closet doors rattle.

Cautiously, Tommy peered between the strips of wood in the closet. The heavily armored assassin approached the far end of the landing first, shuffling nearer Tommy's chosen hiding spot. He could hear the creature breathing heavily as it drew back its arm and punched through the bedroom doors opposite his hiding spot.

The assassin growled in frustration as it tore through the doors like paper, one after the other. It suddenly turned around and slowly headed toward the landing to investigate the rattling noise coming from the closet. Shifting on his knees, Tommy hastily receded from the closet doorway until his back met the wall. The armored assassin stood facing him seconds later, quiet and still. Only thin strips of weak and rotted wood rested between them. The black and steaming steel claw slowly reached for the closet door handle.

Tommy had nowhere left to run or hide. He couldn't help but catch the nightmarish figure from the corner of his eye. Up close, it looked like the creature's armor was piping hot. As the assassin grabbed ahold of the rotted wooden handle, it broke off. In frustration, the assassin smashed a massive fist through the weak set of wooden strips, ripping the entire door off of its hinges. Tommy scurried to the right side of the closet so as to be hidden by the remaining door when the armored creature raised its arm to strike again. Just then, noise broke out from downstairs.

Tommy thought it was music at first, and he was half right. The musical notes came from Jacob's old piano that no one, except for Luther, ever used. The constant banging on the piano keys was enough to convince the armored assassin it was wasting its time searching the landing. The simple distraction was all it took for the monsters to leave. Pushing past each other, the creatures stomped downward toward the piano sounds like a crazed herd.

Tommy knew Luther must have made the sounds to distract the assassins. He didn't hesitate to scarper out from the closet wreckage. Grabbing one of the lanterns, he swiftly ran to the window at the end of the hallway. The glass window had a wooden frame that separated each square pane of glass into nine separate sections. Someone a bit older would surely have had the strength to break through it and free him from the brutal beasts. But where was Luther? Was Jacob already dead?

Tommy's heart sank once the musical sounds stopped. Near the top of the staircase, he could hear the clear hastening of Luther as his mute friend scurried from under the dining table to the dining room door, locking it behind him just in time. The assassins fell over the piano and one another in their desperate pursuit to catch the teenager, but they were too slow.

Within seconds, Tommy stood at the top of the landing, waiting for the assassins to sprout into view when, to his delight, Luther rushed to climb up the side of the broken staircase. Tommy felt relieved to see a friendly, non-threatening face at last.

Luther panted and pointed toward the window, motioning Tommy to break through it.

"It's too tough for me to break," Tommy explained, shaking his head.

Luther grabbed a nearby chair at the top of the staircase and directed Tommy to stand aside as he ran toward the window to ram the chair through it. Luther threw the chair hard and accurately at the glass, fracturing through the wooden frames and creating a large gaping hole. He then hurried to the opening and urged Tommy to look outside or to possibly jump;

Tommy didn't know which.

Below, Benjamin's horse Poppy stood, waiting patiently. Tommy smiled with overwhelming joy at the sight of her. She had come back for them, when all the other horses had fled in terror. Throwing a towel over the shards of glass embedded along the outward frame, Luther motioned once more for Tommy to go through the gaping hole while he held tightly to the opposite end. Luther's nod gave Tommy the go-ahead to climb out the window and lower himself down the side of the manor.

BANG!

It didn't take long for the intruders to break through the dining room door. Both assassins charged through the mess they had left of the staircase, whilst shoving one another back onto the upstairs landing. Luther turned to look behind him as he held onto the towel for Tommy. The hallway seemed much longer and darker than before. Wind blew in from the broken window frame, blowing out the fire lanterns along the hall. Only one lantern kept alight. Tommy let go of the rest of the towel once it was safe enough to land. The assassins hissed when Luther lifted the lantern Tommy took off the wall and held it in front of him. His free hand took a small bag of gunpowder from his pocket that he kept on him for hunting rabbits and pheasants with Jacob.

Luther could barely see the assassins in the gloominess of the hallway, but felt their every step creaking closer to him, until their outline was a crystal clear vision of monstrous horror. The brave hero didn't delay and threw the lamp against the two figures, which smashed at their feet, instantly spreading flames beneath them. Flames increased after Luther threw the entire bag of gunpowder into the thick of the blaze.

Below, Tommy had only fallen a few feet, but it was enough to hurt his ankle. The sudden sight of fire had scared Benjamin's young horse away from the house again, leaving him to hobble after her. *Keep running, Tommy,* he told himself. *Do not stop for a single moment.*

The top of the O'Malley manor exploded into a gust of flames, and the roars of the captives inside traveled across the open field. Tommy couldn't help but turn back to see the awful sight of the burning house. He had run so fast that he failed to notice Jacob lying upon the ground as he passed him.

Fear and disbelief froze him to the spot when he caught sight of the two foes at the manor's main doorway, calmly walking into the open, even whilst engulfed in flames. As the assassins casually marched further, the flames evaporated off their armor until they remained as untouched as when they had first arrived. It seemed nothing could harm or destroy them, not even fire. Luther's courageous sacrifice to destroy them had failed.

Tommy stood there now, unaided and without hope. Every second felt longer when he waited for his own inevitable death he prayed would be quick. His legs couldn't carry him anymore. Even now he wished he had kept running instead of turning back to see the fearful sight.

Bored with the deadly game of hide and seek, both assassins marched past the lifeless body of Jacob O'Malley and quickened their pace to close in on their helpless target.

16

Into the Woods

She was beautiful, graceful, and courageous, but above all, she was fast. Poppy galloped past the monsters too quickly for them to catch her and headed directly toward Tommy. The heavily armored assassin grasped at the tip of her long soft tail, only to grapple at air, unable to touch one strand of her fine hair.

Tommy shed tears of joy and showed a huge smile of relief. "I knew you wouldn't leave, girl," he called out to her, laughing as he used his last ounce of energy to climb up onto the saddle on her back. The glossy auburn animal bolted her way into the forests ahead, leaving the stunned and bewildered assassins behind her.

Poppy's hooves showed no sign of slowing down. Tommy was almost asleep when they reached the forest's depth. The monstrous assassins took flight and soared through the night sky, with their ears attentive, following every sound of Poppy's hooves. Tommy shook at the threatening howls of the flying assassins that kept him awake.

Amidst the trees, the forest seemed like another world; one Tommy didn't fear. So long as he was sheltered from sight, and was far from the nightmarish hunters he'd encountered, he would have settled for anywhere, including the dismal Gatesville. Though they had made good distance, he still feared the monsters would soon catch up. Poppy eventually slowed her pace to stop at a small puddle in the heart of the forest. Tommy lightly tapped her back end to get her moving again, but Poppy stood firm, unwilling to move one more inch.

"Please girl," he said quietly, afraid the airborne assassins might hear him.

Every rapid and random sound from the forest unnerved the two survivors. The hooting of an owl startled him enough to climb off the horse and use her as cover. Peering over the saddle into the woods ahead, Tommy tiptoed around to the front of her.

"Stay," he whispered to the horse before he hid behind one of the trees, patiently waiting for any sign of his friends.

The forest was moldy and moist. Lime scale and moss attached itself to his hands after he held onto the sticky bark. Heavy clumps of mud covered his shoes and clothes, making him dirty and miserable.

Now that Poppy was quite happy to rest at this spot and drink at the small pond of water, Tommy had no choice but to wait for her. Perhaps it was for the best, for they had managed to evade their deadly pursuers, and he and the horse both needed to recover their strength.

But their sense of security was short lived. Tommy caught a fleeting glimpse of the hairy assassin's cloak, flying high past the forest's gap. Fortunately for Tommy, the creature had flown too fast to notice Poppy lingering in the center of the opening. Tommy backed further into the thicket.

He thought he was safe where he loitered, until the silence of the forest was abruptly broken by a crackling noise. The snapping of small branches and twigs became clearer with every step. Even Poppy took notice, raising her head from the pond. The clatter was of human footsteps walking in single file around the circular grove where Poppy had made her temporary pit stop.

Much to Tommy's surprise, the horse wasn't the slightest bit alarmed, even though she seemed curious about the phantom noises. He stood firmly behind the large tree, making sure that his whole body was out of sight when he whispered and motioned to the horse to follow him into the shadows.

Ignoring him, Poppy trotted a little bit forward, tilting her long face to sniff through the air at the strong scent she picked up before lifting her tail in greeting to the new arrivals.

Tommy looked on, hidden by the dark shadows of the trees when the two figures walked into the opening. Sebastian was the first to walk into the grove. His hair was tattered by leaves and dust. Splatter marks of wet mud covered the bottom half of his ruined dinner suit, and his sizeable glasses were cracked and bent to one side. Benjamin stepped out of the shade shortly after. His face was covered in dirt patches, and his clothes were creased and shaggy.

As Tommy lurked in the shade, he noticed that the two of them were calling Peter's name, but there was no sign of the boy behind them.

"Look! It's my horse. I wonder what she's doing here?" Benjamin whispered back excitably to Sebastian while they carefully approached the young steed.

Without wanting to risk reentering the uncovered

grove, Tommy crept from tree to tree, camouflaged by the darkness, and kept a close watch on the dangerous skies above. He waited patiently for Benjamin and Sebastian to approach the black path next to the tree he'd lingered behind. Taking one slow step, Tommy snuck onto the pathway, ultimately frightening the bewildered pair. The scare had been unintentional, causing loud screams from Benjamin and Sebastian to boom throughout the woods like a welcoming beacon to their assassins.

"Shut up! Shut up!" Tommy rasped, running toward them. His shadowed figure caused Benjamin and Sebastian to scream for their lives even more. But before he could even reveal himself in the light, Tommy found himself forced to his knees by an eight-inch dagger, lightly stroking his throat. Confused and terrified, he started to wail.

"I surrender, don't kill me!"

Recognizing Tommy's voice, Peter lowered his weapon and offered to help the shocked lad to his feet. Tommy rejected Peter's hand and brushed the leaves and dirt from his knees as he tried to retain what dignity he had left in front of his peers.

"What is wrong with you?" Tommy shouted at Peter, forgetting momentarily about the assassins that scouted above.

"Quiet!" Peter snapped as he kept his gaze fixed toward the night sky.

"How did you esc—." Sebastian started, but was cut off by Tommy's sudden spark of bravado.

"I fought the savage beasts off. No thanks to you three."

"Weren't you afraid?" Sebastian asked suspiciously at Tommy's exaggerated story.

"Me? Afraid?" Tommy laughed nervously. "I stood up to them, unlike you cowards. But two against one isn't fair, so I had to outsmart 'em and that's when good 'ol Pops came in. We outran them together, didn't we, girl?" He petted the shiny horse on the head.

The horse turned her head and walked away from him, as if she could tell Tommy was lying.

"Where are Jacob and Luther?" Benjamin asked worriedly. Tommy finally stopped boasting when he heard Benjamin mention the names of his friends who had risked their lives to save him. For once, Tommy had nothing to say and shook his head.

"We must keep quiet. We're not out of the woods yet," Peter reminded them as he led them deeper along the black path beside Poppy.

"I can clearly see that," Sebastian sighed, stepping over logs and ducking a few branches.

Tommy lagged further behind the group once they found themselves in a spacious part of the forest where an old bridge, covered in moss and fungi, lay a few feet ahead.

"Nearly there," promised Peter. The group quietly crossed over the small bridge, observing the area around them anxiously. The moonlight singled each one of them out like a stage spotlight. Poppy suddenly stalled, refusing to go any further, which unsettled the group further. Benjamin and Tommy were busy studying the railway tracks they'd discovered ahead of them. The tracks revealed an abandoned old northern line to Birmingham, which ran through the forest. Peter took a few steps ahead of them, glancing in the opposite direction.

"What is it?" Benjamin asked.

"We've been followed. Quick! Gather round me.

We will have to do this here," Peter insisted, lifting a handful of what looked like purple seeds from his side pocket.

"Do what, exactly?" Sebastian asked. Then a flickering light caught the corner of his glasses. Sebastian looked behind the group and caught sight of a horse carriage in the distance, followed closely by a line of people who called out the names of the three boys Peter had taken this far. Sebastian's eyes grew almost to the size of the rims on his glasses when the mob's torches drew closer.

"They've found us!" Sebastian cried out to the other three.

"Who are *they?*" asked Tommy, staring at the orangey glow that lit up the black pathway.

"What is that?" Benjamin whispered to Peter, with an anxious gulp as the multiple dark figures came into full view.

17

The Gateway

The boys were astonished when Peter wouldn't run this time. "Leg it!" Tommy instructed Benjamin and Sebastian, ignoring Peter's motion to stay put.

Bolting in several directions, each boy left Peter to stand alone on the bridge holding Poppy. Benjamin picked a thick dark tree to hide behind. Tommy crawled inside a fallen log furthest from the bridge.

Choosing the quickest option and most subtle hiding spot, Sebastian crawled under the bridge itself.

"Spread out, we'll have a better chance at finding them if they are in here," echoed a policeman. A mob member accidentally dropped their torch down the side of the bridge, causing Sebastian to flinch when it landed inches away from him.

Sebastian stayed well hidden under the bridge and watched a group of men with their torches separate across the woodland like human fireflies.

Tommy could feel his beating heart pulse through his arms as he lay flat on his stomach inside the damp and smelly log. He could only see the soil of the ground through the hole he had climbed in from. He felt the movements of creepy crawlies inside the log the moment several men treaded over it.

Tommy remained like a statue until the sound of feet faded. His relief was brief. Sudden vibrations trembled beneath his body. Tommy knew the sounds that drew near were of a lonesome soul. Not human. Each footstep haunted him. Then, silence.

Out of the blue, the assassin's massive foot slammed down a few inches from his face, directly in front of the hole in the log. They had landed. Tommy covered his mouth to keep himself from breathing too loudly the instant he saw it. The reptilian foot had razor-sharp nails protruding out of each toe, like an eagle. Its nails were almost the size of Tommy's hands and its massive flat foot was bigger than his head and strong enough to crush it.

After a few seconds of lingering and sniffing out the residue of torch smoke around it, the sharp-toothed assassin took flight. Tommy was frozen stiff and wouldn't have been able to move a muscle if it were not for the hand that punched through the bark to grab at his neck.

Several policemen brushed past Benjamin, carelessly overlooking the cowering child that switched trees. He'd caught a glimpse of a lonesome figure that lagged behind, cursing and mumbling to himself in a breathless state. Benjamin couldn't help but wheeze after his eyes caught a sneak glimpse of Mr. Jennings' feet positioned directly behind the tree that covered him.

Without hesitating, Benjamin made a dash to hide behind two trees in front of him. Mr. Jennings reached around the tree with a clawing hand, only to strike his filthy nails into the moss-covered wood before he left to regroup with the police. Now that the creepy principal was out of his sight, Benjamin carefully sneaked his way back to the bridge. He was almost there when he became startled by the gust of wind from a hurdling torch. There was no pain at first contact, for the middle of the stick was light and damp, splitting in two across his back.

Benjamin screamed in alarm, alerting everyone throughout the forest, including the assassins. He grabbed a large, damp leaf from the forest ground to put the orange sparks out, when out of nowhere, Mr. Jennings lunged at him from the top of the hill.

Benjamin darted downward, slipping and sliding his way through the trees until he gained as much distance from the horrid man as he could.

"Help!" Benjamin yelled out to his hidden friends.

Sebastian was the first to react, crawling out from under the bridge to greet him.

The mob charged toward the bridge from different directions.

"Should we hide again?" Sebastian asked, unsure of what to do next.

"Not this time," Peter answered, arriving behind them with Tommy and leading Poppy by the reins.

"Jennings is here!" Benjamin cried to Tommy.

"Stand back," said Peter. Guided by what looked like a real fairy that circled him in flickering light, he sprinkled a single line of purple seeds onto the moss in the middle of the bridge.

"Is that...a firefly?" Sebastian whispered to Benjamin and Tommy. Just then a screaming voice instantly drained his face of color.

"Sebastian Cain!" a woman cried in the distance, past a huge line of torches.

"Oh no! It's them," Sebastian cried. "My parents." He grabbed onto Peter's collar in a desperate plea for mercy. "You said you would take me away from them, you swore."

Peter rested his hand on his shoulder. "I'm about to, Sebastian," came his reassuring reply. Poppy neighed hysterically, lifting her legs in fright. Benjamin tried to hold the reins but it was no good; the horse eventually gave into her fear of the approaching fire and galloped away.

"Poppy!" Benjamin called after her. It was too late. His beloved friend had vanished into the forest.

"Benjamin! No!" Peter called. "You can't go after her…not this time. She'll be safe." Peter stood firm. The pale, white-haired boy now appeared more confident and in control than all three of his peers, who were losing hope fast.

The sound of the mob grew louder, sending their noise toward the listening skies.

"There they are!" yelled another.

"Sebastian Cain! You will pay dearly for this, boy," one man shouted from the crowd. It was none other than Viktor, followed closely by his vindictive wife Greta.

"My runaway pupils!" screamed the all too familiar and horrid voice of Mr. Jennings, pointing a bony finger at them.

"Those flying things will surely hear us now," said Tommy, gawking up at the night sky. Just then Viktor approached the bridge accompanied by a policeman, and Peter motioned for the boys to gather behind him.

"Don't be alarmed, young Sirs, we're here to help," the policeman said, taking small steps toward them. Viktor rudely pushed the officer aside, trudging across the middle of the bridge, determined to get ahold of Sebastian.

"Sebastian, come here," he bellowed in his thick Russian accent, spitting out of rage.

"Stay put," Peter commanded to the three boys before he crossed along the bridge to meet the imperious man.

"Move aside, you little waif," Viktor barked for the whole mob to hear.

Peter confidently stood his ground, blocking the man's pathway.

"How dare you defy your elder, maggot!" Viktor yelled, taking another step toward Sebastian.

Peter took out his dagger and pointed it at Viktor. The three boys stood in pure disbelief while the angry mob began shouting and banging their sticks.

In that intense moment, devilish screeches from the assassins echoed down through the trees and silenced the entire mob below, making everyone look to the skies.

"This isn't for you to see, but you left me no choice," Peter called back at the mob. In one straight line he spread another row of seeds onto the stone bridge and over the moss that grew on it.

The ground shook and the stone cracked, making way for weeds that started to rapidly grow. A great tree followed through the weeds. It shot up in seconds, tearing through the bridge's rocky surface and sending shockwaves through the forest. The tree's long, heavy branches ripped the bridge in half, separating the children from the mob.

"What on earth is this?" shouted Greta.

"Witchery!" Viktor replied, addressing the mob.

"They are the devil's children!" Mr. Jennings screamed hysterically, causing instant panic amongst the crowd.

"Keep back!" Peter yelled as the tree emerged beside him. Soon there wasn't much left on Peter's side of the bridge but a mound of broken blocks of brick and soil.

The top of the magic oak tree sprouted past the tallest tree in the forest, presenting itself to the assassins amidst the skies. Dark clouds formed and wild winds picked up, covering the crowd in dust and dead leaves.

Tommy noticed the persistent and distinctive odor first. The stench filtered through the heavens prior to their appearance. The first assassin appeared from the woodlands behind the crowd. It had used its dark magick to take on its previous disguise. No one seemed to question the odd and sudden arrival of the police Inspector.

"Inspector, thank goodness, we've been trying to find you since that disaster at the Royal Opera House," Mr. Jennings cried out, almost leaping for joy at the villain's return.

"My wife and I will be taking your entire department to court for this, Inspector," Viktor snapped. "You've damaged our business reputation."

Keeping his back to them, the Inspector calmly crossed what was left of the bridge, rudely ignoring the mob. He leaned to one side in front of the magic tree to get a glimpse of the three runaways huddled behind it.

"We meet again." The Inspector smiled, pointing his leather-gloved hand to Tommy when Peter swiftly blocked the Inspector's view.

"Bravo. You made it this far. But enough games. Hand them over," he added casually.

Peter shook his head in silent disagreement.

"Think of how many lives you can save in the long run, if you would but spare these three to me now. There doesn't have to be a war over this. There's been too many of those already. Say, why don't we end this one, before it begins?"

"Okay...come and end it," Peter taunted.

The Inspector's face scrunched into a look of anger and spite. Seconds later, he called out to his co-assassin above him using inhuman sounds.

Greta screamed and fainted at the ghastly sight of the Inspector transforming himself back into the heavily armored assassin he was.

The cloaked assassin dropped from the sky and landed heavily onto the bridge a few feet from the mob.

"What are they? They're hideous!" Mr. Jennings cried from the crowd. No adult had the courage to step forward and help the children after both Viktor and the policeman were tossed off the bridge and into the air by the nine-foot beasts.

Peter calmly lifted the glass ball from his backpack that he'd received from Jacob and raised it up to the moonlight. It immediately absorbed a beam of white light that started to glow luminous colors.

The ball shone its effect on the forest, first with bright greens, and then purples and reds – each color a dazzling and beautiful spectacle. When the colorful light rested on ocean blue, Peter smashed the crystal ball inside the narrow gap on the bridge that separated the children from their assassins.

One of the assassins snickered at Peter's seemingly feeble effort to keep them at bay.

Breathing heavily, the foul assassins traipsed near the gap to reach the boys.

"It is too late for their return," growled the armored assassin, lifting his massive axe from his back. "His Majesty forbids it."

The axe-wielding assassin stood at the edge of the bridge's gap, causing pieces of gravel to fall below. Taking one step over the gap, the armored assassin hovered for a split second. "Prepare to perish, little sorcerer," it said. Just then a loud noise rose up beneath it.

"After you. I insist," teased Peter, as an enormous waterfall unleashed onto the assassin, shooting upward from the gap. The heavy showers soared toward the stars, surpassing the height of the magic oak tree and stalling the armored assassin in the middle of it. It was trapped.

"Into the tree!" Peter commanded.

Benjamin, Sebastian and Tommy looked on in disbelief as the tree's roots morphed into a large doorframe with steps leading into it. The doorway took the shape of a mouth, revealing nothing but blackness inside it. Jagged teeth formed around its doorframe, ready to close and lock out any trespasser.

"It is pointless, you cannot protect them forever; sooner or later, they *will* be ours!" The armored assassin gurgled through the flowing water, thrashing his arms around in a fit of rage before throwing his massive axe through the watery trap. The axe flew dangerously close between the three boys and embedded itself into the magic oak tree that gave out a long deep moan of pain.

"Cross over! Trust me!" Peter pleaded to the frightened boys.

Benjamin was the first to act. He took a quick breath and braced himself to dive into the tree's very core, only too eager to leave the chaos behind him. As he entered, white light beamed out of the gateway. Once Benjamin vanished, the light faded back to darkness. Sebastian followed, giving out a loud scream the second he jumped.

The entire mob fled out of the woods in terror, all but one, whose obsessive taste for revenge clouded his better judgement. Using the forest's thicket for his hiding spot, Mr. Jennings skulked behind.

Once the cloaked assassin took flight, it flew its way around the bridge and went straight for Peter, ready to strike with its needle-like weapon. Peter jumped onto the remaining wall of the half standing bridge to gain high ground.

"Thomas, go through the gateway," Peter yelled, avoiding the constant strikes from the giant cloaked assassin.

"Go ahead, go through. It will only make it easier for us to catch you on the other side, anyway," threatened the cloaked assassin.

Ignoring the assassin's threat, Tommy took a deep breath and prepared himself to run into the gateway. He managed to get an inch away from the gateway when his pace was broken and halted by a swift tackle to the ground. Scrapping fingers wrapped around his neck tightly, causing pain to shoot through his whole body.

"Remember me, you little cricket?" Mr. Jennings yelled into the boy's face as he squeezed his throat.

His enormous grip was strong for a man so deathly thin, and his breath was putrid. He squeezed tighter, digging his filthy nails into the back of Tommy's neck. Tommy felt his windpipe closing speedily as he struggled to fight him off.

"Now, Thomas Joel," Mr. Jennings muttered, "You'll meet the same end as that gullible sod, George Johnston."

You murderer, Tommy thought. Was he lying? Or was the old principal so cruel that he was capable of murder? Of course he was.

"Troublemaker! You're all trouble–," Mr. Jennings began when he was unexpectedly lifted up and propelled high into the air by one of the nine-foot assassins. The armored assassin had broken through Peter's reversed waterfall spell and stood directly over Tommy.

But something stopped the assassin from striking this time. Brambles, branches and intertwining twigs sprouted out from the ground beneath the magical oak tree, protecting Tommy from his deadly assassin.

The tree's branches began hitting and tearing at the armored assassin, preventing its unrelenting attacks. More branches removed the giant axe the assassin had embedded into the tree's trunk. Holding the armored assassin firmly in place, the oak tree generously returned the weapon to its owner, swinging the assassin's axe back at him as hard as its branches could swing. The axe flew at great force toward the giant assassin, lobbing him into the air far from Tommy. But the assassin's armor was so resilient that the oak tree's swing only made a slight dent in the assassin's chest plate.

Tommy ran back and stood in front of the large tree-like mouth, when he caught a glimpse of Peter battling the cloaked assassin in the distance.

Peter dodged the attacks impulsively and carefully with surprising effortlessness. His small stature gave him good speed and balance. The cloaked assassin tried desperately to connect his weapon with Peter, but failed in every attempt. Peter used the remaining bridge walls and woodland around him to back flip and summersault over and through each swipe, using several chances to kick the beast's chest and clip its shoulders.

Peter battled the cloaked assassin into the path of the reversed waterfall. The spell had reached the last ounce of its magic and came crashing back down upon the rubble, casting the cloaked assassin adrift when the bridge finally split in two and fell into the current. Tucking his large dagger into its pouch at his side, Peter walked over to Tommy, steadily and with ease.

"Are you hurt?" Peter asked with great concern.

"Just a little," Tommy replied, rubbing the bruises on his throat where Mr. Jennings had tried to strangle him.

"If you don't do what I say, from here on in, it *will* cost you your life," Peter warned, giving Tommy a hard look.

Wolves started to howl in the far distance, meaning only one thing: they were on the prowl. Peter pointed to the mouth-like gateway at the tree's root. Its broken bits of wood that resembled rows of pointed teeth made Tommy feel uneasy, until a glorious warm light shone out at them.

"Time to go home," Peter said, leading the surviving Gatesville runaway through the gateway. Tommy took one glance back at the old world he was about to leave behind, long enough to see the cloaked assassin rising out from the deep waters, forever on the hunt for him.

18

Brethren of Villains

Mr. Jennings awoke to the rumbling of the ground that shook apart the earthly pit he'd landed in. He was sure he had broken a bone or two. Wet leaves and muck covered his lanky body. His pain and discomfort angered him further. In one desperate attempt, he tried to lift himself up out of the pit, but his weakened state wouldn't allow it. Falling onto his back, Mr. Jennings started screaming in agony, unknowingly alerting the remaining predators of the forest that howled in response.

"Help me! Somebody!" he cried repeatedly in between his grunts and moaning.

Something drew near. The sounds of the wolves' movements and howling ceased as if they'd suddenly evaporated in the mist.

Five wolves silently scavenged, in stealth-like coordination, crawling beside him, until the leader claimed its territory above his head. Mr. Jennings knew they'd found him when he felt warm heavy breaths tickle the few hairs on the back of his balding head. A few crows nested on the towering branches above, goggling down at him, awaiting their meal of leftovers after the inevitable attack. The eyes of the wolves reflected the shimmering light of the moon. Six lights twinkled out of the darkness, revealing three of the wild beasts.

Mr. Jennings couldn't contain his fear any longer and started to weep loudly. Soon, other wolves gathered, snapping at one another over their dinner.

"Please, I don't want to die like this," he cried, after one wolf seized the moment and dared to be the first of the pack to take a bite, sinking its razor sharp white fangs into Mr. Jennings' ankle. His screams were so high pitched they could have been heard over half of Warwickshire.

"Get off, beast!" he screamed, springing to a sitting position.

The rumbling grew louder. Then the two nine-foot assassins marched through the forest toward him, trampling everything in their path. The wolves shifted their attention away from Mr. Jennings to gaze upon the giant assassins. The leader of the pack instinctively bared its teeth at the approaching threat.

Mr. Jennings looked around for any sign of the angry mob he'd led into the forest before realizing their disloyalty was certain. He'd been left to die, to be eaten by wild beasts or something worse.

The leader of the wolf pack charged at the armored assassin to protect his meal. Without much effort (a tap really), the assassin brushed the wolf away from its sight as a human would a fly. The injured wolf fell down and limped into the woods, swiftly followed by the rest of its pack. Mr. Jennings was left to face the deadlier assassins alone.

"Stay back. Stay back, I say." He coughed, trying to climb out of the small grave-like ditch.

The cloaked assassin stomped impatiently over to him and picked the old man off of his feet.

"Don't eat me!" Mr. Jennings yelled, his legs shaking in thin air, trying to kick with what little energy they had left in them. "Who are you? What are you?"

"We want the Children of Aba-*sssin*," the assassin hissed like a serpent.

"Oh, dear heavens, your breath is worse than mine," Mr. Jennings said. "I didn't think that was possible," he added quite boldly, proud of his rotted tonsils.

"Silence!" ordered his capturer, squeezing him by the neck. "Bring us to The Three That Are One," the cloaked beast said while Mr. Jennings gasped for air.

"Three That Are One? I do not teach mathematics, you overgrown bean can," Mr. Jennings wheezed, his ego getting in the way of his common sense.

"Do you know the Children of Aba-*sssin*, petty human?" the armored assassin asked.

"I-I...I can't tell you if you won't release me...bean can," Mr. Jennings muttered, forcing his insult out loud once more.

The cloaked assassin promptly tossed the old man into the clutches of its partner, like a rag doll. This time, Mr. Jennings was held upside down.

"Tell me now or I will drop you on your head," growled the armored assassin as he swung Mr. Jennings back and forth.

"Ah...okay...okay. I don't know them personally. They're my pupils. Please, don't kill me. I can help you find them," he begged.

The armored assassin looked into Mr. Jennings' hard, worn face.

"The Three That Are One...they are students of yours, treacherous human?" it growled again. "You teach the enemy!"

"No, that's not what I meant," Mr. Jennings said.

"Crafts against His Majesty!" snapped the cloaked assassin.

"I'm on your side. I hate the little brats!" Mr. Jennings smiled unconvincingly.

"Liar," the armored beast whispered eerily to his captive. "You teach the Children of Aba-*sssin* to fight against our King."

"No. I wasn't trying to help them...honest. I agree with you charming gentlemen...I mean, gentle-bean cans," Mr. Jennings said.

Both beasts began to cackle at the pathetic captive pleading for his life.

"You don't look as if you would be much use out on the battlefield, human," the cloaked assassin said, laughing.

The armored assassin gave Mr. Jennings a stern look seconds before flinging him back to his original capturer. Held by the scruff of his jacket, the humiliated principal looked like an entangled puppet.

"Now this is just getting ridiculous," Mr. Jennings grunted.

"The children have many powers, foolish human," said the cloaked assassin.

"Powers? My boys? Are you sure about that?" Mr. Jennings giggled.

"Do not mock us, human worm!" the armored assassin warned, pointing its finger at him.

"Well, I could hang around here all day with you chaps, or we could stop babbling nonsense and go find the little scrappers," Mr. Jennings suggested tensely.

At this point the beasts started to talk amongst themselves in a language that Mr. Jennings could not comprehend.

"He's a wasteful human, Thestor, diseased and dying. Leave him for the carnivores of these lands. He's of no use to the Master," said the cloaked assassin, glancing back and forth between Mr. Jennings and its counterpart.

Thestor silently shook his head in disagreement.

"His soul has escaped him, and his heart is empty. I rather like this uncaring, devious excuse for human fodder. If nothing else, he can wash the warts off my back and help with the other slaves in the dungeons, if he survives the transition. He'll be my wart scrubber."

Both beastly assassins looked at the pathetic man and began to laugh at him when the cloaked assassin handed Mr. Jennings over to its counterpart.

"Very well, my ugly pet; I'm sure we can make some use of you...if the Master lets you live," Thestor sniggered.

Unknowingly, Mr. Jennings laughed together with his new villainous brethren in relief that his life had been spared.

In one movement, Thestor abruptly threw Mr. Jennings onto his back, preparing him for their lengthy flight into the unknown. "Make yourself comfortable up there, peasant, you might have to get used to it, if you're very lucky." Both assassins roared with laughter.

"Where are we going?" Mr. Jennings asked in sheer fright, gripping the steel armor on the assassin's back.

Thestor gave a warning look over his shoulder. "Not another word from you, slug," he growled. He took off from the ground at great speed. Mr. Jennings screamed like a little girl (revealing his fear of heights), digging his fingernails into the rusted grip points in the assassin's armor.

The darkened clouds opened their mouths, showing

razor-elongated teeth. A bright blinding light shone out from the gateway, increasing the coldness upon their faces. Mr. Jennings's stomach turned as sulphuric smells flew out at him, attacking his nostrils and clouding his senses. His weak heart slowed to a mere crawl when he slipped into unconsciousness. Luckily for Mr. Jennings, the freezing temperatures had covered the black steel armor in a thick layer of sticky frost that kept his body attached to the flying assassin.

Seconds after his mind faded out of consciousness, the mouth of the vortex opened up, revealing the blinding cold light. Unbeknownst to him, Mr. Jennings was now a prisoner, belonging to the assassin he rode on.

After they entered through the vortex, it evaporated, leaving behind a great patch of gloomy colors in the skyline over Warwickshire. The new brethren of villains had crossed their gateway in pursuit of the three human children who had arrived on the other side of their own gateways...each awaiting his fate.

19

Protectors of Abasin

The transition for Tommy hadn't been anywhere near as hellish as what Jennings encountered. It was comfortably quick, and before he knew it, he stepped out of the same rugged oak tree doorway the very way he had entered it. The only difference was he was now covered in soil and plant roots from head to toe, which clung to his clothes even when he tried to brush them off.

The roots were alive and made Tommy squeamish, as he plucked each one off him. The large gateway door closed over, changing into solid oak again. Once his vision cleared, Tommy gazed in wonder at the most beautiful skies one could ever have dreamed of. Clear purple heavens lit up a beautiful white rock that lay ahead of him.

The thought of discovering this new world excited him. Trees surrounded him, but these were not like the withered and mossy trees that bordered Jacob O'Malley's farmland. These trees appeared to ignite their surroundings like candlelight, reflecting the golden brown leaves that covered their roots. Spectacular colors enhanced the main pathway that lay behind the white rock. Strong, pleasant smells of rosemary and incense rose around him and cleared the remaining residue of stench the horrid assassins had left.

Tommy was exhilarated. The smells grew stronger with every breath he took. His body began adjusting to the atmosphere, when he fell onto his hands and knees, vomiting what little he had eaten earlier in the old world.

"Your body is just adapting to the new air," a tiny high-pitched voice called out.

Tommy slowly got to his feet when he heard the strange voice.

"Who's there?" he asked. There was a short silence, and Tommy found himself wondering what had happened to the rest of the group. Feeling isolated in a strange place gripped him with an unsettling feeling.

Rustling came from the gorgeous woodlands to the right of him along with the sounds of small feet puttering close by.

"Show yourself," he demanded.

The creature seemed to defy gravity the moment it appeared on top of the white rock, leaping gracefully. "Don't be alarmed, we are safe for now," it said, scouting around for any sign of unwanted trouble.

It took a little while for Tommy to recognize his friend. "*Peter?*" Tommy gasped.

Peter's ears stretched into a straight point like the east and west points of a compass, revealing white fluffy hair all over them with the exception of a black lined streak. His hair was whiter than ever, reflecting the forest lights in the background. Tommy noticed that even Peter's attire was different. Sticks, leaves and branches, all finely stripped, made up his clothes, with ripped leggings and brown boots. But the most peculiar characteristic about Peter was in his face. The face now appeared too feminine to belong to a boy.

"What happened to your ears?" Tommy asked.

The creature kicked its feet high into the air and laughed as it rolled upon its back.

"What are you?" Tommy asked, with a light hesitance.

"I'm a nymph. My real name is Ariel," came her soft reply. "I was sent to the old world disguised as one of you, to guide you back."

"What is this all about?" he asked.

"It is not for my lips to tell, little Master...we don't know who could be listening," she whispered. "But you will know everything soon."

"Shouldn't we go back through the tree?" Tommy suggested, pointing at the great oak, only to discover that it had shrunk and changed to a shrub.

"Why would we want to do that?" She laughed. "Don't worry, you'll soon get used to things here," she said, leading the way onto the colorful leafy road. "We must get moving, I'm taking you to the Stained Castle. All will be revealed to you then."

She knelt to the ground and rummaged through several leaves to pull out a living vegetable from its root.

"Where are we?" Tommy asked.

"We're in the new world," she announced, showing Tommy lands as far as he could see from the top of the white rock. "This is Abasin."

"It's so big," Tommy gasped.

"You've no idea," Ariel replied excitably. "Take this, it will build up your strength," she added, handing Tommy the vegetable plant creature. Its legs moved, but the body of the vegetable seemed unresponsive.

"Yuck! What is this?" Tommy asked in disgust, holding one of the squirming tentacles up by the tips of his fingers.

The nymph sighed. "It's food. You have to eat," she ordered, leading the way forward.

"I think I'm going to be sick."

"Just eat, Thomas. The sooner you eat, the sooner you will feel better, and the sooner we can get moving," she called back, impatiently.

Tommy closed his eyes tight and braced himself to take his first bite of the vegetable. The tentacles flopped lifelessly to one side. It had a sweet texture mixed with an incredible savoury taste that took the nausea away from him almost instantly.

"What about Benjamin and Sebastian?" he asked, sounding a little more alert.

"We had to separate you. It's safer that way," came her quick reply.

"But we all went through the same way," Tommy insisted, sounding doubtful. The nymph took another look at the messy boy who had food stains on his chin.

"Like I said, you'll get used to how things work here," she tittered. "Do not fear. There will be other protectors at their gateways to guide them to the Stained Castle."

"What's the Stained Castle?"

"A safe fortress. It once belonged to a great king, long before these dark ages," she explained.

Tommy couldn't help but pose more questions to the nymph, his mind growing ever more interested in the fascinating new world of Abasin. But out of the numerous questions he had buzzing around his head, Tommy Joel knew which one concerned him most.

"How far is it to this castle then?"

***

Sebastian's hands frantically clawed the muddy earth in search of his large glasses.

He'd managed to brush off the soil and squirming shrubs before the new air made him throw up and lose his glasses in the process.

"Where are you?" he cried aloud in frustration until a blurry object appeared, holding his glasses with one finger. Grabbing them, Sebastian quickly fixed the legs of his glasses around his ears.

Once his frames were fixed upon his face, Sebastian could see the grubby fat creature he had so curtly snatched his glasses from.

"That was so rude," came the sharp greeting.

Unwilling to converse with the creature, Sebastian turned around and speedily walked toward the gateway in search of Peter, keeping a close watch over his shoulder. Failing to notice the doorway had already closed, he bounced off the solid oak tree and landed backwards in the sludge. As he hit the surface, his glasses flew off his face and landed back into the hands of the fat creature.

"Well, this is going to be interesting," the creature said, sighing. "I can see you're a right handful."

"Give them back!" Sebastian shouted, rubbing wet splatter marks of mud from his eyes as he swiped for his glasses.

"Give what back?" the creature teased, before it eventually handed the boy his eyewear.

"What in the world?" Sebastian gasped. His jaw

hung open as he studied the offbeat figure dressed in dungarees and gray cotton overalls. Its nose was pointy and it had overgrown bumblebee wings sprouting from its back that glistened in the light. A mop of thick brown hair reached down to its eyebrows to accompany its circular chubby face. The creature was fat, but appeared capable and strong.

"Are you sniggering at me, human?" it asked.

"I do not snigger, I'm a respectable Englishman," Sebastian replied, trying not to smirk.

"Englishman? What is that? I've never heard of one of those before."

"By golly. Englishmen are polite, strong, decent folk, unlike creatures such as...whatever *you* are," Sebastian rambled, showing off his self-educated manner.

"I...my filthy whatever human...am a noble knighted whatever pixie," scolded the creature, speaking with a noticeable but funny lisp.

"Knighted, huh? I see. Shall I call you Sir Pixie then?" Sebastian teased.

"My name is Cecil Baskin," he growled back, but his timid voice and funny lisp spoiled his threatening demeanour. "You have a name, I presume."

"Sebastian Cain," Sebastian said proudly.

"I'm guessing those pillars below your torso work then," Cecil suggested, pointing a funny looking walking stick at Sebastian's legs.

"Of course they do," Sebastian snapped.

"Well then, you will have no problem keeping up with my wings now, will you?" Cecil snapped back. It was clear that they misunderstood one another and this made Sebastian untrusting and Cecil irritable.

"I am not going anywhere with you in this bog,"

Sebastian whined, only to have Cecil Baskin's stick knock repeatedly on the side of his head, which the boy tried to ignore. Sebastian mumbled, trying to excuse himself from Cecil's presence, but instead he was interrupted with a tap on the head with every word he spoke.

"Will you stop that!" the boy finally yelled, boldly reaching out to grab the stick off the agitating pixie.

Cecil's wings began to tire, causing his stumpy body to float lower until he could only muster enough strength to hover face to face with his human companion, panting out of breath. A smug smile crossed Sebastian's mud-covered face.

"You need a diet, Mr. Baskin."

"I've been sent to protect you," Cecil said, as he spat spittle on the swampy ground.

"That's one nasty habit you've got there," Sebastian said.

"You have to come with me...your friends will be waiting for us," Cecil insisted.

"Why didn't you say so? We could've already been on our way out of this dump," Sebastian groaned in disgust as he looked around at the barren wasteland of swamp. "I do hope you're smart enough to get us out of here."

"Of course I am. I'm a Knight!" Cecil said boastfully.

"What does that have to do with anything?" Sebastian sighed, rolling his eyes.

"I...I don't know...but I didn't achieve my Knighthood for nothing...now kick your feet up, it helps when walking through these lands. We have a long way to go, so I guess we'll have to eat soon. I brought some pots and pans with me to make a stew while we camp," Cecil said.

"If you think I'm camping in this wide open hovel with you, you've got another thing coming," Sebastian mumbled under his breath as they moved toward a massive mountain that hung over the entire scenery of swamp hills and mudslides. Glancing over his shoulder to talk to the hovering pixie, Sebastian felt another stinging tap strike his head.

"Eyes front, boy-o, walk while you talk," commanded Cecil.

Nothing seemed to have any life around these parts of the new world. Sebastian noticed the emptiness in the lands afar, after the great oak tree shrunk to a tiny shrub in its place. Pieces of dead trees and rotted logs poked out everywhere from below the mire the further they trekked.

"W-what happened to this place?" Sebastian asked, scanning the wasteland of oozing swamp.

Cecil sighed. "This was once the greatest forest in all of Abasin, before it became the Black Swamp. A wicked politician, betrayed by the False One, was cursed here and his body was transformed into this sludge."

Sebastian glanced below his feet and started to lose his nerve. "You mean I'm walking on—" he cried out, climbing on top of a nearby log as far above the sludge as he could possibly get.

"Not to worry, young Master, I assure you he's a long time dead, or so I've been told," Cecil insisted, reassuring Sebastian with an encouraging wink. "Take my hand, child. I won't let anything bad happen to you, no matter how unfunny you seem to be," he teased.

Sebastian hesitantly took hold of the pixie's warm and prickly hand. With one light tug, Cecil safely lifted the boy into the air and set him down into the sludge.

"Chop chop," Cecil continued, hovering beside the boy as Sebastian pushed and pulled his legs through the deep muck.

"This is revolting. Where are we going, exactly?" Sebastian grumbled, taking long strides.

"To the Stained Castle. That is where your friends are headed," Cecil said quietly tapping him on his head using his stick once more. "Northeast, Sebastian Cain...eyes front."

Cecil pointed, directing the tired and filthy boy across the great swamp toward the overgrown mossy mountains in front of them.

"And to think...this was my only good suit," the boy sighed to himself.

20

Swords Against the Stone

It took Benjamin a while to register where he was when he first awoke. The carcass of a dead nymph lay decaying a few feet away from his face. Benjamin yelped at the ghastly sight and ran toward the edge of an enormous cliffside to get away from it. Dark blue water led out to an ocean far below the thousand-foot drop. Once he noticed an old broken rope bridge that hung over an opposite cliff side, he decided to turn back. The sunset was clear and shone against his face. A low bundle of orange fruit trees covered the area ahead.

Shrubs from the gateway clung and tangled around his arms. He pulled them off him without much effort. His stomach adjusted to the new air instantly. Suddenly, a shadow crossed his. A hairy unkempt creature stood a few feet in front of him. Its lower jaw stuck out like a piranha's, showing a row of sharp teeth that grotesquely chattered.

The ghoulish creature moved its raggedy head from side to side like an inquisitive dog the moment it spotted him.

Benjamin took one step to the left and took an anxious breath when the creature suddenly mirrored his movement. Then, without warning, it started screeching to signal to its leader far away. In a heartbeat, a sword was slung from the fruit vine behind the noisy creature and struck a fatal blow.

The courageous boy slowly stepped over the slain creature to get a closer glimpse past the fruit vine when a young man swiftly sprang out from the thicket. Benjamin jolted at the sudden presence of the man, who seemed uninterested in greeting him. Pulling his golden sword from the creature's back, the young swordsman glared at Benjamin briefly after he wiped the thick bloodstains off his weapon's tip.

He was short for a grown man, and had cropped black hair and piercing dark eyes that gawked from under his thick eyebrows. Benjamin noticed the man's skin was a tan color, much like the Spanish sailors he'd read about growing up. His features were severe, just like a pirate. *Maybe he is a pirate?* Benjamin wondered.

The young man knelt down beside the slain nymph and closed its eyelids with a stroke of his fingers.

Sensing the young man was of no threat to him, Benjamin decided to break the ice. If Sebastian had have been there he could have put off the formal greeting a little longer, but this was the quiet, shy Benjamin, trying to be as direct as he knew how.

"Are you a pirate?" Benjamin asked openly.

"Ask that again you little toad, and I'll show you what I would do to you if I were such a treacherous soul," the young man snapped, pointing his shiny gold weapon at the tip of Benjamin's babyish nose. Benjamin stiffened in fear.

"I hope you were referring to the human," a voice gurgled from the bushes.

The young man swung his sword toward the shaded cliffside where a little man that resembled a toad-like mutant crept out from the trees.

"Lower your weapon, bounty hunter," the toad-man instructed, followed by an unsettling gurgle.

"Well, if it isn't the infamous Trump," replied the young man. "Still in that horrible body?" he teased. "It must be hard knowing how beautiful you once were, having to wake up every day to the thing you are now. At least now the outside of you matches the inside."

The toad-man named Trump was repulsive to look at. Slime dripped off the stubborn amphibian and there was something about the shifty look in his fishy eyes that made Benjamin uncomfortable.

"Don't pay any attention to him, Benjamin, he's bounty hunter scum," Trump gurgled.

"How did you know my name?" Benjamin asked with suspicion.

"My boy, you are known to everyone here in Abasin," Trump said gleefully.

"Abasin?" Benjamin asked.

"Yes! All you see around you is Abasin. Welcome to the new world," Trump gurgled and smiled. "You are very famous here."

"I am?" Benjamin gasped, smiling in shock and excitement.

"I'm taking the boy to the Stained Castle," the bounty hunter interrupted.

"My orders are to stay here and wait for the other protectors to arrive," Trump argued, scowling suspiciously.

"Really?" the bounty hunter asked, disbelievingly. "I'm changing those orders. It's too unsafe here. Screams of a sea guard will not go unnoticed. Not from these heights," he continued, brushing past the toad-man. "We go to the castle."

As Benjamin sat carefully studying the unusual pair, a sudden strange change in the color of Trump's skin caught his eye. In a matter of seconds Trump's color changed from lime green to light orange, revealing his mood of irritation.

"I can't leave without my friends," Benjamin insisted to the pair.

"Your friends are safe. I'll take you to them." With one sharp stroke the bounty hunter pointed his sword at the dead nymph. "I've been sent to replace your protector." He then handed Benjamin a large dagger and a heavy bag of food. "I trust you are strong enough to carry these?" the bounty hunter asked, raising his thick eyebrows in hope of a positive answer.

"The boy is too small to carry all that. He'll slow us down," Trump grumbled, hopping in front of the bounty hunter's path.

"Are you deliberately trying to slow us down before we even get started, Trump?" the bounty hunter asked, folding his arms. "I have a better idea. Since you're so concerned about the human's ability, you can carry the food and the water too," he ordered, throwing the heavy bag into Trump's slippery hands.

Benjamin stuck close to the bounty hunter to escape the sour company of the cursed toad-man.

"So, what's your name?" Benjamin asked.

"Cassius," the bounty hunter replied unenthusiastically while they waited for Trump to catch up. Slogging with the weight of the small bag on his slimy, disease-ridden back, Trump's complaining finally stopped.

"Move it, Trump, we'll vanish with hunger by the time you get across these fields. Hop to it," Cassius shouted.

"You don't like him much, do you?" Benjamin asked quietly so Trump wouldn't hear.

"I don't trust him," Cassius corrected, holding an old bronze timer and compass up to the sunset. "It's as I feared. We're already behind the others."

Cassius led the way across a beautiful landscape of greenery and fruit patches that ran parallel to the moss-covered mountains. Close by, but a few miles west of them, Sebastian and Cecil Baskin continued to make their own way through the Black Swamp.

Benjamin's excitement grew the moment the Stained Castle became visible. His legs were almost worn out from walking in the evening heat. "Can we rest and eat now?" he asked.

Cassius pointed to a cluster of large rocks that rested on the top of a gigantic hill. "We shall rest once we reach those rocks," he said. "It's safer upon high ground."

Trump's pores oozed with enough slime to make his own pond by the time they reached halfway up the hillside. Cassius paused for his companions to catch up every time he climbed too far ahead of them.

"You're almost there, Benjamin," he called down from the large rocks above them, once he'd made it to the top.

Suddenly, the sound of marching footsteps emerged nearby. Cassius jumped to the highest point to get a better view. A horde of twenty soldiers swarmed over another hillside and briefly halted when they spotted Benjamin and Trump.

They were the royal sea guards of the new world; vicious amphibian fighters that served the False One; each cursed with their own unique form of mutation that resembled various sea life.

Cassius took out his sword and called down to his companions to climb to the top as fast as they could.

A dented patch in the hill caught Benjamin's next step off guard, causing him to lose his balance on the dangerous hilltop and roll back to the bottom. The soldiers were only a few yards away when they began to close in on him.

Cassius leapt with his golden blade high in hand ready to greet his enemies below. He wasn't afraid to take on the entire regiment in combat; rather, he was more worried about reaching Benjamin safely in time without making a clumsy mistake in his attempt.

Nearer the top, Trump had saved his own slithery skin by hiding behind one of the large rocks, shying away from the oncoming tribe that was prepared to seize the hillside. Grabbing at clumps of grass, Benjamin managed to stop rolling a few feet from the bottom. Cassius leapt over Benjamin's head, landing directly in front of the swarming sea guards.

"Lemis!" Cassius growled, gawking at the hideous chief sea guard. A simple signal from Lemis halted his troops.

"You be a warlock, young one?" Lemis asked Benjamin, who cowered behind Cassius, terrified by Lemis's razor-sharp under-bite.

"Do not speak with him," Cassius warned.

"Your brains are in your boots, young bounty hunter. Civilian trespassing on the King's land carries the death penalty," Lemis hissed.

"Just try it," Cassius snapped back, swiftly raising his sword to swipe and causing the entire group of sea guards to flinch.

"I've heard a rumor from the witches that a powerful warlock is in the making. You civilians should beware these Children of Abasin you have been sent to protect," Lemis rambled. "One of these thorns will bring a prickly end to you, the witches say. They are destined for darker things."

"A rumor from a witch is hardly trustworthy, fool!" Cassius mocked.

"Ah...now I remember you. You be young Cassius Shark. I thought I recognized you. The pirate's son turned rebel bounty hunter. How you've grown...*a little*." Lemis jeered alongside his troops, poking fun at the bounty hunter's height. Cassius sighed and gripped his sword handle tightly.

"I'm big enough to see you fall this day, *accursed*," Cassius announced for all to hear.

"Such bold words. There are too many of us to fight this time," Lemis promised, regarding the False One's world forces.

"There's only one child, and he's too small," one villain shouted out.

"Is he really one of the three? A human?" another sea guard spluttered.

"We can take him," a squid-faced trooper muttered from the group.

"He's *new* to this world. I can smell his human stench. It is him; he's a thorn, the cursed spawn the Master spoke of," one whispered amongst several of his fellow troops.

"Give me the child, bounty hunter, by order of the King of Abasin," growled Lemis, pointing his rusted black sword at Benjamin.

Cassius instantly struck Lemis's chest with a mighty boot, kicking him to the ground in front of his soldiers.

"Saul is not *my* king!" Cassius roared.

As Cassius battled the large group of soldiers by

himself, Benjamin clambered his way to the safety of the rocks above, pursued by several troops at Lemis' command. Cassius fought his way through a large number of sea guards, hacking and slaying each villain through one fatal move of his golden blade, until Lemis struck hard and fast behind him, stabbing the bounty hunter deep in his side. Cassius clutched his wound in pain and warily retreated to the safety of the rocks.

Benjamin finally made it to the top of the hill, ahead of his pursuers, and scaled the rocks to reach the peak. "Trump, where are you?" he called out. But Trump didn't respond.

"You're going to the King, my little prisoner," one sea guard cackled when it arrived at the top of the hill.

Benjamin screamed in shock when another sea guard snuck in front of him. In a flash, the pintsize monster fell off its rock and plummeted down the hill, screeching.

Cassius began shooting his arrows wildly now, using the edge of the hilltop as his perfect vantage point to shoot more charging guards below. Within seconds the numbers grew. Troops of twenty increased to thirty until over fifty soldiers swarmed the steep hill. They had answered the screeching calls of their chief sea guard, General Lemis. Cassius was slowly but surely running out of ammunition while the remaining sea guard in pursuit of Benjamin climbed onto the top rock and moved in for the capture.

A fireball hurtled through the swarm of arrows toward the hilltop. Cassius made a dash for cover behind a gigantic rock before the burning boulder slammed against it.

Benjamin held on for dear life. The vibrations shook through the rocks and almost thrust him and his pursuer to the ground. Another fireball hit the same huge stone that protected Cassius.

During the launch of a third fireball, a sleeping beast was abruptly awoken from its long slumber.

The movement of the rock shook the foundations of the hillside. Benjamin sensed the rapid elevation. The second movement was unceasing, taking him higher from the hilltop.

The gigantic creature had awoken, tearing off half of the hilltop while it rose, growing taller to an almost ridiculous twenty feet in height. It looked like a giant tortoise when it fully stood straight up. A massive shell of rock covered two thirds of its body, including its entire back and most of its head. Its front was swathed in dark soil and earth. Clumps of rock plummeted off its chest and fell toward the army, squashing several troops below. The gargantuan rock-shelled creature flicked Benjamin's assailant off its shoulder with a single finger.

Lemis gasped in horror and ordered his troops to engage in warfare with the mighty creature. "Attack!" Lemis commanded, pointing a solid finger at the stone giant. Immediately the entire army of sea guards charged at the rock-shelled giant. The giant creature swiftly turned its rocky back on the oncoming fireballs, arrows and swords, all with Benjamin clinging to the top of its stone head.

"Don't look down, don't look down," Benjamin told himself.

Weapons had no effect, ricocheting off the creature's stone shell. Most of the arrows fell back down, puncturing several sea guards, while a few swords recoiled, piercing those that threw them. In one ingenious and skillful move, the rock-shelled giant had managed to wipe out more than twenty soldiers by their own artillery.

Cassius backed out from under the giant's legs. As much as the young bounty hunter was strong and courageous, he could never have matched this vigorous display of power. Cassius feared for Benjamin (now trapped on top of the beast's head), when the rock-shelled giant unleashed its attack, charging toward Lemis and his army.

21

Molo the Savior

Catching a fireball with its bare hands, the rock-shelled giant bowled it back, demolishing all in its path. Scooping up a handful of sea guards from the ground, it swiftly closed its massive fingers, crushing their bodies tightly together until they fell lifelessly from its palm.

"Stand down!" Lemis shrieked, unaware that his surviving troops had deserted the battlefield. The giant's large eyes fixed upon Lemis once the chief's flying servant, a black omnicorn, swiftly swooped down to rescue its master.

It was a horrible sight, unlike Poppy or a normal colt. This black brute was greasy and tatty with two black horns pointing from its forehead. Its black leathery wings revealed arrow holes and a bizarre pattern of scars collected from previous battles. The omnicorn kept flapping its grotesque wings rapidly in mid air as it shot past the giant's eyes. Its teeth were not like that of any normal horse for they were small and razor sharp.

Lemis pointed his slimy finger straight at Benjamin the moment he saw the boy on top of the giant's head. Benjamin knew the wicked grinning fiend now singled him out.

The twenty-foot giant swiped at the flapping omnicorn above its head, grazing the creature's hooves with its stone fingertips. Lemis screeched in fright and kicked the sides of the omnicorn, sending his hellish pet into the heavy fog that swept across the blood soaked fields.

Cassius clutched the wound on his side and slung his water carrier and weaponry over his back. He stealthily crept over to a trembling Trump, who had scarpered behind a large piece of debris, hoping the rock would conceal him from the giant's huge, watchful eyes. Fear had rapidly turned Trump's skin color to a luminous blue, which glowed brighter by the minute.

"Relax," Cassius whispered, while he slumped beside the toad-man, keeping his back to the rock.

"What is that...*thing?*" Trump whispered after an anxious gurgle.

"Isn't it marvellous? I haven't come across anything this ancient before. I don't think *they* had either," replied Cassius pointing his sword at the dead army around them.

"It's going to kill us!" Trump whimpered, crouching low.

"No. It's just a bit grumpy, that's all. Something tells me it was sleeping here for a long time before we came," Cassius whispered calmly.

"Of course, why am I worried? I too wipe out an entire field of Saul's troops every time I wake up on the wrong side of the swamp!" Trump scoffed, rolling his eyes at the injured bounty hunter, his body turning light orange again.

Cassius dug into his goat-skin satchel and lifted out two potion jars, one containing a miniscule hurricane and the other a dancing fairy that represented good health. He opened up the second jar, letting the potion flutter in the air in the form of a fairy before it settled itself on his wound. Cassius hissed in pain as the fairy shape melted into its original form of liquid medicine and filled his wound until its red glow burnt out. Brushing the remaining ash off his healed wound, the brave bounty hunter slowly stood up to face the rock-shelled giant.

Trump's body turned luminous blue again, glowing his fear for all to see, while trying to remain hidden. "Stupid bounty hunter, you're going to be the death of us."

"Someday...maybe," Cassius replied quietly, smiling down at Trump.

The evening had dropped in temperature, and the thick fog masked the open fields. Benjamin kept still, clutching onto the head of the unwitting giant. Cassius called out his name and approached the rock-shelled giant. Taking one look at the armed bounty hunter, the giant pushed out its chest and charged toward him. Cassius held up his hands to surrender whilst carefully stepping over the patches of dead bodies, but it was to no avail; the rock-shelled creature couldn't tell the difference between friend and foe.

"Hold it! Wait! Halt!" Cassius pleaded after dodging a frighteningly lethal blow from the giant's monstrous rock-covered fist. In one solid strike, the enormous creature smashed a massive chunk of earth out of the field that disintegrated into smaller bits of dried dirt next to Trump. The toad-man hopped out from his hiding spot and swiftly opted for a pile of dead sea-guards to shield him from the flying lumps.

"Run!" Benjamin called down to the bounty

hunter. Cassius lunged through the giant's open legs facing in the direction of the cliff side. The rock-shelled giant chased after him all the way back to the same spot where Benjamin had crossed through his gateway. By a quick tug of its arms, the rock-shelled giant uprooted each fruit tree near the cliff's edge. Cassius had nowhere to hide.

Skidding to the edge on his side, the bounty hunter covered his face as the rock-shelled giant slammed two enormous fists deep into the earth at either side of him. Cassius held his hands up in surrender and plucked up enough courage to speak to it, cautiously taking his time and choosing his words and tone wisely.

"I mean no harm. I'm a friend. Ally!"

The giant flinched back in alarm when Cassius sat up straight. Its striking brown eyes stared curiously at him until Cassius felt it was safe enough to call Benjamin's name one more time.

The small boy stood up as steadily as the giant's wavering allowed and called out to his protector below, cupping his hands as he shouted.

"I'm up here," he cried out, faintly.

The giant opened its mouth in surprise and spun around to see where the little voice had come from, flinging Benjamin to the front of its head by its rapid movement. Benjamin's birth blanket slid off the giant's head and fell past its huge eye before Cassius caught it below. Once the rock-shelled giant realized the boy was resting on top of its head, it began to swipe. Benjamin held on for his life as the creature ran back and forth, slamming its hands on its head in order to shake the boy off.

Benjamin flew between its fingers and yelled in panic as he fell. His chest hit a hard earthy surface.

Digging his fingers as deep as he could into the damp soil, the startled boy heaved forth, climbing up the nose of the giant, only to reach a set of mammoth eyes that glared back at him. His initial terror was soon replaced by sleepiness from the hypnotic effect of the giant's gaze. Benjamin felt a strong sense of powerlessness. He struggled to keep awake as he felt his wilted body slide off the giant's muddy nose. The giant creature smoothly scooped Benjamin into its right palm before the boy hit the ground.

Cassius stopped dead in his tracks, watching in horror as Benjamin's legs dangled lifelessly between the giant's fingers. If it had so wished, it could've crumpled the boy. And this knowledge made Cassius's face drain white.

"No!" Cassius bellowed and ran toward the rock-shelled giant. He immediately stopped in his tracks when it flattened out its massive hand to reveal the unconscious boy unharmed.

Cassius paced around its hand slowly until it motioned for Cassius to take the child from its hand.

At first, his instincts told him that it was an obvious trap. But the more he studied the creature's eyes, the more he felt at ease by their calming effect. As he approached the giant's hand, it knelt down to greet him. Cassius quickly nudged Benjamin from his sleep and helped him down.

"You dropped something," Cassius laughed lightly, handing Benjamin his maroon blanket, revealing the distinct two-headed snake and crown emblem.

"Get out here, Trump."

The slithering amphibian took his time hopping over the pit holes across the demolished fruit patch, his skin still beaming blue – the color of his fear.

"He seems friendly enough, don't you think?" Cassius muttered to Trump, giving the toad-man an encouraging wink.

"Oh yes. I bet his stomach is dying to meet me," Trump replied sardonically.

"Somehow, I don't think he's French," Benjamin added openly, forgetting for a moment the new world he was now a part of. The two protectors frowned at Benjamin, which made him feel awkward.

"French! The French eat frogs in my world. Get it? Never mind," Benjamin mumbled and blushed, the red color showing his embarrassment, which Trump keenly noticed.

"I am not a frog, I'll have you know," Trump gurgled back.

Disinterested in the three weird creatures mumbling by its feet, the rock-shelled giant took a few lengthy steps back toward its hibernation spot.

"Wait!" Cassius called back to the creature, running in front of its path.

"What on earth are you doing, bounty hunter?" Trump protested.

Cassius ignored the blustering toad while he attempted to communicate with the giant. "Where are you going?" Cassius asked, looking up to its bulging eyes.

The rock-shelled creature appeared to understand Cassius perfectly as it pointed to the hillside. "What's over there?" Another point in the same direction followed an enormous yawn.

"That's your home?"

The creature shook its head in disagreement and yawned again but Cassius couldn't interpret its body language.

"He's telling you he wants to hibernate," Trump

interrupted.

Cassius turned back to the giant and frowned. "Is that it?"

The giant simply nodded in agreement.

"No. You can't, I mean...don't you know what's going on?" Cassius continued, hoping it would listen to him.

Puzzled by the question, the giant shook its head. Trump gave a long sardonic sigh as Cassius explained to the creature about the dark war in their world, about Abasin's new false king and his plans to destroy every good and wholesome creature in it.

Cassius felt bad for the rock-shelled giant. It looked like it hadn't seen daylight for centuries. The giant stood scratching its head as it thought about what Cassius said.

"Will you help us?"

It was most unusual for Cassius to beg for help, but to gain the powerful rock-shelled giant as an ally was too good an opportunity for him to miss. His approach took less time than he'd expected. Even Trump was surprised at how eager the rock-shelled giant was to join them in their adventure.

"What's his name?" Benjamin asked.

Using its index finger, the giant scraped through the soil and drew massive letters in the ground next to them. Cassius and Trump gathered around the boy to look at what the giant had written.

"Uh...pleased to meet you, Molo." Benjamin smiled, lifting both hands to shake the creature's fingertip.

It was near dark when they gathered up their equipment to cross the foggy fields to the Stained Castle. Cassius led the way into the thick fog, while the rock-shelled giant named Molo strolled steadily behind them, looking out for any dangers that lay ahead.

22

Jennings' Ultimatum

It was dark and wet inside the grimy cell. The dungeon's executioners appeared no bigger than four feet tall amidst the gloom. Each pint-sized monster gawked at the prisoner through their red beady eyes and sniffed his human scent using the long, flopping trunks on their tiny faces. Bristly hairs covered their faces, reminding Jennings of the spikes on a porcupine.

One grotesque executioner sneakily shifted closer toward the old man before poking him with a small pole to get a lively reaction.

"Stop, you little vermin!" Jennings shouted.

A voice came out of the dark. "Enough!"

Immediately the group of executioners scurried off. Jennings started sobbing as a black silk handkerchief floated down upon his knees.

Jennings picked up the beautiful crafted silk material and ran his scarred fingers along its smooth texture. It was the nicest thing he'd felt in what seemed a very long time, ever since his fateful experience in the woods of Warwickshire.

"They can be the cruellest of all living creatures, can't they?" came the patronizing voice from the shadows.

Jennings eventually gained the courage to look

up at a well-suited knight walking into the dim yellow moonlight. His gray hair reflecting the moon made him look eerily older in contrast to his youthful complexion. He was richly dressed in the best of boots and had a layer of steel covering his entire left hand to resemble a glove.

Jennings squinted at the knight, confused as to what he was talking about, until he answered Jennings' query for him.

"Children, I mean," the knight grinned with a dazzling smile.

He was indeed very handsome and charming. But something in his character reminded Jennings of himself, which made the old man uncomfortable. His piercing black eyes were as cold as Jennings' but held a burning fury inside them that he kept well hidden.

"Children...those monsters?" Jennings asked in surprise, backing away from the knight in fear for his life.

"May I...?" asked the knight, politely gesturing toward an old wooden stool that lay on its side next to Jennings's chains.

Without uttering a word, Jennings nodded enthusiastically, all too willing to please the eerie knight. Demonstrating a simple spell of dark magick, the knight dragged the stool across the wet stone floor without lifting a finger.

Jennings gulped. "H-how did you do that?"

The knight smiled with a different grin, a devilish grin, as he trailed the stool back beside Jennings, whose body sagged on the wet concrete floor.

"On second thought, you should have this seat... you need it more than I," came the knight's soft reply.

With shaking legs, the frail man managed to stand

up, only to slump his bruised body onto the stool.

The knight walked around his prisoner, staring at the hole in the stone ceiling above them.

"I've heard one of my trusty assassins would like you as his personal slave." He laughed gently. "Would you like that? I could have my ogres build you your own personal oubliette."

"What do you want, young man?" Jennings asked.

"Young man? I like that Jennings...I wish that were true." The knight sighed, kneeling down to stare closely into his prisoner's old worn black sockets.

"That's *Mister* Jennings," Jennings corrected, causing the knight to snigger.

"Titles must be earned in this place, old man."

"Wait...how do you know my name?" Jennings whispered in horror.

The knight's laugh shuddered through Jennings' ringing ears, giving him chills. "Let's just say...it's complicated."

"Who are you? I demand to know," Jennings cried, losing his patience.

"I speak for the King of Abasin," the knight said pompously.

"Who runs this place?"

With a sudden smile, the knight folded his arms with glee. "I do," he said boastfully.

Jennings looked the man up and down in disgust before uttering a long sigh of despair.

"Do you believe in destiny, *Mister* Jennings?" asked the knight.

"Yes, I believe in one's fate," replied Jennings.

"I asked if you believed in *destiny*," sighed the young knight, standing back upright.

"Is there a difference?"

"Vast. You cannot change fate. Purpose, on the other hand, well..." the knight tittered when the lock around Jennings's bare foot came undone by another simple use of magick. "You *can* change that."

"What is this all about?" Jennings pleaded, rubbing his bruised ankle.

"Destiny, Mister Jennings. Three destinies to be exact...each in need of changing. The Children of Abasin are prophesied to overthrow His Majesty and rule this world together," the knight explained.

"You mean, my runaways?" Jennings gasped in awe.

"Come!" the knight ordered bluntly.

"Where are we going?"

The knight turned his head to give Jennings a glowering look. "Or wait here for Thestor's nightly back scrub."

Jennings shuddered at the screams of prisoners echoing from the dungeons as his captor led him out of an enormous underground torture chamber.

Outside the air smelled of burnt charcoal, and dust filled the stale atmosphere. Jennings breathed in deeply to adjust to the cold temperature. Then he caught sight of the ghostly vision before him.

It was a castle, but unlike any castle he had ever seen before. Land encircled it but the castle had no solid foundation beneath it to hold it in place, as it magically hovered in the middle of an everlasting pit. The awkward positioning of this ingenious creation was obviously to protect it from enemy sieges. The castle itself appeared no more than a mere monumental building of rocks, which twisted and changed position continuously. It seemed to be alive.

"Keep moving," the knight ordered, leading the

way along a narrow and dangerous path built on the better half of a bridge. Jennings looked between the cracks in the bridge at a frightening, everlasting pitfall of nothingness that made him feel dizzy. They walked out from the root of Saul's great castle and travelled to its top in a massive lift that had been built on a steel structure of winding chains and rusted pivots. It was a long ride to the top of the castle. Towering over the landscape several thousand feet above the ground around it was enough to give Jennings a strong wave of vertigo, causing him to sway back and forth before he lost all sense of balance. Jennings leaned over the edge of the unshielded lift when the knight tugged at his tie, saving him from a fatal fall. "Grab onto something if you must," the knight said coldly, rolling his eyes. The lift cranked into place. The shuddering halt caused Jennings to stumble out onto the floor. The ground felt different. It was smooth in texture; similar to the handkerchief the young knight had given him earlier. Only this wasn't a handkerchief but a royal carpet. "This way," the knight instructed, stepping over him.

They were at such great heights that Jennings could touch the very clouds that were now within reach, inches above his head. Rows of statuesque warriors glistened in the dark behind pillars that held half of a marble roof over them. They seemed to be a decorative row of statues until Jennings caught sight of their glowing cat-like eyes peering back at him.

The knight reached the enormous steel gates to Saul's chamber room. The gates metamorphosed into black smoke as the knight moved through them, disappearing down a tall dark corridor, leaving the old principal to wait behind.

The freshly faced knight entered the circular floor inside Saul's great throne room. The throne itself was made of pure blue flame. Whatever dark magick this fortress carried, it was certainly of the most powerful kind. On either side of the flamed throne stood an assassin that had been sent to the old world to kill Benjamin, Tommy and Sebastian. "Jodo Kahln," whispered a voice from the flaming throne.

Stepping through the flaming throne seconds later, the False One greeted the knight. The False One was a beast-like creature. A white velvet shroud with a bronze-plated mask that concealed his face covered his body. He was tall, but only a few inches smaller than his assassins that stood guarding him on each side, and none the less grotesque. "We have a problem, your Highness," Jodo, who remained kneeling, began.

"Ah yes...the human wart scrubber. He is your problem now, as you are his," Saul said slowly. His mask started to change to an aggressive expression that matched the face that leered behind it. Saul's voice soothed Jodo as much as it frightened him. "What shall I do, Sire?" Jodo pleaded to his fierce and powerful ruler.

"It is a very uncommon dilemma you are in with this captive; one that only you can judge, Jodo Kahln. My finest knight of knights," Saul complimented as he approached the kneeling servant, his mask now a contorted smile. "We have more important matters at hand. The threat to my throne has finally arrived. The children have returned to take it from me, you understand?" Saul spluttered, resting a beastly hand upon Jodo's armored shoulder.

"I will do what is asked of me, Highness," the bold knight stated, looking up at his master through hardened eyes. Saul knelt to face his trusted knight and spokesman, taking off his mask for only Jodo to see beneath it, which terrified the evil knight.

"Their Brotherhood will become the greatest thorn in our sides. It is the same future that has been foretold by the witches," Saul growled. The knight kept his gaze upon the ground. "You know, thorns are much easier to pluck from the flesh when they are small, Jodo. A little pick and scratch is all it takes to heal the wound. But let them grow, and some can become big enough to cause a fatal puncture, and together...demonstrate nature's power, more lethal than steel."

"What would you have me do?" Jodo replied with a serious and stern look, hiding any signs of fear.

"Shake my lazy army out of their rut. Go to the Goblin City and lead Borland's lot to the Stained Castle," he ordered, sitting back upon the blue flamed throne. "*Civilians* are protecting The Three That Are One. Their capture will require much force now. My Nockwire will aid you."

With one gentle nod, Saul motioned for his two assassins to accompany the knight.

The two assassins, Thestor and Scythas, towered over Jodo Kahln, when they marched on either side of him, snarling at each other as they left Saul's chambers to recruit their destructive army of goblins.

Thestor lifted Jennings onto his back before the group flew off the marble balcony outside Saul's palace chamber. Flying at high speed, Jodo led the Nockwire assassins and Jennings toward several glowing mountains concealed in radiant blue mist, at least forty miles away from Saul's castle.

"Where are we now?" cried Jennings when they landed on one of several thousand high bridges built between the mountains and their caves. The rope bridges each intertwined with every other in an enormous spider's web-like maze.

Jodo Kahln's eyes blazed in anticipation as he stared back at Jennings. "This is the entrance to the Goblin City. We're now in their den so be careful where you tread...for they fly too."

23

Crossing the Shoe Tree

Brisk winds picked up when Ariel and Tommy reached a grove near the edge of the sharp mountainside.

"Can we get by that?" he asked, pointing to the bunch of brambles and trees.

"I'm not sure. This used to be a clear way to the Stained Castle. I say we wait here for the others. They're bound to come this way soon," she said, resting a hand on his shoulder.

Instead of heeding his protector's advice, the stubborn boy moved her hand away and proceeded forth into the grove until he felt something swipe at his head and miss.

His eyes darted around the grove, but he was unable to spot who or what was responsible for the unprovoked strike. Trees of different shapes and sizes made up the grove. There was one in particular that caught Tommy's attention most of all. Molds of humans in various postures decorated its bark alongside creatures unfamiliar to him.

The girth of its trunk was three times larger than the oak trees that neighbored it. Its roots sprawled over most of the area and claimed the entire ground.

Casts of ill-fated pixies, goblins, and children

patterned its wooden surface. High above, hundreds of different shoes dangled from laces attached to its floppy branches, some in even pairs, others in odd pairings, and a few single shoes hung alone. Flats, heels, riding boots, snow boots, dress shoes and dozens of other types of footwear hung lifelessly and motionless, as if part of the tree's decoration.

"What are they?" Tommy asked as he stood gawking at the disturbing spectacle.

Ariel placed her finger over her lips, signalling him to be silent. As Tommy took a step out of the tree's domain another swipe came at him, but this time it didn't miss. As the lace wrapped around his wrist, its tugging grip spun him around.

"Get it off me!" he yelled.

Another lace wrapped round his waist. Together, the laces hauled him deeper into the grove, out of Ariel's reach. Tommy yelled as loud as he could, muffled by the laces that had ensnared him. It was difficult for Ariel to spot him inside the mass of living shoes.

A web of shoes quickly formed in front of her, attempting to block her path. Slicing through, Ariel threw herself into the den, fighting off every swiping attack with her trusty dagger. The nymph flipped backwards and forwards fluently, missing every assault the shoe tree made toward her. Hacking her way through the thicket of entangled shoelaces, Ariel saw the tree open its gaping mouth, ready to swallow Tommy whole after it took the boy's shoes off his feet and added them to its eerie collection. But Ariel wasn't going down without a fight.

"Thomas, get ready to grab hold," she called out, anticipating the next striking shoe and dodging its attack. Using the tree's predictable pattern to her advantage, Ariel grabbed a tight hold of one lengthy lace and speedily climbed it to reach a suitable height. Once she had Tommy in her sights, the acrobatic nymph began swinging from shoelace to shoelace, effortlessly slipping through the multitude, and cutting down every shoe that got in her way.

"Fight it off, Thomas!" she cried out seconds before she reached the lace-covered captive. The tree's tongue was made of shreds of wood that aggressively tugged at the boy to pull him into its mouth. Over a dozen shoes waged a relentless attack on both of them, without mercy. It was like trying to fight smoke.

After the attack left both cocooned, the tree instantly settled, but not until Ariel had managed to wedge the tree's tongue to its bark with her dagger, sealing its mouth from gobbling them up.

***

Sebastian approached the last half-mile of the Black Swamp. Ripping his way through the shallow end of the thick dark sludge, his stamina weakened with each gruelling step, unlike his protector who kept urging him forth.

"You can do it, boy, a little further...that's all it takes, remember," Cecil rambled.

"I know, I know, *eyes front,*" Sebastian interrupted, frowning at the pixie's unrelenting encouragement.

The night was closing in. Sebastian could feel the chill nip at his clothes from the gusts of wind beating down upon his mud-covered back.

"You're almost there; that a boy, keep it going." Cecil kept imploring with much restlessness in his voice.

"I'm trying my best…if I could buzz around so easily and freely as all you *buzzing pixies* do, believe me, I wouldn't still be in this blasted blobby bog," Sebastian scolded before he laughed at the shocked expression on Cecil's face.

Cecil giggled a little in return, until his ears perked up, recognizing a distinct cackling laugh that joined theirs, chilling him to the very tip of his wings.

"Run like lightning, Sebastian," Cecil ordered in a faint whisper. He took hold of the boy's hand and began pulling him through the swamp. Cecil flew as fast as his little wings could carry them both.

Sebastian kicked his legs out of the murky sludge, sensing the awful seriousness of their predicament. Someone was heading toward them. And judging by Cecil's reaction, it wasn't someone friendly.

"Don't let go," Sebastian begged, loosening from Cecil's grip.

"Grab hold with your other hand," Cecil yelled, almost reaching his top speed. Sebastian obeyed the pixie's order and stretched his free hand out to get a tighter grip. Holding on for his life, Sebastian shut his eyes tight until he couldn't feel the swamp underneath his feet anymore.

Cecil flew hastily and erratically, swerving left to right. Rapidly gaining more momentum, the pixie started their ascension to the top of the cliff.

They were almost at the highest point, a few thousand feet in the air, when an airborne assailant jumped from a flying omnicorn onto Cecil's back, separating Sebastian from his protector. The boy quickly grabbed onto a bundle of weeds protruding from the cliff side, which slowed his descent to a desperate halt.

Taking a vicious grasp of his back, the tenacious fiend tried to snap the bones in Cecil's wings. The sudden and unprovoked attack sent both crashing into the mountainside.

Cecil's fairy awoke and flew into the eyes of its master's attacker, blinding him with its powerful beam of light. Taking advantage of the fairy's attack, Cecil pulled the villain off his back and slammed him into the wall. It only took one of Cecil's free hands to hold the attacker in place and reveal his identity.

"General Lemis!" Cecil rasped. The pixie's strong grip tightened, causing the chief sea guard to choke and splutter.

Lemis tried to kick and punch his way to freedom, but he proved no match for the pixie's natural strength.

"What is that? You want me to let go? Very well," Cecil teased, scowling, before he dropped the sneaky villain off the mountainside. Lemis called out to his omnicorn for help.

The steed seemed confused as to whether it should pursue Cecil or save its master. Cecil tried to antagonize the omnicorn to fight him, so it would fail to rescue Lemis in time.

"Come on, pretty pony. I dare ya." Cecil growled under his breath at the hideous creature seconds before it dipped its wings and shot down the cliff.

Following suit, Cecil retracted his own little wings and bolted toward Sebastian in a downward spiral.

Lemis swiftly shot past Sebastian a moment before the dangling boy joined him.

"Cecil! Help me," Sebastian beseeched as the

unstable weeds snapped away from their weak roots. Cecil instantly sped, catching the boy by a thrust of his strong wings.

The omnicorn had succeeded in rescuing its master a few feet from the swampy ground. Without deliberation, Lemis ordered his flying pet to turn around and soar after their targets.

"They're coming back again!" Sebastian cried out in panic as he kept his glasses from falling off his face.

"We're almost there, boy," Cecil reassured, picking up the pace in a dangerous vertical ascent whilst playing his part in the risky game of tag.

Lemis pointed his rusty black blade straight up at Sebastian, baring his twisted grin.

"Where do you think *you're* going, human?"

A few more feet were all they had left to cover before they reached the top of the cliff, but the omnicorn was a faster and more agile flyer than Cecil Baskin, for the creature's very wingspan and aerodynamic structure was designed for reaching tremendous velocity.

"Faster Cecil! Faster!" Sebastian called to his protector.

The omnicorn flew inches away from his feet. Its hellish jaws opened up to show its razor sharp teeth as it snapped at Sebastian's shoes, missing each time the boy lifted his legs to avoid contact.

"Hang on!" Cecil ordered.

After several efforts of retaliation, Sebastian lifted his left leg and thrust it hard against the omnicorn's face, wedging his shoe between its upper and lower jaw. The omnicorn shook its head violently from left to right in order to unlock its mouth from the child's foot while the four ascended in a single chain.

But it was to no avail. The omnicorn was stuck in

a knotty position now, as was its prey. Lemis shuffled along the monster's neck toward Sebastian, ready to separate the two of them using his rusted sword.

"Cecil, get us out of here," Sebastian pleaded, twisting and turning away from each swiping attack.

By chance, Sebastian's free leg managed a lucky kick to Lemis's chest.

The chief sea guard failed to grab the reins several times while he tumbled off his beastly pet. The dark creature neighed in pain when Lemis grasped onto its tail, saving himself from a second fall.

Cecil ordered Sebastian to take the stick that was strapped to his side. With a free arm, the boy unbuttoned the pixie's pouch and raised the stick as high as he could. The stick glowed bright red and felt alive with magic. Sebastian struck the omnicorn's long and disfigured face. Fearful of the sudden blast of magic, the steed bit down hard, tearing the shoe straight off Sebastian's foot while it trailed its rider into the fog-covered abyss.

"You did it, lad!" The pixie laughed the instant they flew past the top of the massive cliff's edge.

"Woo hoo!" Sebastian yelled, ecstatic from his near-death experience and relieved that they'd both survived the terrifying battle to tell the tale.

"We're near the Stained Castle now, Sebastian, but first I need to rest these old wings," Cecil panted, at the same time his speed had decreased rapidly.

"And if they come back?" Sebastian asked.

"Just let them try," Cecil replied, gazing back down to a calm fog thousands of feet below them. "Best we rest further away from the edge, I think."

"That looks as good a spot as any," Sebastian said, pointing down at a small patch of woodland nearby. In one swift halt, Cecil's flight took an unplanned pivot, lightly crashing into a strange and unfamiliar grove. Cecil's fairy dimmed its light and disappeared back inside his chest pocket.

As Cecil rested to catch his breath, the one-shoed boy limped to the front of the grove, investigating his surroundings further. Walking into the gloomy patch, Sebastian noticed that it was made up of many strange and frightening-looking trees, with one in particular that immediately caught his eye.

It was the largest of the grove and rested dead center amongst its neighbors. The tree revealed a large face from a distance that was made up of many bodily shapes. Its deep dishevelled crevices resembled large eyes that appeared to look straight at him. Multiple shoes hung immobile against the light breeze as Sebastian took a step further.

"I sure hope there is one in my size," he whispered to himself, staring down at his single bare foot.

24

March of the Troll

Cecil dug through his pouch and guzzled a bottle of his trusty healing remedy. It was the perfect time to rest up. "Stay in sight," he ordered from over his shoulder, wheezing heavily to get his strength back.

Sebastian tried to run to his protector after the shoe tree fired out one of its closest shoes toward him.

"Mr. Baskin, I really think we should..." Sebastian called out, his voice trailing off.

"Boy?" Cecil called, irritated at the unfinished conversation. "Sebastian Cain!" he called again like a father would his son.

The pixie struggled to get back on his feet then spun around to face the grove, groaning because of the painful state his overused wings were in. With each trailing step, Cecil dragged his tired feet toward the largest tree. He noticed something struggling in front of him the instant he entered the grove.

"Sebastian?" he asked cautiously, flabbergasted at the sight of the knotted shoes and laces that enfolded the boy. "Let go of him!" Cecil bellowed, trying to take flight to avoid a sudden attack. It took only a few shoes to get the better of the stout pixie. Laces tightened and knotted themselves around his bruised wings and brought Cecil's bumpy flight to an instant halt. The boy and his protector had now become two more unfortunate casualties of the ruthless shoe tree.

In unison, the shoe tree finished wrapping its captives up by binding their arms and legs together so that they were unable to move an inch. Sensing danger, Cecil's fairy instantly shot out of his breast pocket in time and sped through the web of laces in search of help.

It had only been a few minutes since their capture when heavy stomping shook the ground. Trees rustled from afar in opposite waves, disturbing the creatures that lived in them as their nests cracked and fell. Each captive caught glimpses of a wide hairy creature that approached. It was terrifying, for only their eyes remained uncovered. They'd expected to see something enormous, but what emerged was surprisingly nothing of the sort.

The troll lunged out of the woods and leaped directly within firing range of the slinging shoes.

"Oh, I smell you," he threatened. His humungous nose sniffed the different scents in the air. The shoes wasted no time in their persistent attack, but the hairy troll effortlessly brushed them away, dodging several more that attacked from both sides. He moved with elegance, reaching Tommy in seconds. In one flick of his razor sharp fingernail, he promptly cut the boy down before taking his first prize away from the shoe tree's den.

The troll leaped out of reach of the tackling shoes and unravelled the petrified boy, slicing off the smothering laces. Tommy was so glad to breathe normally again that he failed to focus on whom and what had freed him. When he finally studied the troll's daunting features, Tommy scurried backwards, fleeing from the ugly sight. It was a miniature troll, just over a century in age, and had tiny pointed ears with no hair to cover them (unlike Ariel's). His bright yellow eyes were his most distinguishing feature next to his large nose and his round, blunt teeth.

"Where do you think you're crawling to, little scamp?" the troll asked.

"My goodness, does everything in this place talk?" asked the boy. It wasn't the smartest of questions one could ask of a troll, especially a troll that had just met a human for the first time.

"What are you? Stand before me," growled the troll, stomping the ground while he marched over to the boy. Tommy scarpered along the dusty ground and withdrew toward the shoe tree. "Don't go back in there," the troll commanded, pounding his large hairy feet on the damp earth.

"Better those things than being eaten up by... whatever it is you are," Tommy cried.

"Ha! Be my guest. I don't eat ignorant silly bodies anyway," the troll sneered back. Tommy paused to look over his shoulder at the mass of shoes hanging lifelessly and almost in range of him. "If you go back in there, I won't follow after you," the troll warned.

"Let me be," Tommy snapped.

"Relax, human. I'm not like the giant trolls from the Bothopolis Forest, I can tell you. They'd already have you cooked for breakfast by now. My name is Cackerin. Ban Pan Cackerin to you," the troll snapped, spitting over the boy's face and pushing his nose against Tommy's.

"Are you a villain?" the boy boldly asked, trying to get straight to the point.

"That all depends from where you're standing, chap. Do you see a villain?" the troll grunted, before marching back into the grove.

It took the troll even less time to retrieve the others from the intertwining mess of laces. Ariel was the last to be rescued. Flapping her arms to break free, the delirious nymph accidently whacked the troll on his big nose, which wobbled back and forth. "Nice to see you too," Ban Pan said sardonically, helping Ariel to her feet.

"Oh Ban Pan, I'm so happy it's you," she sighed, hugging the troll.

"Of course it's me. What else has my smell?"

"My old socks," Cecil answered.

"You don't wear any socks, Mr. Baskin," Sebastian sniggered as Cecil raised him out of the laced sheath.

"Precisely the reason." Cecil winked back holding his nose.

Tommy and Sebastian laughed at Cecil's remark before they noticed each other. Taking a deep breath in disbelief, Tommy gazed at the familiar face of the posh boy he had briefly met in Warwickshire and was overjoyed to be in company with someone human again.

"Hey! Silver-spoon head!" he called to Sebastian and gave him a welcoming handshake.

Sebastian smiled, fixing his large glasses with one hand while greeting Tommy with the other. "Thomas, right?"

"What in heaven has happened to Peter?" Sebastian asked. A baffled look showed on his face, until Tommy explained the nymph's real identity.

"*Extraordinary!*" Sebastian circled Ariel, studying her face at every angle.

"What is *that* thing?" Tommy asked, pointing to Sebastian's appointed guardian. The tired pixie gave Tommy a grouchy stare, offended by the boy's disrespectful tone.

"That's my protector, Cecil Baskin. He calls himself a knight but I've never seen one like him before."

"I thought for a while I was dreaming this whole thing. But now you're here, it's really real. I can't believe it," Tommy replied.

"I can. I've seen this place in my dreams," Sebastian whispered, staring out at the evening sky.

"Let's go talk to big stinky here," Cecil joked, humoring the boys as they approached the troll.

"Sir Cecil Baskin, I'm glad you made it," Ariel smiled as she bowed her head to the knighted pixie.

"We're lucky to be alive after the attack we encountered," Cecil went on, coughing as he told Ariel the story of his horrendous ordeal.

"And Lemis? Is he dead?" Ariel asked.

"I can only hope," Cecil replied, hissing from the excruciating pain still throbbing at his tiny wings.

"What about Benjamin?" Ariel asked.

"Nothing yet," frowned Cecil.

"You are the first friendly faces we've seen since the Black Swamp," Sebastian added.

"Black Swamp?" asked Tommy, turning to Ariel for an answer.

Cecil interrupted, pushing the boys away from the grove by a tap of his stick. "Never mind all that. Come on, less chatter boys and more wander. Legs forward and eyes front."

"This smell is rotten," Tommy blurted out loud, holding his nose as he stepped away from the troll.

"That's right. Nothing smells as bad as us trolls. Not

even the pixie's footwear," grinned Ban Pan proudly.

"Tell that to the Nockwire," Ariel mumbled, joking privately beside Cecil Baskin, who let out a strong and abrasive laugh.

"You're kind of grouchy, aren't you?" Sebastian asked, sneering back at the brazen rescuer.

"You're lucky that's all I am. Not all of us trolls are as tame as I," Ban Pan warned.

"How did you find us?" Ariel asked the troll, her excitement and wonder evident.

"One of your fairies sought my help. When my nose perked up, I just knew it was you," he said assuredly as Cecil's fairy fluttered back into the pixie's breast pocket.

"I'm so glad to see you. I thought you had been killed in the battle at Bothopolis," Ariel said smiling with relief.

"Done for? Ban Pan Cackerin?" the troll said indignantly. "Don't be ridiculous, why I'm the only one I know of who can make it through shoe trees without getting entangled," he rambled. "By the way, I suggest you find another way to your destinations. There's no way beyond that shoe tree even if you could get by it. Its forest is too thick and dangerous."

And with that, the troll simply turned his back on them and marched away without even so much as a goodbye.

"Where are you going?" Cecil demanded.

"To the Stained Castle, of course. The trolls have been summoned there for an emergency meeting."

"Everyone has," Cecil added.

"That's where we're going. We might as well go together," Ariel called.

"Ha! Travel with other kinds? Now that I do not

do," the troll scoffed, marching away.

Ariel looked to Cecil for support. "Well, what do you want me to do? He doesn't travel with other kinds," he whispered back to the anxious nymph, holding out his hands. "No troll does."

"You're the knight here," Ariel said, encouraging the pixie to exercise his authority over the stubborn troll.

"I'm just a protector, not a negotiator," Cecil insisted.

"Order him."

Giving out a long groan, Cecil rolled his eyes and fluttered his little wings, taking small flying leaps to catch up with the stomping beast.

"Wait, Ban Pan, there is something I forgot to mention," Cecil said finally.

"You're welcome, now quit pestering me," Ban Pan muttered in reply.

"No, not that," Cecil insisted.

"Ha! Talk about ungrateful. What is it then, ungrateful knight?"

"This human is the reason we have all been summoned to this emergency meeting," Cecil explained to the troll, pointing to Sebastian.

"And Tommy, too," Ariel added.

"Let's not forget Benjamin," interrupted Tommy.

The troll instantly paused in his march and turned his massive hairy feet back round to face the mixed group.

"So, they *do* have names," the troll scoffed, gesturing to the group to come closer. As the four approached him, Ban Pan bent down to face the guardians and whispered. "There is a better way to the Stained Castle than this one, but first you must give me something, something of reasonable value."

"I knew you were a villain. And a cheat at that," Tommy accused.

Cecil swiftly knocked Tommy on the head with his trusty stick to prevent the mouthy boy from insulting the troll further.

"That's enough lip from you, boy," Cecil insisted while Sebastian covered his mouth to keep himself from laughing at his friend's sudden chastisement.

"Are we bargaining, Ban Pan?" asked the nymph.

"Of course we are...I wouldn't be much of a troll if I didn't."

"We really don't have time for this nonsense," the pixie suggested, the flutter of his wings showing his exasperation at the troll's stubbornness.

"Zip it, Gramps," Ban Pan mocked. Cecil screwed his face up at the annoying creature. "I cannot believe that the Council chose you two to protect the Children of Abasin. Good grief, of all the civilians they could have picked," Ban Pan continued.

"You know of the Children of Abasin?" Cecil gasped.

"Every soul in Abasin knows about The Three That Are One. I don't know of one who hasn't heard of *that* prophecy," sighed Ban Pan, frowning at Cecil and the two boys.

"What is he talking about?" Tommy asked, looking between Ariel and Cecil for an answer.

"You mean to tell me you boys don't even know about your own future?" the troll began to tease Tommy, chortling to himself.

"Why don't you shut your trap, you big furry fungus, before I help you shut it," Tommy barked. Cecil and Sebastian reached out simultaneously to hold the boisterous lad back.

Ban Pan pointed at Tommy while laughing loudly. "You, my boy, are hilarious...look at the size of you and still you would dare take on a troll." Ban Pan laughed a little longer until he shot back a serious look that frightened Tommy to his core.

"You, scamp, are this world's last hope," he muttered slowly. "The prophecy foretold three human children would return from being cast out of Abasin and come of age to kill the False One and take over this kingdom. This makes you three the most important people in this entire world right now, as well as the most hunted. And you don't even know it." Ban Pan chortled again and shook his head.

"Well, we weren't told anything until now," Tommy admitted, turning his blameful gaze toward Ariel and Cecil.

"My dreams," Sebastian whispered to her.

"I told you they were true," Ariel muttered.

"You didn't tell me about the killing part," Sebastian snapped back.

"That's enough!" Cecil roared at the troll. "You're scaring the boys."

"If they're scared now, what use do you think they'll be on the battlefield? The way you two are mollycoddling them, you would do better to hand them over to Saul while you can and pray for a quick death," the troll replied.

"I'm not scared," Tommy declared, interrupting both creatures as he walked toward the troll with courage and conviction.

"Then I think Abasin maybe in luck with you at the helm, chap." The troll smiled in respect to Tommy.

"I-I'm not afraid either, I just wrestled a bull horse

with wings, you know," Sebastian added after a few seconds of awkward silence.

"That a boy." Cecil smiled to Sebastian, motioning for him to keep his large glasses from sliding off his nose again.

"You will lead us to this castle, no bargains necessary." Tommy barked his order as if the ability to command came from somewhere deep inside him.

The new world was already changing them and they could feel it. Tommy's eyesight had altered and his confidence was growing to an almost fearless high. All Ban Pan could do with the bold little human was obey his orders.

"Very well...*Prince of Abasin*," the troll replied, placing his claw on his heart.

"Um...before we fulfil any prophecy, we're going to need a decent pair of shoes. I'm a size six," Sebastian spoke up, motioning the troll to cut down a new pair of shoes from the grove.

Tommy kept close to the troll as the group began their journey together. The others trailed behind along the edge of the enormous cliff side Cecil and Sebastian had flown up.

The edge stretched into the distance as far as the eye could see. The road was tiresome and dangerous, but if they were lucky enough not to be deterred from it, its route would eventually lead them straight to the Stained Castle, just as Ban Pan had promised.

25

Goblin Versus Goblin

Lemis fell off his omnicorn when it crashed onto the castle's top balcony, shredding through a large piece of royal carpet. In a flash, the chief sea guard found himself surrounded by members of Saul's guards.

"Wait, I'm General Lemis, I'm the chief sea guard of Denasin. I'm a servant! I am a servant!" the pathetic creature protested as the royal guards pointed their glistening scythes and glowing staffs at his throat.

"What brings you?" one of them hissed.

"Please! I seek the favored Knight, *Jodo Kahln!*" Lemis shrieked as the royal guards left him to resume their stance in a militant line, confident that he was no longer a threat.

Without warning, an undertaker who worked in the prisons far below appeared at the top of the lift shaft.

"Lord Lemis, I have some of your surviving troops waiting for you outside my dungeons, if you please," the disease-ridden creature said smoothly, coaxing the new arrival to join him on the rickety and grimy elevator. With what little dignity he had left, Lemis brushed his armor and jumped back on top of his omnicorn. Saul's royal guards were infamous for killing unannounced visitors and Lemis knew how lucky he had been.

"We'll make our own way, rat," he spat back at the undertaker, before he flew off the edge of Saul's castle toward the few remaining troops below. "Give me news," he demanded.

"Jodo Kahln has gone to counsel the king of the goblins, Lord Lemis," said one mutant sea guard.

"Borland," Lemis whispered back in shock. "Stay here and wait for my return. I must consult with Jodo Kahln," he barked at them as he prepared to take flight into the black skyline.

* * *

The Nockwire stood on higher ground to keep watch for any foul play or unwanted attention a gremlin or goblin would inflict upon Jodo Kahln and his new baggage.

"Keep up, old man. Lose track of me and you'll never get out of here alive," Jodo warned, walking confidently across one bridge of many thousand.

"Indeed, you wouldn't want to get lost in a place like this...something worse could happen to you than scrubbing my back," taunted Thestor.

"I doubt that very much," Jennings muttered under his breath, amusing Jodo who'd been the only one to hear his insult.

Jodo walked steadfast across each of the descending bridges that led toward the city below the blue fog. As they got lower, Jennings noticed little shacks, shelters, and half houses welded onto the rocky cliffs on either side of the inlet. Screeches from goblin families fighting their neighbors penetrated his ears.

"Trespassers!" one goblin growled out through the mist of the mountainside.

"You're not welcomed here!" another goblin creature yelled down at them.

"I smell human stink," an elderly goblin mocked.

"Call the goblin guards," one older goblin screamed.

"Fresh meat! Fresh meat!" chanted a group of young goblins.

"Kill them!" another random goblin called out.

"Gobble their skin...gobble them all up," screeched a cackling female.

As Jennings studied the grotesque creatures, he noticed how well their houses and shacks had been built and how closely they resembled the stone walls. It was inventive camouflage. Even Jodo couldn't tell the difference between some of the crafted houses. It was obvious to Jennings that these goblin folk were creatures of intelligence. The threatening jeers failed to intimidate the knight and his Nockwire assassins, which reassured Jennings that he was in safer company than he realised.

They had only crossed the entrance to the Goblin City, and already an inconspicuous goblin guard flew silently above the weakest target. Its dangerous claws reached for Jennings' withered neck while it landed discreetly behind him.

Jodo Kahln didn't have to see the trouble brewing, for the powerful knight simply sensed the threat. Using his dark magick, Jodo pulled the scrawny man away from the creeping goblin. When he landed at the feet of the unconcerned Nockwire, Jennings realised

Jodo had safeguarded him from harm.

The goblin fiend cautiously hopped back a step and crouched, squinting at the young warlock.

"You're intruding here," it hooted.

"King Saul may permit your kind to live here, but may I remind you that this city still belongs to him. And since I have jurisdiction, it is *you* who are invading *my* path, goblin," Jodo explained, approaching the goblin guard.

"King Borland never mentioned your arrival, human," the goblin insisted.

In one strike, Jodo's blade penetrated the stubborn goblin's gut, finalizing their discussion.

The goblin's eyes rolled back in its head when Jodo released his blade. Its life slipped away instantly.

"You, *human!*" beckoned another voice. "In what name do you spill goblin blood?"

Jodo turned to face four new goblins that blocked the connecting bridge that lead to another. "By order of your true King, Saul of Abasin, I demand to meet with Borland," Jodo called out to them. The goblin quartet huddled together to deliberate their minimal options.

"But you are human," one goblin tittered in disbelief (for no human had ever graced their kingdom before that night). Using his magick, the knight levitated the dead goblin and threw the carcass across the bridge until it tumbled toward the group of goblins.

"You want to end up like him?" the brash knight threatened, winking back at Jennings and his Nockwire assassins.

"Follow us...you're obviously daring enough," another goblin sneered.

The quartet of guards jumped off the bridge

and took flight. Without hesitation, Jodo took hold of Jennings by the scruff of his neck and threw the weakling over the bridge, then jumped overboard to join him.

Jennings screamed, trying to dodge each rope, chain and plank that zoomed past him. A large piece of mountainside came into clear view and was seconds away from breaking his fall when Jodo grabbed hold of the man's collar and pulled him aside.

Jodo and Jennings flew past goblin buildings and factories when they broke through the fog to the gigantic goblin city beneath.

The Nockwire watched over them from above when Jodo and Jennings followed the four flying guards into a cheering crowd made up of thousands of goblins, hobgoblins, and gremlins surrounding a cage fight.

The grisly spectators screamed chants as they watched a cage fighting match kick off between two large and dangerous hobgoblins.

"You wanted to meet with our King, there he is," the leading goblin guard told the human pair, pointing to a large sheltered booth at the very top of the stadium's center. "Just so you know, only the disobedient are summoned into His Majesty's presence without invitation. I find it amusing that you request to meet with King Borland, uninvited. You humans are as crazy as the stories I've heard," the goblin leader snickered.

"I like that word. *Crazy!*" Jodo laughed, patting the goblin on the back while he pushed Jennings in front to lead the way, brushing past the four goblin guards in defiance. "Oh, there is one story you haven't heard about us crazy humans, my brute," Jodo continued, turning back and leaning to whisper into the goblin guard's ear. "I was the craziest."

Magick poured out of the knight's steel gloved hand, splashing over the goblin's face. The cursed creature started to scream. "Please stop!" the goblin leader begged while the dark spell gradually changed his form.

"What have you done to me?" the goblin leader wailed in horror after it looked down at its new amphibious form.

"The same thing I did to the last jester that found it funny to mock my humanity. I guess we humans are just spontaneously crazy," Jodo teased.

Goblins and gremlins licked their lips, surrounding the transformed creature. To goblins, frog and toad creatures were a much sought after delicacy. The sniggering knight took one look at his cursed creation and turned his back. The ill-fated creature tried to slither away but it proved impossible. The feeding frenzy erupted. Creature upon creature fought amongst the ever-growing crowd for a bite; like a school of flesh eating piranhas. The feast lasted merely seconds.

Jodo and Jennings made their way through the scary crowd of vicious and raucous goblins. The knight turned to point his finger at the old man.

"Keep close to me; we're in unfavorable company. If you lag behind, I'll leave you behind. Do you understand?"

Not wanting to upset him, Jennings simply nodded his head in silent agreement. Jennings felt a new fear of the knight and was only too glad to stay on his good side, if there was a good side to stay on.

Rows of hideous faces watched the unwelcomed humans walk through the large gathering that circled the cage. Most, if not all, were astonished, for no human had ever dared to step foot inside the Goblin City before, never mind two of them. To the goblins, what their uninvited human guests had done was nothing short of suicidal. For a goblin to even spot a civilian near the outskirts of the city was unheard of, and now two humans, thought to be extinct, walked amongst the thousands of goblins inside their city.

Roars became screams. Screams became yells, and then the yelling turned to mere whispering chatter. Jennings kept close to his captor. The silence made the old man's blood run colder than usual. Even the fighting hobgoblins peered out from the large cage to catch a glimpse of the human guests that had brought their match to a standstill.

Impervious to the hostile atmosphere, Jodo confidently marched up the steep steps toward Borland's private booth, only to meet a row of specially armed goblins at the top. As the knight ignored their request for a body search, the row of armed goblins stretched out their arrows. By a powerful display of magick, Jodo Kahln triggered every arrow to backfire onto each goblin, in sync. One by one, their bodies collapsed and lifelessly toppled down the narrow steps toward the stage cage. The rattling sounds broke the dead silence around the stadium.

"Who is the fool who disturbs our Ruler's game?" barked a scrawny gremlin from Borland's lavish upper circle.

"You only have one leader. Or have you forgotten His Majesty already?" Jodo snapped. "You need to remember your allegiance. All of you do. You have rotted in this derelict devil's pit too long. Look at you. You're a disgrace to your true King. You've been too busy getting fat and slothful on King Saul's offerings while our enemies grow strong. This charade stops now."

"Shut that human up!" the scrawny gremlin ordered from its safe spot on Borland's balcony. A crowd of hobgoblins surged around the knight, scraping their weapons along the concrete steps in an attempt to intimidate Jodo into submission.

Jodo calmly kept his eyes on the scrawny spokesperson, showing a confident smile the moment his two Nockwire assassins landed behind him, breaking large chunks out of the stone steps. The mighty tremor lifted the surrounding hobgoblins off of their feet. Several hundred goblins pushed one another back to keep a safe distance from the nine-foot beasts.

The two cage-fighting hobgoblins began to quietly flee in opposite directions at the sight of the Nockwire, climbing out of the cage ring in haste.

"Forgive us, my Lord, I see now the seriousness of the situation," the scrawny spokesperson muttered timidly.

"Walk with me," Jodo smoothly ordered Jennings. The Nockwire stood patiently still upon the steps, watching for any would-be renegade that dared stir up a lynch mob.

Jodo and Jennings strode between the remaining guards and gate crashed Borland's private and luxurious VIP lounge. The morbidly obese Goblin King lay in the comfort of a troll-furred rug that was draped over his throne chair, keeping his back to them.

"What is this travesty? Where is my game? Why has it stopped?" the Goblin King sputtered at several female goblin servants that pampered him, waving his legs and arms in the air like a spoiled child throwing a temper tantrum.

"My Liege, we—that is I...err," stuttered his scrawny spokesperson.

"Stop your mumbling in my earhole. Korrell, take care of this fool," Borland said to the wall. For a moment, Jennings thought the Goblin King to be a loony that talked to imaginaries, until a camouflaged figure appeared out of the darkness.

The cloaked figure crept upon the scrawny gremlin and put it to sleep with a single stroke of his blade. Jodo confidently raised an eyebrow at the masked, cold-blooded killer, inspecting him as a possible threat. Korrell's mask had an optical design that resembled the eyes of a fly or wasp. Its mouth area revealed rectangular shapes on either side that represented the fangs of a viper snake. It was a sinister and ghastly visor, which sent quivers all over Jennings' body.

Borland slowly turned round in his luxurious chair to lay his beady eyes upon the dangerous soul who had interrupted his most favored game.

"Well, well. If it ain't the knight of all knights...Jodo Kahln. Your reputation fits you...like a steel glove," Borland teased, joking amongst his servants as they laughed at Jodo's steel gloved hand.

"Still predictable though," he added. Borland licked his huge lips and spat into a bowl held by one of his female goblin servants. "If my mind serves me, you were the only human I had the unfortunate task to work beside...a long time ago."

"Well, that *unfortunate task* has reached a critical level, Goblin King," Jodo said as he stepped aside to reveal the frail and pathetic looking Jennings who stood in silence, embarrassed by the sudden attention.

"What? Another human?" gasped Borland, spitting out liquid substance over his new carpet. His hands and feet began flapping around in excitement again. "Not possible! I thought you were all extinct," he puffed at the befuddled old man.

"Extinct?" Jennings asked, feeling both perturbed and bemused at the thought.

Borland groaned in discomfort and wriggled out of his chair onto his fat feet.

"Where does he come from?" Borland demanded, staring at Jodo.

"He's not of this world," Jodo confirmed.

"He's a son of the old world?" Borland guessed. "For a moment I thought humans still existed somewhere we had overlooked." Borland laughed with relief. "At least we can be assured that you cannot procreate by yourself," he spat back at Jennings.

"I've always admired you, Jodo. For one to betray one's own kind so easily and without a sense of guilt or remorse is a trait even we mere goblins do not have the heart for," Borland sighed.

"That is because you are not born with hearts, my Lord," Jodo wittingly replied.

"Ha! And all the better for it," Borland sniggered back.

"King Saul requests your help. I'm here to take your goblins with me to the Stained Castle," Jodo said.

"May I ask why?"

"Our enemies are to gather there. They carry a weapon that could destroy us if we don't stop their illegal meeting in time," Jodo said loudly, pressing the issue.

"Interesting. This weapon they possess, what is it exactly?" Borland casually asked.

Jodo sighed, frustrated at the goblin's persistent pestering. "If you want my co-operation, Jodo, at least tell me what it is for."

"The Children of Abasin have returned," Jodo said slowly.

Borland immediately commanded his servants to leave the room. "The Three Thorns? Ha! Not possible. They were killed at birth...you must take me for a fool," Borland rasped.

"With all due respect, I did not come all this way to waste my time insulting you. I am telling you the truth. The Three That Are One live," Jodo insisted.

"How can this be?" Borland demanded.

"Simple. They were misplaced, Sire," Jodo corrected politely.

Borland eyed the young man up and down before his irritation got the better of him. "You mean *you* misplaced them, more to the truth," Borland mocked.

"Either way you look at it, they've survived." Jodo clenched his teeth and stared back at the Goblin King, hate and murder filling his thoughts. "If we could focus on the problem at hand," suggested Jodo through gritted teeth, his tone increasingly belligerent.

"Very well, you may take what troops you need. Try to finish your job instead of sweeping it under the carpet this time," derided Borland, rudely turning his back on the human pair.

Borland sent Korrell to gather his top soldiers when a familiar voice spoke through the entrance. "I have my own troops standing by. We're ready to follow you, my Lord," the voice rattled.

"Who dares enter my quarters...*again*?" Borland yelled.

Jodo turned and smiled gleefully when his eyes

locked upon the menacing face of General Lemis, stepping out of the shadows.

Clicking his fat greasy fingers loudly, Borland motioned for the attention of his servants inside the room. "When Korrell returns, have him send for my security staff...so I can do more than just fire them," Borland snarled.

"I wouldn't worry about your inadequate security, Sire. I already took care of that for you when I came in," Jodo interrupted, smiling from ear to ear.

26

The Council Collates

The troll led the group along the cliff side's narrow route. Sebastian tapped Tommy on the shoulder to get his attention when the tip of the Stained Castle came into view. Overgrown shrubs tampered by barbwire and knotted thorns pushed the group dangerously close to the edge. Luckily for them, Ban Pan was a master of untangling such material, clearing huge sections of pathway in a few minutes.

"Watch your step. I wouldn't have the strength to hold you all if you started dropping on me," Cecil warned, steering both children away from the edge he hovered beside.

The landscape had an abandoned feel to it, and the Stained Castle itself looked dilapidated and rickety at best.

"Why do you call it the Stained Castle?" Sebastian enquired, interrupting the daydreams of his companions.

"Because of the stains on the walls it accumulated from war. Dark spirits of dead soldiers hung around this place long after it was deserted," Cecil said, only to be interrupted by the arrogant and boorish troll who took it upon himself to continue the story.

"I remember the building was at least three times the size it is now when it was first built. It was indeed glorious before it was seized and destroyed," Ban Pan muttered.

"What happened to it?" Tommy asked.

"The true King of Abasin was betrayed by his closest advisor."

"Saul," Sebastian thought aloud.

"Will we see any of these dark spirits inside this place?" Tommy asked in a soft whisper so that nobody but Cecil could hear him.

"Only if you indulge them, so keep your eyes front, and don't look to the walls or mirrors. Dark spirits like to linger in dark areas. They attack with the only thing they can use," Cecil explained.

"Which is?" asked Tommy.

Cecil frowned, tapping his chubby index finger at his temple. "Your mind, dear boy."

"Do not worry too much about them, dark spirits rarely appear in large crowds anyway," Ariel reassured.

Pushing through the half hexagram-shaped door, Ban Pan led the group into the Stained Castle toward another set of doors.

"That's the room," Cecil whispered, pointing. Without replying, the troll marched ahead of the group along the ivy-infested marble hallway until he reached its end. The rest followed him, taking their steps slowly and cautiously.

Ban Pan didn't notice anything unusual until a loud snore startled him. In order to get what looked like a sluggish and scruffy faun awake from his slumber, the sour-faced troll took one heavy breath and covered his mouth, then positioned his humungous nose over the faun's head.

"Watch this," the troll whispered.

Ban Pan's nose sounded like a trumpet when he blew it, covering the faun in troll snot.

Yelping out of his deep sleep, the faun chastised Ban Pan, poking the uncouth troll in the chest with its small horns. Tommy and Sebastian couldn't help but laugh at the comical sight.

"I thought that might get your attention," Ban Pan joshed.

Cecil and Ariel shook their heads at the troll's rude behavior and tried consulting the snot-drenched guard. Its ears were not pointy like a normal faun. Instead they curled up at the tips, much like a piglet's tail. The faun guard was less hairy and smaller than a usual faun.

"Are you a baby faun?" Ariel asked.

"Ha! How dare you? I am twenty years old, though you wouldn't know that, would you? Typical ignorant nymphs," he ranted.

"Where is everyone?" Cecil asked.

"They are waiting for you latecomers inside," the faun moaned.

"I don't hear anything," Ariel added.

"That's because they have used the silencer spell, silly. Surely you didn't think a meeting as important as this would be without one, did you?"

"They could have at least informed us first," Ariel said.

"Well, if you all weren't so late," reminded the faun. "Wait one moment and I will open this door for you. Stand over there," he instructed, urging the group to step aside. He then took a golden key that hung from a chain around his neck and carefully positioned himself a few feet away from the wooden double doors.

"What are you doing?" Cecil asked.

"Opening the door, dummy," the faun snapped, mumbling numbers under his breath and shuffling his hooves in sync with every count.

"You mean those doors in front of you, right?" Sebastian muttered.

"Hush! I'm concentrating, human. I've never met one of you before. You smell terrible."

"The doors are over there you little–," Ban Pan growled at the same time the faun lifted the key over his little head and turned it counter clockwise to unlock an invisible door above him.

"It's an illusion, so we don't get any unwanted visitors," the faun said proudly, gesturing for each visitor to enter the room. Ariel walked through first, followed by Tommy and Sebastian, then Cecil and lastly Ban Pan.

The room was marvellous. Dusk beamed through the massive windows that lined the left wall from floor to ceiling, showing lands afar and glorious oceans boarded by greenery and snow-covered mountains. The Stained Castle's left side rested on an enormous cliff side, which was visible below the windows.

"That's a long way down," Tommy whispered, walking past rows of different creatures. Elves, pixies, nymphs, trolls, white witches, warlocks, wizards, sorcerers, knights and fauns all conversed, murmuring so Tommy and Sebastian couldn't hear. No other human inhabited the room.

Tommy caught sight of lurking spirits from the darkest corners of the ceiling. Smiling faces soon changed to devilish grins and nightmarish frowns, turning aggressive in nature. Tommy's multi-colored eyes glowed brighter toward the spirits. When he looked to Ariel and Sebastian, their faces suddenly transformed into angry creatures he did not recognize.

"Eyes front, boy." Cecil's voice quickly distracted Tommy's mind from the spirits.

Ariel appeared normal again as she led the group to a panel of politicians sitting behind a high table at the end of the marbled room. Struggling to concentrate, Tommy rested his eyes upon a royal panel of five peculiar creatures that glared down upon them from an elevated table that exhibited a symbol of a two-headed snake entwining a crown.

"I know that symbol." Sebastian whispered into Tommy's ear.

"Children of Abasin. You have returned to us...at last," announced an older faun on the panel.

"Where is the third of the Brotherhood?" asked a lady dryad. Ariel and Cecil looked to one another and frowned.

"He is with his protector, as you requested," Ariel muttered.

"Brotherhood?" Tommy asked.

Whispers and chatter increased amongst the large gathering of civilians at Tommy's sudden outburst. The dryad politician raised her hand to appeal for silence.

"Yes child, the foretold Brotherhood - the offspring of our last King," the dryad continued. "You are that offspring. The first born of three."

"And the others?" Tommy asked, before Ban Pan sneakily pointed to Sebastian behind Sebastian's back. "This is wrong. You've made a mistake, we're not brothers or Princes," Tommy tittered nervously. "We're not anything." Sebastian nodded his head in agreement whilst still in shock, staring back at his supposed brother.

"The Council does not make mistakes," the elf politician insisted.

"I find that hard to believe," Sebastian muttered in a snooty manner, fixing his huge glasses from sliding off his nose again.

"This can't be real. He can't be my brother," Tommy persisted. "It's impossible."

"Not to mention improbable," Sebastian giggled.

"We have followed the three of you since birth, make no mistake of it," the elf added sternly.

"But, surely not him?" Tommy gasped.

Sebastian's cheeks grew redder by the second when the embarrassed boy retorted. "You think I would want *you* of all people as my brother?"

Hovering in between them, Cecil quickly prevented a physical conflict, pushing the children away from one another. "Boys, hush now," Cecil commanded.

Forcing his hand, Tommy pushed the pixie aside to invade Sebastian's personal space in an attempt to intimidate him.

"Do you find something wrong with me, posh boy?"

"I can't find anything right with you. You're nothing but a cowardly little bully," Sebastian yelled.

Tapping both on the side of the head with his stick, the pixie snapped, exerting his authority that echoed across the room.

"Enough!"

The gathering muttered and whispered once again.

"We should have been told this before," Tommy cried out in frustration, unable to look Sebastian in the eye. A strong grip of emotions made his eyes water.

"Not until you were ready, child," said the faun politician.

"We're ready now. We need to know the truth if you want us to help. You do need our help, don't you?" Sebastian asked, speaking as loudly and as clearly as he could.

The brave boy approached the creatures that sat on their seats like the judge and jury of a courthouse. The panel of politicians fell quiet for a moment and glanced at each other in silent agreement. All five of the panel nodded before the eldest of them, a troll, broke his silence.

"That is why you have been brought back," the troll began in his deep and soothing voice.

"Tell us everything," Sebastian muttered, keeping his eyes fixed on the troll.

"Since the beginning of the new world there has been conflict between our kind, the civilians, and human kind. That conflict ceased when your Father fell in love with a Royal civilian. Your Mother was an elfling. Their love was forbidden by our laws but it gave the new world of Abasin hope for peace between the two kinds. So it was permitted. It wasn't long after your parents were ordained King and Queen that there was outrage from certain civilians for having a human as their King. To prevent another war, your parents turned to an ancient cherub for help and made a pact with it to end the on-going feud between humans and civilian creatures. The cherub, Sowl, offered great magic that had the power to bring world peace in the form of a very formidable spellbook. Because of their love for Abasin, to spare it, your parents were deceived into abdicating their throne in exchange for this book. In turn, Sowl craftily offered the throne over to your Father's brother on the condition he honored the new world's peace treaty. Seven years went by peacefully, nevertheless, Saul's heart became embittered and consumed by his own pride," explained the troll politician.

"He craved more power and sought to reign over both the humans and civilians by giving the new world its first collective government and solitary King. But the humans rebelled to Saul's dictatorship, bringing Abasin its first dark war. The humans were not prepared. This dark war eventually wiped humanity off the face of the new earth. Once Saul had broken the peace treaty between civilians and humans, a curse of mutation fell upon him and all who served his corrupt monarchy. This curse can be broken by the powers that reside in that spellbook," the troll continued.

"The False One refused your Father's request to abdicate the throne in trade for the spellbook, believing he could have both," the elf politician added.

"In order to hide the spellbook, its spells were transferred into each of you. When Saul found out the spellbook could no longer be used by anyone else, he ordered your deaths as a way to end his curse. Consequently, your Father instructed us to cast you into the old world for your own safety," explained the troll in his husky slow voice that almost sent his own panel nodding off. "So great was Saul's jealousy that he unleashed his wrath against humanity, who had shown allegiance to your parents and their efforts for peace. Sadly, both Saul and your Father were played against one another by the ancient cherub," the troll explained seriously.

"*What* is that?" Tommy asked in a fearful tone.

The faun politician quickly cleared his throat and broke the sudden silence of the court.

"He is an immortal being that governs all sorcery

and magic. Sowl is no ally to anyone but himself. Be warned; he knows you have returned. He will try and stop the Brotherhood at all costs from bringing Abasin peace. He may try and tempt you like he tempted your parents, but do not deal with him, or you will end up accursed like your Uncle, or with a similar fate that befell our King and Queen," the faun politician warned.

"What happened to them?" Sebastian asked.

"Saul ordered the public execution of your Mother. Your Father went missing soon after the dark war had begun. Some say he escaped Abasin to follow you into the old world, others claim he was exiled to the Barronlands of this earth. No one truly knows," the troll said. "I am sorry."

Tommy stared down at his feet, unwilling to look up at the Council further whilst Sebastian wiped a tear from under his large glasses.

"What is it you want from us?" Sebastian asked.

"You have tremendous magic inside you. Soon, you will be able to use that magic to fly, change your appearance, adapt to strenuous conditions, and even go through time. You will advance further than any before you," the elf said.

"So, you're waging your bets on this spellbook to overthrow the King?" Sebastian asked.

"Not exactly," the dryad interrupted. "It is foretold that your Brotherhood shall defeat the False One together and uncover the Shield that can save the new world."

"Shield?" Tommy asked curiously.

"Can we not just kill him?" Sebastian asked.

The five politicians looked at one another and shook their heads.

"The threat to Abasin is more grave than that.

There is a Shield of Life that has been lost since the new world began. If it is not found in time, all will die, both the evil and the good. Our bodies are failing too," said the faun.

"If no one has found this Shield yet...how do you know it's real?" Tommy asked.

The troll politician sighed. "Because, we civilians were the ones who lost it. If you don't help us, no one will be able to stop the False One. He will take those he sees fit to serve him and leave the rest destitute. We cannot make you help us. The choice belongs to the three of you. But know this; the three of you must become as one. Should one of you decide to leave, the rest of you will fail. Your combined power is the only chance Abasin has against Saul's dark magick," the troll said.

"So, where is this spellbook?" Tommy demanded.

"Your parents hid it from Saul. Fortunately they placed a tracking spell upon one of you. That means the spellbook will track down the one with the tracking spell upon him," the dryad explained.

"I wonder which one of us it is?" Sebastian whispered to Tommy.

Sebastian noticed Tommy twiddling his fingers and biting his lip while he gave serious thought to such a heavy burden.

"Are you sure you have the right people? I mean, what if there's some kind of mistake here?" Tommy asked.

The faun was the only one to laugh from the panel before he gathered himself. "You are the children of the true King. We've been keeping a close watch over all three of you, every day of your lives," the faun insisted, leaning forward over his chair to look Tommy in his unevenly colored eyes.

"If we say yes, what do we have to do?" Tommy asked.

The troll smiled, giving both boys a warm look. "Once the third child of Abasin arrives, your assigned protectors will take the three of you together to a hidden sanctuary. There you will meet two of your own kind, the last remaining humans in Abasin. They have been allocated by your Father to teach you the magic you will need to search for the Shield."

The troll politician spoke out softly and caringly, treating each boy with a sense of respect and courtesy that the other members on the panel failed to show. "I commend you, Children of Abasin, for your willingness to help."

"Wait, we haven't agreed to anything yet," Tommy said.

"He's right, we still have to wait for Benjamin to come to our final decision," Sebastian added.

"You won't have to. He will help us too. I can see clearly your hearts have already said yes," said the reserved hobgoblin politician, speaking his only comment on the matter. A respectful bow followed his words before he silently left the Council's panel.

Sebastian peered around the room filled with hopeful faces that gazed in awe of them.

"Suddenly London doesn't seem so bad anymore," he mumbled.

27

The Accumulation

Casting a magick spell of silence ended quarrels between several goblins when Jodo Kahln's army entered the Stained Castle. Jodo instantly noticed the sleeping faun and strode toward him without hesitation.

"Well, at least he's *on* the job," Jodo joked, sniggering alongside his horde of goblins and what remained of General Lemis's battalion.

Unable to hear a thing, the ill-bred faun snored loudly, causing more laughter and mocking within the goblin tribe.

"Disgusting creature," one spat.

"I hear they make good stew," said another.

"Not much of a security guard is he?" Jennings noted, causing the goblins to heckle at him.

"No, my horrid human, they're not. The real talent of a faun lies with their minds, which contain the blueprints to create the best illusions." Jodo grinned. "Wake him," he ordered.

Clutching the faun's throat, Lemis hoisted the guard up against the oak doors until Jodo gave a slight nod to release the captive. The startled faun hit the floor, struggling to catch his breath.

Jennings felt slightly sympathetic, but he ignored this feeling when he sensed Jodo detect his human emotion for the faun, as a shark would smell blood from wounded prey.

The knight coolly knelt down and offered the faun another one of his dark navy silk handkerchiefs, only to be refused by a slight push of the hand.

"Suit yourself. Well, let's get down to business," the knight said, forever showing off his cool mannerism. "We're here for the meeting," he said with a smile as the faun sat up to stare the knight out.

"You missed it, by a day or so now," the faun lied, grumpily.

"Oh! Well...that is rather...upsetting," Jodo sighed dramatically.

"Heart-breaking for you, I'm sure," the faun sneered back, showing a half-hearted grin that seemed to crawl under Jodo Kahln's skin. But to the surprise of many, Jodo didn't do a thing to harm the gatekeeper. Instead, the young knight smiled back in response.

"Okay," he said casually, nodding. "Did you know, my furry friend, that this lot have an unwavering craving for faun?" Jodo badgered the scared faun, causing him to look on in fright at the gnawing teeth of the monstrous creatures around him.

"I know...I find it quite disgusting myself. I suppose one has to have a goblin's palate for such a menu. But, next to frog, boiled faun is quite the treat. You see, fauns, I am told, are much like lobsters...they're always better when they're cooked alive and screaming!"

Jodo rose to his feet to address his troops lining the hallway from outside the Stained Castle's main entrance. "Second helpings, anyone?"

The chanting of the crowd almost turned into

another frenzied brawl when numerous goblins scrambled to reach for the faun.

"I'm telling the truth, check the doors yourself. There is nobody inside these walls," the faun pleaded without realizing that he had given his secret illusion away. "H-here's the key," the faun stuttered as he lifted an old rusted black key out of his trouser pocket and held it over his head in a gesture of surrender.

Jodo Kahln raised his hand and motioned his soldiers to halt. "Arrogant little fool, do you think such powers as I yield would find need of a key for those doors?" he laughed as he imploded the two large oak wood doors behind them by a flick of his steel gloved hand. The doors flew heavily off the hinges at great speed, crashing into the room that revealed a large deserted hall.

"You see, I told you the truth, you're too late," mumbled the faun.

"As I was saying, I do not need a key for *those* doors," Jodo insisted as he leisurely opened his right hand, revealing the golden key the faun had kept hidden from him.

"How did you–?" the faun began to ask. A moment later Jodo took a hold of the faun's hair and dragged him through the group of goblins.

"No doubt you would have made a worse goblin than you did a faun. Such an unconvincing little liar you are. And with all that mindless nattering...it just goes on and on. It's enough to make one ill with headache."

Jodo rambled loudly, stopping a few feet from the damaged door space. "I only need your eyes, faun. That's all. Show me where they are or you will suffer at my hand," he threatened, revealing his steel gloved hand in front of the creature's pudgy face.

"Alright...but I need you to give me the key back," the faun said.

Slowly and gently, Jodo handed the faun his golden key. Anticipation grew as each creature watched the baby faun's every movement.

The moment he turned the key to the invisible lock, the faun wasted no time and scurried through the visible doorway to the chambers of the Council as quick as a fox. He had only enough time to save himself and not enough time to lock the door behind him, leaving Jodo and his brigade the perfect opportunity to enter the doorway after him.

Missing a step through the entrance, the faun guard tripped and crashed through the chamber doors.

The eyes of the Council followed the unorthodox entrance as the faun slid upon the chamber floor. His little hooves slipped on the shiny marble as they scrambled toward the panel. His face was drained of all color and his whitened lips could barely utter a word.

The chambers fell anxiously quiet when they heard the creaking sounds from both doors at the far end of the courthouse. The creak stopped. Silence was broken by a few dreaded knocks that teased and intimidated the human children.

"You, there! Yes, you that cowers in the dark. Come forth," yelled the troll, standing amongst the panel and pointing a finger toward the blackness beyond the doorway. But there was only a mocking laugh in return that made Sebastian's skin crawl.

"Jodo Kahln," whispered the troll politician. An inspecting faun guard was pulled into the darkness at the open doorway.

Suddenly the ill-fated faun guard's head came rolling out of the dark all the way up the aisle. The rolling head had been thrown hard enough that it crossed the entire aisle, reaching Tommy and Sebastian's feet at the far end of the massive room. Tommy and Sebastian weren't aware of it, but Cecil knew it had been deliberately aimed at them. The entire room gasped in utter disbelief, a prelude to the rumbling that had abruptly emerged. Having seconds to prepare for what was to be unleashed upon them, each white witch, elf, dwarf, warlock, faun, sorcerer and bounty hunter joined together to form a double line facing the breached doorway.

"They've found us!" Cecil gasped, signalling Ban Pan and Ariel to join forces with their fellow fighters just as three huge ogres leapt through the doorway, tearing apart its very frame.

Some slipped through the chaotic stampede more easily than others, but all had the same intent: to kill and destroy everything inside the room that protected the human children.

Chains and hooks were thrown into the crowd, rapidly snapping unfortunate victims up into the air. Several more were snatched away from the security of allied fighters as the hooks tossed them into the deadly pit of their opposition.

Tommy and Sebastian cried out in horror at the unexpected war that had broken out. The remaining panel of politicians swiftly joined the defensive line of protectors to battle the oncoming attack.

Between hundreds of creatures, including goblins, gremlins, hobgoblins, ogres, and sea guards, a few dozen warlocks and elves stood firmly together, creating a wall between the monsters and the human children, all ready to fight to protect the Brotherhood.

As magic spells and wonders were released in bright flashes and different forms of light, Tommy and Sebastian witnessed each damaging effect the spells had on their targets. Each spell was individually crafted by its maker, making the battle before them such an entrancing spectacle to witness.

Some forms of magic targeted Jodo's army faster than others. Spells of flying creatures and four legged beasts made of flame swallowed groups of goblins and spat out their skeletons. Another spell hit a few sea guards and caused the rapid decay of their bodies. Other spells changed their mutant skin to wood so that they stiffened up and cracked like branches from a tree. Creatures of light were unleashed, leaping upon the backs of ogres and blinding the gigantic beings, while every protector's fairy distracted their assailants by nipping at their faces and stinging their ears.

More spells were cast, until each white witch, wizard, and warlock had to reserve their energies and regroup, while the rest of the fauns, elves, and bounty hunters continued fighting by the standard method of hand-to-hand combat. The strength and endurance of the good civilians was put to the test.

"What are they doing?" Sebastian pointed to the large circle gathering of sorcerers that included the Council of politicians.

"There's salt in the air. Listen to the hissing of the bubbles. Alkaline...can you smell it?" Cecil asked.

Sebastian and Tommy could feel the ocean's cool breeze. The smell of the ocean had reached their nostrils amidst the chaotic violence and spellbinding war between light magic and dark magick, calming their senses.

"Clear your thoughts and keep close," Cecil cautioned.

The smell of the ocean grew stronger and changed, for there was electricity in the air now. For some reason he could not explain, Sebastian knew what was about to happen next.

"They're making a storm. A storm is brewing, a giant wave will come...wait...how do I know that?" Sebastian asked excitedly.

"But the ocean is way down there," argued Tommy, impatiently pacing toward the windows and back again.

"Your talents will soon be shining through. It's a glimpse of your own powers, Sebastian. The power of prophecy," Ariel said reassuringly.

"You are a sorcerer in the making," Ban Pan added, whilst he finished beating a goblin to the ground.

When Tommy and Sebastian glanced up at their furry ally, they witnessed an abrupt and mighty lightning spell toss the heavy troll back into the thick of the fighting crowd. Jodo Kahln took responsibility for the foul attack with pleasure, applauding himself as the troll fell. The crashing of the troll's heavy body shook the ground beneath everyone, crushing a few gremlins in his way. Thankfully, the troll's body armor had taken most of the lightning's impact. Without much effort, Ban Pan pulled himself back onto his feet, ready to aid his allies against the oncoming horde.

Standing disrespectfully on top of the Council's table, Jodo eagerly antagonized Ariel to fight him.

Ariel took no chances and hastily charged at the knight, pointing a spare dagger ready to strike him. The experienced knight moved effortlessly to avoid her blows, launching into his own planned retaliation seconds later. Making sure her arm was joined with the strap of the dagger by magick, Jodo willed the well-crafted instrument high off the ground and embedded it deep into the marble wall behind the panel.

Ariel struggled fiercely after being catapulted into the air, but nothing seemed to work; she was trapped, dangling and vulnerable. Jodo appointed two gremlins to stand below her, blocking her only avenue of escape if she broke free.

"Watch that one," Jodo ordered his gremlin guards as he stared up at her. "I'm coming back for you, my sweet. So, just hang on."

Jodo strode across the Council's bench with his arms behind his back, shaking his head at Cecil Baskin and tutting at the two boys.

"Run to the end of the room, stick to the windows and keep low, go now," Cecil ordered under his breath. Before the knight had gotten too close to Cecil, Tommy and Sebastian scurried off, picking up speed as they rose from a creeping position into a full sprint.

The knight stepped off the table to stand in front of the protective pixie, towering above him in height. Uncomfortable with the arrogant knight glaring down at him, Cecil fluttered his wings in defiance and raised himself up off the ground to meet his opponent face to face.

With a flick of his steel gloved hand, Jodo shoved the brave protector against the enormous glass windowpane. The impact caused a large crack in the window's bottom half. Cracks in the window started to increase as the evil knight held the honorable knight in position.

"I want you to watch this, I want to see the look on your face, pixie. When the Brotherhood dies before your eyes, and you hear their screams for your help, then you'll know your King wasn't a real prophet but a stupid farce," Jodo threatened, nodding at the two gremlin guards standing below Ariel to leave their posts and pursue the two humans. "You should have joined us, Cecil Baskin," Jodo hissed.

The pair of gremlins rushed toward the end of the room. Each kept close to the windows and quietly followed Tommy and Sebastian.

From Ariel's high point of view, the villainous army looked like an infestation of cockroaches scuttling through every nook and cranny, outnumbering and overpowering the rebel sorcerers.

"Help the humans!" Ariel called out when the gremlin guards crept inches away from Sebastian and Tommy. Tommy's sky blue-colored eye caught a glimpse of the gremlin's advances. He swiftly pulled Sebastian aside, saving his brother from the fatal swipe of a rusty blade.

"Thanks!" Sebastian said.

Eyeing around them for some escape route, Tommy jumped onto one of the huge window ledges in order to get a better viewpoint. But there was nothing he could find. No escape route. Nothing. It seemed nobody could save them now.

Ready to do their rightful duty for their King, each grotesque gremlin climbed up on the window ledge, gripping the stone with their sharp instruments.

"What now?" Sebastian asked, when something caught Tommy's eye once more. It was the spirits he was told about, the ones that he had seen earlier that lay in the darkest corners of the Stained Castle.

Tommy watched their erratic movements diving into the fighting crowd. Every time a goblin or soldier of Saul was killed, a black spirit from the stained walls would sharply descend toward their bodies and pull their darkened spirits out. Sometimes the spirits of the Stained Castle would take a dead creature's soul so fast, the new soul would instantly become a part of it. It was an accumulation of dark spirits that waited for their own opportunity to strike at the dead.

Tommy's concentration on the accumulating spirits was broken when Sebastian lifted a dagger that had landed on the window ledge after being thrown to him from the middle of the room by Ban Pan. Tommy suddenly took the dangerous instrument off his brother just as the gremlins stood in front of them.

"We have no choice," Tommy yelled to his brother.

Sebastian nodded eagerly when they both ran against the assailants that charged back at them. But the nearer they got to their attackers, the more Tommy could see the gremlins for what they really were. In a frantic skid and desperate tug at Sebastian, Tommy managed to stop both of them from making a grave mistake.

"It's a trick, get back," Tommy explained.

"But they're smaller than us," Sebastian started, his heart beating with newfound bravery. "We can take them."

Tommy quietly shook his head and moved against the window as he studied the clever illusion. "No they're not. I see them," he whispered to Sebastian.

"See what?" his brother asked, confused.

"Watch!" gasped Tommy while pointing back at the gremlin guards in front of them.

The two guards had already begun to shed their brilliant disguise the moment Tommy's piercing eyes saw through it. Real armory reappeared, ripping through the skin of the gremlin costume. Both villains started growing in stature and changing in size, until everyone saw what Tommy's eyes could see through their dark magick. It was the Nockwire.

The assassins Tommy had been dreading since the moment he'd first laid eyes on them had finally returned for them in the new world, like they had promised. Baring their needle-like weaponry tight in their grips, both assassins took thudding steps in front of them, pinning each boy to the window.

Sebastian faced the bushy haired and cloaked assassin Scythas, whilst Tommy faced the heavily-armored beast Thestor for his third time. It was in that hellish moment, without warning, that Tommy finally unleashed his first new worldly power.

28

Weapons of the Elements

Cecil struggled to turn his head when Jodo pinned his face hard against the cracked window. The evil knight stared obsessively at his assassins, waiting for them to strike a fatal blow.

Spotting a trickle of sweat roll from Jodo's brow down his cheek, Cecil was sure the evil knight had his focus elsewhere. He released his own light spell from his glowing staff. The sudden surge of electricity caused an instant separation between the pair. Jodo was flung a few yards from Cecil and landed on the ground in a firm combat pose, watching his faithful and trusty Nockwire assassins bully the children into a helpless position.

Amidst the bedlam, all Sebastian could do was cover his eyes like a scared animal preparing for the worst, when the heavily armored villain lifted his brother up by one strong hand.

As Thestor prepared to kill his human captive with a fatal stab, Tommy found himself staring directly into the assassin's face. His fire-lit eyes saw past the monster's cursed form to who the Nockwire assassin was before: a man.

Suddenly, Tommy's shining eyes caught the

attention of the dark spirits and attracted them. The blackened spirits that were invisible to most civilians, the souls Cecil Baskin had warned him not to indulge, Tommy now openly embraced. They noticed his stare immediately and swarmed to him, only too happy to claim another pitiful life.

The Nockwire didn't know what had hit them when blackness of each dark spirit engulfed their senses, shrouding their faces from everything around them. The attack caused each assassin to stagger to his knees, making the marble floor shake.

"The child, get that human child!" Jodo called to Lemis, who was still fighting off the defensive barrier that the bounty hunters and elves had successfully sustained.

One whistle from Lemis signalled his trusty omnicorn to breach through the ceiling of the enormous room. Amongst the endless fighting of the two armies, Lemis led the omnicorn and several of his last remaining sea guards to Tommy and Sebastian.

"Now is our chance. Let's wipe these parasites out," Lemis called back as he rode the horribly diseased and greasy creature in the direction of the two children. Once again, Tommy and Sebastian found themselves cornered, this time by different and equally dangerous assailants. The pursuit for their lives was unrelenting.

At first, Cecil thought it had been the combined weight of both the Nockwire falling to their knees that sent the minor shockwaves through the ground. Ariel had hoped it was the storm spell the warlocks had yet to complete.

The intense display of Tommy's inner powers had left him drained. His blazing eyes turned their focus onto what approached beyond the Stained Castle's walls. He could see what had caused the sudden shockwaves.

The second tremor came with a vengeance. Loud thudding steps totalling eight in a row vibrated through the floor. The dark spirits scattered once Tommy's eyes turned away from them.

Lemis and his sea guards encircled the boys like a pack of creeping monsters from some horrible ending of a nightmare. Slowly but surely, the Nockwire rose to their feet to tower behind Sebastian and Tommy.

Instead of stepping back from Lemis and the Nockwire, Tommy pushed Sebastian to the ground and leapt out of the way of the oncoming terror he saw charging toward them all, long before anyone else had.

Ripping a massive hole straight through the six-inch stained wall, the mighty heroes made their grand entrance. The giant rock-shelled monster kept up its amazing momentum, trudging through dozens of enemy troops before it sped across the room, unable to stop.

Molo slid left and right in an attempt to slow down, whilst kicking and stepping upon several goblins he'd scattered around the room like pebbles.

The gigantic rock creature abruptly changed course the moment he noticed Lemis assailing toward the human children, alongside the Nockwire assassins. Instead of kicking his heels in the floor to steady himself, Molo sped his charge, heading directly for the small band of sea guards and gremlins that enclosed the two boys. He had no choice but to keep charging, for time was of the essence.

"My friends are over there. Help them, Molo," a tiny but rowdy voice called out from above the crowd. Tommy instantly recognized his brave brother resting on top of the giant's head. Benjamin pointed at the deadly assassins who looked unprepared for a sudden and mighty impact.

Molo's momentum proved too strong for the Nockwire's feeble attempts to shield themselves. His rock-shelled body repelled every shabby arrow and sword fired at him. Trump slithered closely behind each giant step, avoiding any contact with allies or foes as he kept a close watch on Benjamin.

Cassius rushed to the aid of his allies at once, joining the other bounty hunters in battle and striking fatal blows to any enemy that stood in his way.

Molo thrashed his way through an entire group of fiendish assailants within seconds, simultaneously stomping upon Lemis's sea guards below his feet while he tackled Thestor between his huge stone arms. Grabbing a steady hold of the Nockwire's neck by one of his gigantic hands, Molo reached for the tail of Lemis's omnicorn above his head before twirling the flying steed in circles.

Molo was unbeatable. Scythas did not hesitate to protect his companion and dove onto Molo's rocky back to restrain the giant. But his sly attack was not enough to stop the rock-shelled giant. Benjamin's words of encouragement only fuelled Molo's determination to keep charging.

He rushed Lemis and the Nockwire against the enormous courtroom windows. Unable to slow down, Molo stormed through the glass and plunged down the side of Stained Castle's cliff side, taking Lemis and his omnicorn along for the ride, to their deaths. Scythas had just managed to help Thestor break free from Molo's fierce grip, and flew to safety seconds before the rest crashed.

"Benjamin!" Tommy yelled when he ran to the window and looked all the way down. "I can't see him."

"That's because I have him," Cecil called out, flying overhead, carrying Benjamin nearer to the ground.

"You made it!" Sebastian called in surprise.

Tommy couldn't withstand his excitement either, greeting his brother with a tap on the back. Benjamin didn't seem to notice nor care at first. His concern for Molo drowned out the commotion around him. Pushing past Sebastian and Tommy, Benjamin rushed through the broken glass to lean over the middle of the gigantic window ledge.

"Molo! He saved you both." Benjamin snivelled, turning to Sebastian and Tommy as his lips trembled. "*He's gone!*"

"He looked strong enough to survive the fall. I'm sure he did, boy. Legs forward, we must leave this place," Cecil instructed, as he flew onto the panel to help each boy up onto the platform.

"Who are you?" Benjamin gasped.

"Cecil Baskin at your service my Prince," Cecil panted.

Just then Jodo Kahln appeared from behind the desk and took a sly kick at the pixie's back, bruising his left wing. Cecil gave out a painful cry and fell head first onto the floor, knocking himself unconscious.

"Mr. Baskin!" Sebastian screamed in horror.

"Well, well. Look at you all. You've gotten so big." Jodo sniggered, stepping closer to the three boys. "You really shouldn't have come back here. As you can clearly see, it's quite upsetting for everyone," he continued, thrusting the boys toward the window by his magick. "Let's start with the first born."

Tommy slammed first against the same window

that had a large split in it from Cecil's dent, followed closely by Sebastian then Benjamin.

A sudden strike from behind sliced Jodo's holey, shredded black cloak in half, causing the knight to stumble off the panel. Once Jodo was back on his feet he set his eyes upon a stocky and rough bounty hunter; a hunter he immediately recognized from his own past.

"Cassius Shark, I watched you die," the knight jeered, as he manoeuvred his way around the bounty hunter.

Cassius didn't hesitate to attack the devious and unpredictable knight. After spinning one of his crystal balls toward Jodo's face, the bounty hunter fired his dagger to his imprisoned friend, slicing through the tightened strap that entangled Ariel's wrist. The strap tore loose, disjoining her from her own weapon, which was embedded too deep inside the marble stone wall to be removed. The knight shielded his eyes from Cassius's blinding light spell and staggered away from him.

Ariel fell to the ground and rushed to pick up Cassius's dagger that had set her free. Equipped with the new blade, she jumped behind Jodo, blocking his exit while Cassius obstructed the knight's path at the front. As both protectors closed in on him, Jodo Kahln took out his own weapon in great haste and raised it high above his right shoulder, gripping the handle tightly, and eager to make his first strike. Jodo showed amazing agility and balance during his assault, until Cassius carved a prominent mark upon the knight's armored breastplate by his golden blade in one close hit. Sparks flew off the knight's weapon as they continued to duel.

The cracked window finally smashed under their weight. The three boys grappled to avoid a dangerous fall over the window ledge. Broken glass covered them. Tommy pulled his two brothers away from the ledge, and then ran to Cecil's aid. Lifting an arm and a leg each, Tommy and Sebastian instructed Benjamin to secure the pixie's wings as the three brothers struggled to get Cecil back onto his feet. He did not look it, but Cecil Baskin was extremely heavy for a pixie.

It was only a few seconds later when they felt the dead weight of Cecil abruptly lift from their shoulders. Stumbling to look behind them, they noticed their large troll protector, Ban Pan Cackerin, relieving them of the burden. Ban Pan flung the unconscious pixie over his massive shoulder and motioned to them.

"This is a job for the troll," he barked proudly, leading them through the mess of broken weaponry and carcasses of horrid goblin creatures.

The horde of villains grew rapidly. More goblins entered the fold while dangerous ogres and evil hobgoblins stormed through the hole in the castle's wall.

Just as the enemy crowd had overpowered the last of the defending elves, warlocks, bounty hunters, and faun soldiers, the Council's witch circle finally released their powerful spell.

Rain poured from the ceilings inside the Stained Castle, stirring up a massive oceanic wave spell. An enormous wave rose over everyone, before crashing down on all the armies.

"Here it comes!" Ban Pan roared, holding onto the three boys and the unconscious pixie to protect them from the mighty wave.

Jodo Kahln had been smart enough to take his exit

while he still could, but not before having the last clash of his sword. He fought the two daring protectors until they had successfully cornered him near the windows. Using his magick, the powerful warlock knight melted both of their instruments of steel. Jodo took full advantage of his position, striking his blades at the unarmed warriors. Cassius and Ariel retreated toward the huge hole Molo had made in the Stained Castle's wall the moment the wave broke.

Remembering his trusty new slave, Jodo rescued Jennings from one of the hidden corners of the courthouse. It hadn't taken the faint-hearted man long to run away and hide from the ongoing battle; he didn't have the strength to withstand the fight that would have been required of him.

Trump swiftly slithered his way toward the evil knight and begged to be taken with him.

"You still have a job to finish, toad. Camouflage your skin and follow them...that's an order," Jodo called back through the howling winds.

Using the destroyed window as his only exit, Jodo took Jennings and withdrew from the storm, followed by over a dozen goblin troops that took flight in time. In a flash, the gutless duo left the rest of Borland's soldiers to their own fate.

Every ally and rebel to Saul was tossed by the massive wave that covered the entrance like a cold gray blanket, swallowing its victims inside its powerful current, until nothing was left of the room but a stormy sea, unfit to be inhabited. The waves crashed on top of the Council of politicians and circle of sorcerers that had created it.

Trump's amphibious body adapted easy to the water current. He swam low and deep to keep out of sight and danger while he tracked the Brotherhood above him.

Ariel and Cassius fought their way through each goblin creature when the wave washed over them.

Like a large fire hose, a huge part of the wave smashed against their backs, pushing each protector off of their feet and out of the large hole in the wall with enormous force. Now a heavy river, the spell's mighty current swept everyone downstream and away from the flooded Stained Castle, spreading across the route Jodo Kahln had previously taken to reach it.

29

Victory of the Thorns

Cassius drew his sword out of the water when enemy figures emerged from the murky depths, swimming round him. But the bounty hunter didn't have to strike a single blow, for other allied bounty hunters had survived the current and fought off the foes for him.

"Protect the children, get them out of here!" a white witch screamed as she shot out of the stream to battle a flying goblin.

Nearby, the rest of the protectors had regrouped with the children, looking wet and miserable as they waited eagerly for Cassius to appear.

Thrusting his large claw back into the water, Ban Pan grabbed the struggling bounty hunter and pulled him through the heavy current to dry land.

"That's some arm you've got there, Master Troll," Cassius spluttered.

"Don't expect my help again. I'm not here to protect the protectors, especially pirate scum," Ban Pan griped.

"Ex-pirate scum," corrected Cassius, flashing the troll a cheeky smirk.

"Take them to the hideout!" a chief faun ordered,

and with that, several armored faun guards escorted the Brotherhood and their band of protectors away from the continuing battle, followed by the baby faun guard the group had met at the Stained Castle's entrance.

The battle itself had only begun to fizzle out when Borland's reinforcements infiltrated what was left of the Stained Castle.

The chief faun joined the large group and led the way to a secret doorway under the mountain the Stained Castle rested on. All were safe and accounted for. The air grew quieter as the chief faun continued to guide the Brotherhood and their protectors down an enormous set of steep stone steps. They descended a thousand feet before reaching the secret door to the Stained Castle's belly.

The chief faun cast a spell upon a gigantic area of stone, which uncovered the door and handle that protruded out of the rock. A few faun guards pulled the massive stone door open and led the group through its doorway before the door merged back into the mountain.

Another enormous staircase stretched upon the inner mountain for miles, spiralling downward toward a living society below them.

When the fauns guided the group to the bottom, they continued to lead the way through what appeared to be a marketplace consisting of large, rounded tables that were fully dressed with feasts. There appeared to be a celebration about to commence, but at close range it was clear the fauns were only storing food for the long migration ahead of them.

"What's all this food for?" Cassius asked the chief faun.

"We've kept ourselves hidden for years, since Saul's dark war. But ever since the Children of Abasin have returned, we have been preparing for our own trip to Reethwood."

"You're going to Reethwood, too?" Ban Pan asked, panting as he held the unconscious pixie upon his back.

"We've heard it is one of the last untouched places on this earth. Too long have we fauns been in the caves, homeless. We long for daylight and to be amidst the trees again. Our hooves have not been exercised enough here. This habitat is for cave dwellers and dwarves, though this particular area has done us favorably," he said, smiling.

"I need to get home to the Bothopolis Canyons," Ban Pan said. "We've still to hold our fortresses. I must warn my people."

"That is the problem. We have not banded together like we should have. Most of the dwarves have fled across this earth, only to protect what is theirs," the baby faun mumbled as it passed the chief faun.

"He's right. You need to stay with these chosen protectors and help guard the children," the chief faun leader said, nodding.

"A mixed band of protectors? Preposterous! We aren't equipped or prepared. We don't have the same skills!" the flabbergasted troll yelled.

"Maybe, but this is more than a civil war, Master Troll. Come this way," the chief faun said quietly. He brought them through the market place filled with saluting fauns.

"Where are we headed?" Benjamin whispered, but nobody seemed to hear him.

The group walked another half mile across a

marbled land. Statues of dwarf kings and queens on the cave walls loomed over each passerby, stretching several yards to a dead end.

"Must be another one of those faun illusions," Ban Pan whispered to Ariel. The nymph nodded in agreement when she saw the chief faun had unveiled another massive door and opened it sideways.

The chief faun smiled, addressing the children while leading them into a brightly lit room. "I was saving this transportation spell but you need it more. Besides, I'm sure our army would like to meet you."

The strong sunset outside pierced through the windows of the stone room and filled it with a warming orange glow. The children looked in awe at the two thousand faun soldiers that knelt in their presence.

"This gateway has taken you far from the Stained Castle," the chief faun said mildly. "We must part ways now," he continued. "If you leave this mountain, you will find the hidden sanctuary upon the opposite cliff, beyond the bridge. The Council requests that we leave the children in your care. We have duties and allies to aid on our journey. It would be much too dangerous for the humans to travel with us."

"I understand." Cassius sighed, frowning back at his small group of friends. "It looks like we're stuck with each other."

Passing the multiple lines of kneeling troops, each boy and protector couldn't help but look at the sheer magnitude and precision of the secret faun army.

The window at the end of the stone marbled room opened up, inviting them to walk through. After Tommy and Sebastian waved goodbye to the faun guard leader, the boys' protectors took a tight grip of their hands and led them into a new area of Abasin.

After the dusk settled, Ban Pan and Cassius built a small fire to dry off the children. No one knew what region of land the faun's doorway had led to, but it soon became too dark to contemplate moving on further without one's bearings. Ariel had begun sewing the wounds on Cecil's wings shut, aided by her fairy's light.

The fire was beautiful and the ember glow gave off just enough heat to keep members of their band warm without attracting attention. A rustle from the bushes behind him woke the sleeping troll from a deep sleep, startling the beast to raise his claws in defense until he saw Cassius appear, carrying a young ox over his shoulder. Cassius threw the carcass down in a bundle next to the fire and made the surviving group gasp in horror at the butchered animal, but everyone felt too exhausted to argue with the bounty hunter's untraditional ways.

"Your bellies will thank me," Cassius insisted.

Sebastian sat beside a sulking Benjamin, who had his back to the fire, facing away from the group as he stared into the starry night sky.

"Why so quiet?" Sebastian asked bluntly, encouraging him to reply with a little push.

"Tired." Benjamin let out a slight cough, whilst rubbing his arms to keep himself toasty warm.

"Face the fire, Benjamin," Ariel suggested, but Benjamin ignored the advice. The worried boy kept his eyes fixed on the night. Tommy searched along the ground and found a few pieces of living earth food for the boy to eat. Carrying the plant over to him, its tentacles jumped from Tommy's arm and wrapped themselves around Benjamin's hand, feeding off the boy like a parasite.

"Bon appétit, I guess," Tommy tittered nervously.

Benjamin raised the dancing vegetable up to his mouth until a tug on one of the tentacles sent the vegetable flying into the camp's fire.

"Don't eat anything that grows out of these lands. They're poisonous and feed off your blood... understand?" Cassius chastised, pointing at the three boys. Tommy and Sebastian nodded their heads obediently in agreement while Benjamin sat in silence.

"Proper food will be ready shortly," Cassius assured them after he headed back to skin the rest of the fat off the dead ox.

"He's only trying to help," Benjamin finally muttered, fiddling his shoelaces between his fingers. The quiet boy kept his back to the fire when Tommy joined him to feast upon the juicy, tender bits of ox fillet later that night.

"I'm sorry about your friend," Tommy muttered between bites, rudely chomping his meal.

Cassius raised his head up from the dead animal, awaiting Benjamin's reaction as he kept carving more meat off of the carcass.

"Why are you sorry, Tommy? You didn't kill him, did you?" Benjamin mumbled. He finally rested his head by the fire and took what rest he could get for the day ahead.

***

The protectors awoke to the sounds of Ariel rustling through the brambles. The thicket surrounding them was swiftly torn apart, revealing the enormous cliffs and the bridge that cut across them. In daylight they could see the whole cliff drop they had camped dangerously close to. The bridge was still very much intact. The sun was shining brighter this day, and humming birds filled the bushes around them. Cassius busied himself helping the boys equip their own utilities and baggage for the journey when he heard a call from Ariel.

"Are you sure we're not on the enemy's path?" she asked.

"It hasn't been tarnished by them yet. Notice the footprints are faun," Cassius said, pointing toward the markings and scraping the sandy ground with his blade.

"Very well, so this is the way to the hidden sanctuary?" she asked, seeking confirmation as she looked toward the bridge.

"Yes, that is where we must take them." Cecil's voice caught everyone by surprise when he stirred from his slight coma. "I know this place well." The haggard pixie used his stick to rise and lead the way forward with a ranting that had even put the rowdy troll in his place. Everyone smiled in relief and felt comforted when they heard the commanding lisp of the plump pixie. "The Council didn't expect a cowardly ambush yesterday. Let's stick to their wishes. We take the Brotherhood to the hidden sanctuary...end of discussion. I don't want to hear any more on the matter. Time to get moving," Cecil rambled.

The rocky dirt path formed into a minor cliff edge – half the size of a cliff one hundred yards opposite it. The taller cliff blocked the sunlight and cast the whole group in shade.

"Bounty hunter, watch our back," instructed Cecil, pointing his staff at Cassius.

Cassius hung back to follow the group as Cecil Baskin took charge, fronting the way to the bridge ahead of them.

"I like your ears, Peter," Benjamin said suddenly, causing Sebastian and Tommy to start sniggering behind Ariel's back.

"Very funny, you three. I'm very proud of my ears. They can hear better than all of your ears put together," Ariel informed, teasing the giggling boys behind her. "My real name is Ariel."

"Cassius," Benjamin called out, watching behind him to see his protector guarding the group.

"Yes?" was the bounty hunter's one word reply.

"We've lost–," Benjamin began, but Cassius finished his sentence for him.

"Trump...I noticed. You can't lose those who are already lost, Master Benjamin."

It took a mere second for Benjamin to understand exactly what Cassius was implying. Benjamin kept his eyes peeled as he hiked beside his friends.

"What's a Trump?" Tommy asked, taking the leading spot in line from Sebastian to have a closer talk with his reunited brother.

"Trump is their friend, dolly daydream," Sebastian answered, rolling his eyes back at Tommy. Tommy immaturely stuck out his tongue in response.

Cassius could tell Tommy's question had unsettled Benjamin, so he answered on his behalf.

"He was a companion who travelled alongside us to the Stained Castle," the bounty hunter informed bluntly.

"My word, so you've lost two friends instead of one," Sebastian began.

"Trump is a traitor and one we are better

without the company of," Cassius added, closing the conversation once and for all.

"We're here," Cecil called out, panting while he stepped his little foot onto the bridge. Shaking his leg up and down to test the durability and safety of the tied rope, the pixie gave them one of his reassuring winks. "She's safe to cross alright."

Bright morning sunlight broke through the hollow cave from the other side of the cliff and shone on the bridge.

"It's a cave tunnel. Look!" Tommy gasped.

"More like a shortcut. It's just a tunnel to the other side," Ariel explained. "What do you think, Cassius?"

Taking a gulp of water from his animal skin strapped water pouch, Cassius simply gave a rude shrug and kept a lookout behind them.

"Let's just cross it," Ban Pan grunted, taking his first step onto the bridge. The troll's large, hairy foot caused the supple bridge to sway from left to right.

"Wait, I think we should start with the lightest first," Ariel suggested.

"And that would be?" Ban Pan asked, offended by the nymph's suggestion.

"Nymphs are the lightest to carry," Cecil muttered.

"What are you really trying to say?" Ban Pan blurted out, discomforted by the heat of the sun that blasted directly in his face. "That I'm too heavy?" he continued.

"Now's not the time for petty squabbles. Cassius can accompany the children across while I fly Ariel over to the other side," Cecil instructed.

"And I'll just sit here and work on my tan I guess," Ban Pan retorted.

The sharp reply was only to be expected from the

uncouth and impatient troll, but Cassius was in no mood to wait around arguing. Lingering there would inevitably risk a chance of another ambush.

"You may cross when everyone else is safe on the other side, Ban Pan," Cassius explained, turning his back to the troll as he took his first step upon the bridge.

When Benjamin reached the middle of the bridge, he paused for a brief moment to smell the fresh morning air that hit his face. The swift breeze made the boy's head feel a little light as he held onto the rope with both hands.

"Benjamin! Look at me," Cassius ordered sharply, but the boy's shaking legs only worsened the moment he looked down at the thousand-foot drop.

"I-I can't let go," Benjamin called out, afraid of the daunting size of the cliffs around him. Tommy was next in line to pass Benjamin when they heard a horrible screeching noise. It was a noise that could only have come from a flying beast or an animal nearby, and it didn't sound at all tame.

"What is it?" Tommy shouted up to Ariel and Cecil.

"Just keep moving," Cassius shouted back while he made his way closer to Benjamin.

The small youngster had now slumped to his knees, which leaned out past the bridge's ledge. All the while Benjamin kept his hands gripped onto the guiding rope – the only thing that was saving him from a deathly fall.

"I'm almost there, Benjamin, hang on," Cassius yelled.

Just then, several thousand bats soared out of the dark pit below them, covering the entire bridge in a cloud of wings. Through the thickness of the flesh-biting night creatures flapping their way blindly in between the group, Cassius managed to grab hold of Benjamin, rescuing him from a fatal fall.

Sebastian hastily pushed against Tommy's carefully placed steps in panic. "Quit pushing!" Tommy hollered while they tried their best to cover their faces from the flapping wings of the bats.

"Don't rush, or you will fall," Cecil called down to both of them. "Let's see if we can distract the colony," he suggested to Ariel. Ariel keenly nodded in reply and climbed onto the shoulders of the old knight.

As they flew higher over the two boys who were struggling to beat the bats off themselves, Ariel made high pitch whistling noises to attract the flying rodents. The colony of bats reacted instantly, smashing holes through the bridge's dry wooden spots in pursuit of the whistling sound.

"Fly, fly, fly," Ariel repeated anxiously, when the flesh-eating bats flew toward them.

"Hold on, I've done this before," Cecil yelled over his shoulder, swooping up and down and side to side in an attempt to out manoeuvre the snapping swarm.

A bite to his chubby bare foot caused Cecil to accelerate his speed and increase altitude. He took the swarm vertically as far as their little wings could carry them in an attempt to wear them out, freezing many in the process. Several hundred bats froze up and fell out of the sky like stone raindrops whilst the remaining swarm dispersed and flew away.

"That was close," Cecil wheezed deeply. His impulsive actions had cleared the entire bridge and provided a clear passage for Tommy and Sebastian before Ban Pan could cross without much distraction or danger, for he was considerably the heaviest of the group.

"Come on, old troll," Cassius teased.

"Don't call me old," Ban Pan snapped back, taking his time.

Flying high, Cecil and Ariel were able to see a much bigger part of the landscape. Judging by the darkened lands around this new area of Abasin, it was apparent the bordered roads around them lay near enemy territory. The two airborne protectors also got a close glimpse of what appeared to be an armada fleet, crossing the blue seas hundreds of miles away. Whether friend or foe they could not tell, but it was a scary sight to behold nonetheless.

During the swarm's sharp descent through the bridge and into the deep, Ban Pan noticed a gigantic black wing, at least sixty feet long, shimmering in the slight light that pierced a corner of the darkness.

In the same moment he had noticed the vast wing crawl past the opening, it quickly vanished into the dark. Ban Pan was unable to make out what it was, at first, but its size was enough for him to fear it.

"Ban Pan?" Cassius called over to the befuddled troll that kept his gaze upon the rocks below.

"Something's down there. *Something big*," Ban Pan warned, shifting his pace from baby steps to full speed ahead, rocking and jolting the bridge from side to side.

"What did you see?" Tommy asked, wide-eyed and worried. Ban Pan saw the utter fright in the boy's eyes and didn't have the heart to scare the child any further by telling him the truth.

"Oh, nothing. I-I was just worried about the bridge being able to hold such a big troll like myself, that's all," Ban Pan added with a nervous chortle. It was a fib well thought out enough to convince Tommy and

Sebastian, but not Benjamin, for he had seen the same haunting glimpse of the enormous wing below and was also afraid to talk about it.

"Let's move," Cassius sighed, frowning at Ban Pan and Benjamin as he walked into the cave. "Where are the others?" Cassius asked, noticing the absence of the airborne protectors.

Out of the blue, Ariel and Cecil flew directly into the cave's entrance in complete disarray. Cecil let go of Ariel, dodging a shooting arrow that grazed his side and made him swerve and crash into the cave's sidewall.

"What is it now?" yelled Cassius, ducking low to the ground whilst sliding out his golden blade, already prepared for any challenge set against them.

"Enemy trolls!" Cecil panted in between deep breaths. "They came out of nowhere. As soon as they spotted us, they opened fire."

Ban Pan was the first to notice a small band of his own kind that had already begun to cross the bridge. Cassius hastily pushed him aside. Chopping his blade against the main rope around the left pole that was embedded into the cave opening, the brave bounty hunter tilted the entire bridge onto one side, causing a small number of trolls to slide off.

Some trolls were persistent enough to hang on and continue their pursuit of the boys by scaling the tilted bridge. Cassius hacked at the remaining rope tied around the right pole that was embedded in the stone of the cave's entrance. It was the only thing that kept the bridge horizontally attached to the cave. Gaining ground, the enemy trolls climbed over each other, shuffling between wooden plank and rope to reach Ban Pan and the children at the opening of the cave.

"Help me, for goodness sake," Cassius snapped, desperately sawing as fast and as hard as he could. But the thicker rope around the right pole was almost impossible for one person to conquer.

For the first time since the shoe tree, Ban Pan showed his true talents for cutting through such ropey situations. In one fell swoop, the troll had made the difficult decision to hack through the slanted bridge. With one stroke of his right claw, Ban Pan tore through the area of rope that Cassius had been frantically hacking at. Ban Pan watched on as several trolls plummeted into the pit below. Others who had held onto the bridge swung back toward the opposite cliff.

Two surviving trolls had carefully reached the front of the group the moment the bridge snapped. Scurrying ahead as the bridge fell, one troll grabbed onto the right pole, while the other dove into the cave's entrance and landed inches away from Sebastian.

"Child of Abasin," it snarled at Sebastian after picking up his human scent.

The evil troll had made the jump only to be greeted by Cecil Baskin's fat foot.

"Sniff this!" Cecil's mighty kick hit the troll square on his nose and sent him sliding back past the cave's entrance and over the edge.

The remaining troll used the pole to climb into the cave before it thrust Cassius against the cave wall and sprang onto Ban Pan's back.

After a long wrestle with the savage creature, Ban Pan finally clutched its large nose and picked the smaller troll off of his back. In one fast move of his right arm, he threw the attacker into the abyss in full view of his fellow trolls that had climbed the vertical broken bridge to safety upon the opposite mountain.

"Ban Pan Cackerin...the traitor," announced one of the surviving trolls, smearing Ban Pan's name. "You are a dead troll walking. No canyon or forest will ever be safe for you now," another troll threatened as they marched off.

"Thanks," Cassius uttered, out of breath. He tapped the brave troll on his hairy shoulder while both continued their journey along the brightly-lit cave tunnel.

"I'm a traitor," Ban Pan sighed, slowly dropping to his knees.

"Don't listen to them...they chose to serve the False One," Cassius said caringly.

"Cassius is right, Ban Pan, they've made their choice. They chose Saul...if anyone is a traitor, it's *them*," Ariel insisted, putting her arm around the troll's huge furry neck.

"You did a brave thing, Master Troll. You fought for us against your own kind and protected the Brotherhood," Cecil commended, smiling down at the saddened creature. "You stood up for what is right."

"And what is that? Betraying my own kind?" Ban Pan suddenly asked, brashly wiping away a tear, as he brushed by both protectors so no one would see.

"It's not about that no more," muttered Cassius. "What species we are...it no longer matters, Ban Pan. It's only us...and them."

Giving out a long sigh, Cassius hesitantly strolled behind the group through the narrow tunnel. The bounty hunter failed to notice a trail of toad slime directly above him, dripping onto his footprints as it followed his tracks. The group paced hastily toward the light without pausing for rest, oblivious of the toad-man that lingered above them, lurking in the shade with his body now camouflaged amongst the rocks. For once, the detestable traitor didn't try to hide his current mood, for it fitted hand in glove with his plan. It was his only mood that shielded Trump from sight — deviousness.

30

Meeting the Pompertons

Cassius shielded his eyes from the sunlight with one hand. It was a lot brighter on this side of the mountain and the area itself was a safer place to travel. If only they could find a way down.

"This is great; what now?" shouted Ban Pan.

"I'll have to take each of you to the bottom, one by one," Cecil suggested, stretching the muscles within his stitched wings, preparing them for the busy task ahead. "The hidden sanctuary lies across that lake. We're lucky the fauns brought us this far."

"Your wings can't take that amount of strain in their current state, Cecil. You'll risk permanent damage," Ariel said.

"Plus, there is no way you can lift Ban Pan," Cassius agreed, raising his hands to the grumpy troll. "No offense, big guy."

"I'll have to take that risk. We've no other choice," Cecil insisted. A nervous twitch caused one of his wings to flutter and spasm. Cecil hissed in pain, shying away from the children in embarrassment. "On second thought, he'll have to jump," he added, pointing to Ban Pan.

"We all will," Cassius suggested reassuringly,

smiling at all six of them. "We jump!"

"What do you mean? Even at this side of the tunnel, that drop is nearly one hundred feet, and you expect us to just cut over the rocks," argued Ban Pan. "You don't even know if that lake is shallow or not."

"The water is deep, and the wind current will give us more than enough room to spare. I'm certain," Cassius replied.

"You're certain. Well in that case, let's all go for a dip then, eh?" the troll grunted back.

"Ban Pan, stop bickering," Ariel scolded, leaning over the cliff's edge in order to better judge the distance between land and water.

"It will save time, time we don't have," Cassius explained.

"You've been here before, Cecil. What do you suggest?" Ariel asked, giving the pixie his chance to speak.

"It was a long time ago, but I don't recall ever coming this route before. The hidden sanctuary is an island shrouded by overhanging trees. Certain faun illusionists have fooled many passers into believing it is nothing more than an empty ravine," Cecil said, speaking softly and keeping his finger pointed in the direction of the far lake and his eyes on Cassius.

"What is your point?" Ban Pan asked curiously.

"If we swim there and are unable to find anything right away, we could drown...that is...if we make this jump in the first place," Cecil warned.

"We'll make it. Boys, you ready?" Cassius asked, hopeful for a positive reply. But instead, all three of them looked at one another and shook their heads.

"What are you talking about? *I* can't swim. I've never even been to the seaside before," Sebastian gasped.

"Don't know much about it either to be honest, gaff," Tommy added.

"I've never tried either, apart from the flood at the Stained Castle, but that was thanks to Ban Pan," Benjamin reminded.

Hearing three unsure and poor explanations, Cassius started to laugh out loud, much to everyone's surprise. Cecil was clearly unimpressed by the bounty hunter's sudden humor, which he mistook for mockery at the children's expense.

"And just what do you find so funny about that?" the pixie retorted while his wings fluttered irritably.

"They can't swim?" Cassius asked, calming his laughter to a light titter.

"All the more reason to think of another plan," Ariel insisted, lifting a heavy pack of Cecil's kitchen equipment Benjamin had been carrying off his shoulders.

Without warning, Cassius snatched the bag of Cecil's crockery and tableware from the nymph and threw it overhead, hurtling it into the air a few feet away from the edge. The protectors gasped in disbelief at the sudden and unexpected action the bounty hunter had just taken to prove a point. The wind current pushed the bag several yards away from the rock filled land before it hit the water.

"Our entire world rests on three human boys that don't even know how to swim. That calls for some urgent training, wouldn't you all agree?"

"The water's dark...that means it's deep. It has been left to us to get the Brotherhood to safety. That means we must trust each other. And ourselves. You understand?" Cassius pleaded to each protector. Peeking over the ledge, Ban Pan suddenly made a loud grunt as he took a second or two to think.

"Who's going first?" Cassius asked.

"I will," Ban Pan replied, to everyone's surprise. Gawking back at Cassius's stunned expression, the troll screwed up his face in offense. "What, you think I am afraid to do it?"

Unwilling to cause further upset or engage with the feisty troll, Cassius simply shook his head and made muffled noises from his throat that comically described a yes answer, much to everyone's amusement.

Tossing over anything that would cause him injury or jeopardize his fall, Ban Pan followed the bounty hunter's example, until he was the first to take the leap of faith. Ariel called out in fright to prevent the troll from nose-diving off the edge, but after only a few running steps, Ban Pan flung himself into the air.

Like clockwork, the troll was pushed further away from the rocky bottom by the current of the wind. Splashing several feet into the lake's deep pit only confirmed that Cassius's belief in his plan was right. It took a few intense seconds for the troll to resurface to a cheering round of applause.

"Right then, who's up next?" Cassius asked, reaching out his hand for one of the unnerved humans to take the plunge with him. "Don't worry, I won't let you drown," he promised, showing sincerity and faith that made Tommy take hold of his hand.

"I'll see you losers at the bottom," the frightened boy nervously joked to his peers.

Seconds later, Cassius charged fast toward the cave's edge. It would have been funny if Tommy's girl-like screams were the result of an experience Benjamin and Sebastian didn't have to share next. Instead, Tommy's shriek of fright made both boys quiver on the spot.

In a few seconds it was over. When Benjamin peered down at the lake, he noticed Ban Pan swimming to collect the bags. Since he was the biggest, and some would argue the strongest of the four protectors, Ban Pan took it upon himself to carry the burden of each protector's personal items and weaponry while they swam across the water.

Cecil Baskin held Sebastian in mid-flight whilst keeping himself out of sight, making it appear that Sebastian ran in mid-air from a fast sprint. It was a little prank to lighten the mood, but nobody seemed to find the childish sense of humor funny, especially Tommy who was now finding the water colder than he'd expected it to be.

"How come he gets the easy way down?" Tommy called up to Cecil, but the pixie pretended not to hear the boy's complaint and carefully lowered Sebastian onto the rocky dry land yards away from the lake. "Because I'm not a silly sausage," Sebastian teased.

"Are you ready?" Ariel's question instantly broke his wondering mind out of its daydream. The turn to jump seemed to come too soon for Benjamin to prepare himself.

Ariel took a tight hold of his hand and pulled him toward the opening. Daylight had made everything white the second they leapt out of the cave's entrance. As he fell toward the dark blue water he shut his eyes tight.

Air bubbles surrounded him while he frantically attempted to reach the lake's surface. But it was of no use. The blanket of cold water had already engulfed him. Benjamin proved to be the worst swimmer. He could see the light above his head silhouetting the figures of his friends at the surface. The sudden drop in temperature gripped him. It was the cold that strained his movements the most.

Ariel and Cassius dove after Benjamin. Tommy and Sebastian grew anxious when Ariel was the only one to re-emerge seconds later. Cassius had yet to come up for air since taking his first and only search dive and hope for Benjamin's safe recovery was almost lost.

"I knew this was a bad idea. Nobody ever listens to the troll," bellowed Ban Pan.

Meanwhile, below, Benjamin sank near the lake's bed. Twelve foot dangling sea plants surrounded the area where he awoke from his frozen trance. Benjamin kicked his feet and waved his arms in several directions, but it didn't get him anywhere. He couldn't hold his breath any longer, inhaling deeply while his lungs gasped for air.

Water filled his throat, turning almost lighter than air by magic when he breathed it in. Pure oxygen filled his lungs. He hadn't realized he had been breathing all along as the transition in his inner body converted the intake of water into unfiltered oxygen.

Laughing out loud, Benjamin sent a huge trail of air bubbles floating up out of the tiny sand dune that acted as the perfect beacon for Cassius to spot him. Before Benjamin could bask in the sun-kissed underwater garden and appreciate his new miraculous and magical talent, Cassius's strong grasp disrupted the moment and pulled him away from the amazing experience – for the protector needed air himself and was running out of time. Holding on tight with one arm, Cassius used the first rock he'd landed on as a springboard to help both of them reach the surface quicker.

Cecil and Sebastian cheered and clapped when

they saw Cassius punch his way out from the depth, pulling Benjamin beside him.

"Don't you ever try something like that again, you 'ear me?" Tommy shouted, splashing water over his brother's face.

Ariel sighed in relief, giving a nod of gratitude to Cassius, who quickly returned the gesture, then proceeded to swim toward the sanctuary with Benjamin on his back.

Ariel helped Tommy across the lake, teaching him the breaststroke manoeuvre, one of the most important and basic lessons essential for swimming long distances. Tommy took to the swimming faster than Ariel had imagined was possible. He also impressed Ban Pan by overtaking him several times during their swim to the shady coast at the lake's far side.

Cecil and Sebastian hovered across most of the water, but at some intervals, especially when Tommy was tired, Cecil would let Ariel train Sebastian to swim so that Tommy could take a rest. Before they reached the hidden sanctuary of the lake, the two boys had learned all the basics of how to swim and keep afloat in the water.

Benjamin, however, managed to stay quiet enough to avoid any of the lessons. Having nearly drowned earlier, there had been no pressure put on him throughout the journey. Therefore, Benjamin kept his newfound underwater power a total secret. So far, Cassius's rescue of Benjamin had fooled the rest of the group into thinking Benjamin had nearly drowned. All save one.

Cassius thought it to be of much irony that this special gift was bestowed upon one so helpless in the water, but decided to keep his opinion to himself, giving Benjamin the option to share his experience when he was ready.

***

It was late evening when they arrived outside the overhanging branches of the hidden sanctuary and the sun had almost set. Cecil lifted Benjamin into the air when it was his turn to take a flight, relieving the bounty hunter to enter through the leafy curtains alone to make sure all was safe.

"I've found it. It's only a few yards away," Cassius explained after he popped his head out to them.

Smells of petrol, gas, and other fumes mingled with the glorious fragrance of blueberries and cinnamon in the evening air. The bizarre fusion penetrated their senses. It was the strangest combination of scents the human children had ever smelled, which made Sebastian's sensitive stomach a little queasy. The group gazed silently in amazement at the large island surrounded by the exquisite, shallow, light blue waters. Furious noises of roaring engines and clanking metal were enough to put anyone off an actual visit to the island. As for appearances, the area looked rather inviting, but the sounds warned, "Do not enter."

"Follow my lead," Cecil ordered the group. The pixie gently glided across the shallow lake toward the roaring sounds of active machinery while the rest of the group was forced to navigate through soggy mud hills that made up the figure eight border around the lake.

Drawing closer to the island, the boys noticed a towering house shaped like a cottage beyond the thin circle of factory smoke that cloaked it. It was quaint and had an antique look about it. The thatched roofs seemed tough, especially the bell tower above it that peaked into a sharp point.

Smoke soared from the chimney tops and other various parts of the giant cottage. It was obvious that some form of machinery development was taking place inside. Mechanical sounds kept drowning out any noise that the group made.

"What kind of hidden sanctuary causes this much racket?" Ban Pan asked, stepping his foot upon the island.

Keeping close to Cecil, the group approached the island's front entrance, which lay below a massive ringed bridge that stretched on for miles around it. The sound of a loud throat clearing startled everyone as they stepped onto the island.

Leaning on the low oak bridge, a weird figure with patches of wiry gray hair sprouting from his head greeted them with a loud and bubbling laugh. Sebastian noticed the man was wearing one pair of oval shaped glasses on his face and several more pairs on the top of his head. His second pair of glasses looked more like a miniature replica of his first pair, which made the old man look crazier.

As Cassius stepped in front of the group to talk to the eccentric figure, he was stunned by an electrical shock to his chest that bolted from the old man's glasses.

"Stop that!" Cassius snapped, drawing his sword in a warning stance.

"You are trespassing. Who are you?" The old man glared with suspicion.

"Friends," Ariel declared.

"A nymph, a troll, one pixie, and a pirate...what type of a troupe are you, *the all sorts?*" The old man began to laugh at his own joke while Cassius gave him an unimpressed look.

"I'm not a pirate," Cassius insisted, nursing his chest.

"Well, you are...sort of," Ban Pan teased.

"Button that big mouth for once," Cassius sighed, shaking his head at the troll.

The old man didn't seem to take any offense of Cassius's sudden outburst after he'd set his sights upon the charming nymph.

"Well, suit yourself. Pirate or not, I don't care. What's next, humans I bet?" the old man shouted sardonically, patting his legs while he laughed louder.

"You bet right," Cecil Baskin interrupted, bringing the old man's laughter to an abrupt halt. The old man immediately took his electrifying glasses off his head.

"Show me!" He fumbled to reattach a larger, more idiotic looking pair of glasses onto his face. With a clumsy drop of his scientific instruments, the weird old man promptly climbed down from the wooden bridge and puttered around each boy, fearless of the other protectors that watched his every move.

The old man rapidly lifted pieces of random technical equipment from inside his heavy coat. One wacky piece of apparatus looked like a tiny metal claw that opened and closed by the simple push of the button.

Gently approaching Sebastian's side, the mad scientist used the claw tool to look through the child's ear. Sebastian instantly pushed the device away. One springy gadget was next on display for the group to see as the old man hopped toward Tommy. When the snake type mechanism was switched on, it shone a bright light on its tip, which the old man used to shine into the boy's eyes, directing it with a remote control.

"Yes, he has the eyes, he has the eyes. You're the first born," the old man insisted.

"Hey, get that thing out of my face," Tommy snapped, belting the irritating contraption away from his eyes and into the lake.

Taking off his silly looking spectacles to look at the human children with his own eyes, the crazed scientist then crept to Benjamin and spotted his maroon blanket protruding from his jacket. After politely asking to see the cloth, the old man unwrapped it and shone a light onto the two-headed snake emblem entwined with a golden crown.

"Exceptional! Oh, this is a discovery indeed. The Brotherhood has returned to seek out my help, as it was foretold. Oh, how marvellous. I had hoped this day would come, and not a minute too soon. Permit me, my little Masters; I am Senior Pomperton of the Scholar Ishtar Pompertons," Senior Pomperton rambled, clapping his hands while the unresponsive group stared back at him.

"You haven't heard of me?" He sighed in shock, disappointed as much as dumbfounded. It was evident that Senior Pomperton had been oblivious of the outside world for a very long time. It also came as no surprise that the zany old man hadn't left his post on that island for most of his quirky life, and judging by his eagerness to have new company around, he rarely had visitors.

"I do apologize for the slight taser, pirate," Senior Pomperton said to Cassius while he puttered around the rest of the group, studying them with several appliances that he kept well attached to his belt of tools. "You can't be too careful in the new world. I'm afraid you've caught me in the middle of moving home."

Cecil gasped. "You're leaving already?"

"Huh? No, I'm going nowhere. I'm simply *moving* my home," the crazy old man giggled, pointing to another area a few yards away where he was planning on relocating his entire cottage. "What do you reckon?" he asked the bemused group. "My front door will face the sun."

"Very noisy for a simple move, is it not?" Ban Pan asked, drawing their attentions to the vibrating sounds coming from inside the massive house.

"Oh goodness, I forgot; those are my experiments. I must get back to work. Please, this way. Welcome, welcome," Senior Pomperton yelled excitedly. "Iris, Iris, get out here quick, we have guests," he hollered as he ran ahead of them and into the entrance of the house.

Taking their time, the group cautiously approached the booming noises. An old, petite lady revealed herself in a small, slanted doorway, holding a fresh batch of tea and cups on a large tray.

"Welcome, my darlings, come forth, come on," she smiled, beckoning each of them forward to follow her into her lavishly designed garden.

Stepping into the back garden, the nice lady led them along a path filled with little stone slabs until the group made their way into a half open and half sheltered garden. The garden was rich and filled with the most bizarre and beautiful plants that no one in their party had ever laid eyes on before.

Benjamin was first to notice the plants were

moving by themselves.

Taking the tray from Iris's arms, the plants separated the teapots and cutlery for her while several of their free stems intertwined and formed a large table and a few chairs.

"I was wondering where we would sit," Sebastian whispered to Cecil, who gave a slight chuckle in reply.

"Sit, please, sit, sit, sit," the old lady rambled, every bit as overjoyed to have guests as her husband was. Ban Pan's eagerness to quench his thirst overtook his manners. Grabbing a hold of the teapot, the parched troll rudely started to chug the pot of tea without waiting on the others or using a cup. A slapping of the wrist from the disgruntled Iris Pomperton caused a few quiet laughs between the boys.

"If you please, I'll do the serving once we're all seated," Iris scolded.

Basking in the half-sunlit, half-shaded conservatory, the new visitors took their first rest since their long journey earlier that morning. Benjamin sat beside Ban Pan, avoiding the grumpy troll's eye contact at all times, while the old lady poured a fresh pot of tea into individual cups next to them.

"You were sent by the politicians, I presume," Iris said to Ariel, still unable to take her reverent eyes off of the human children before her.

"It was the Council's wish for the boys to be brought here," Ariel explained, sipping gently at her fresh brew.

Cecil Baskin cleared his throat and with a nervous flutter of his wings, he began to talk.

"There was an ambush, at the Stained Castle," Cecil explained, gently hovering a few feet above the ground now.

With a kind offering of more tea, the old lady tried to settle him.

"Please Mr. Baskin, have a seat, you are in a safe place now," she said gracefully. Her words were soft like a velvet cloth and clothed the tension within the overwrought group. In a moment Cecil's battered wings ceased to flutter, as he sat down to continue his account.

"You know my name?"

"Of course. I remember you from long ago. Forgive my husband...he's never been one for remembering brief encounters, but I never forget a face. Besides, we're not totally kept in the dark about things around here, especially things that concern us. I have my own methods of retrieving information."

Iris smiled, petting one of her plants on the head before it recoiled back into the ground beneath her. "Although most information these days is becoming too dangerous to obtain, and I wouldn't risk any of my darlings unless it was absolutely necessary," she continued, smiling at her nest of plants. "Please continue, Mr. Baskin. You mentioned the Stained Castle."

Iris sipped at her tea as Cecil gave her more reports to help her understand what had gone wrong.

"A meeting of political figures was announced several moons ago and important militia from all areas of Abasin attended. Warlocks, wizards and white witches showed up in abundance. We were just the protectors. Our job was to convene with the children and escort them to the meeting safely," Cecil explained. "Their return was kept secret for the most part."

"But one of you were followed," Iris guessed with a sharp whisper as she sipped at her cup.

"Not that we knew of. We were extremely careful," Ariel admitted before taking one last sip at her tea. Without her having to ask, one of the plant's long spindly and bendable stems lifted up the pot and refilled the nymph's cup.

"An informer!" was the old lady's next guess. Benjamin's eyes shifted off his lukewarm tea to Cassius, who stood quietly at the corner of the conservatory.

"Trump," Cassius muttered, before rudely walking away in silence to patrol the island.

"I'm glad to see some of you have manners," Iris joked full-heartedly.

"Trump! That sneaky toad! I always knew he was a traitor ever since Jodo Kahln turned him into that slimy creature," Cecil spat, his flustering wings readily showing his contempt for the exposed traitor.

"We all have our own part to play in this, Mr. Baskin...even the fallen knights of this new world. This Trump character was not the first, nor will he be the last treacherous soul to try and lead the Brotherhood astray," Iris warned each protector. "For whatever unknown mysterious reason, it has fallen onto each of you to protect them now, as it had fallen onto us Pompertons to shelter you. It was foretold that these boys will grow into a mighty force," she insisted with her kind words of wisdom, capturing the attention of each human child. "They need time to develop their magic gifts before the search for the Shield continues."

"Why would the Council send the Brotherhood to two crazy loners in the middle of nowhere?" Ban Pan asked, embarrassing both Cecil and Ariel because of his insolence.

Iris Pomperton was a woman of great patience and knew all too well the regular ill- mannered behavior that accompanied a troll's nature, so much so that she calmly smiled back and gave the arrogant troll his answer without taking offense.

"The Council made a promise to King Anamis to protect the Brotherhood. Senior and I made the promise to teach and train them. It was the wish of their Father." Iris sighed, taking her last sip before resting her cup back on the tray.

"Father?" Benjamin's frail and emotional voice broke through, as he lifted his head, wide eyed in total fascination by this one word she spoke. Each guardian silently stared back at the other, waiting on one who would break the truth to Benjamin when Iris answered innocently.

"Why, yes, don't you boys know that you are brothers...by blood?" Iris asked.

"Brothers?" Benjamin whispered, keeping his eyes fixed on Sebastian and Tommy.

"Oh dear, don't tell me no one has told you boys who you are?" Iris gasped.

Noticing the uncomfortable looks Sebastian and Tommy fired back at one another, Benjamin realized he had been kept in the dark. "J-just me, it seems," Benjamin stammered. "Brothers? *Us?*" Benjamin asked both boys, pleading with them to answer him.

"Triplets. Born on the same day, the day you were cast out of the new world," Iris rambled.

Benjamin stood up to take the shocking news in, whilst Sebastian and Tommy nudged one another to answer him.

"Say something. Speak!" Benjamin snapped, raising his voice.

"We already knew," Sebastian finally admitted.

"That much is clear," Benjamin barked.

"We were told everything by the Council before you arrived late to the Stained Castle, we forgot to tell you," Sebastian whispered uncomfortably.

With a stunned look spreading across his face, Benjamin quietly nodded. His mind raced. "You forgot?" he asked, feeling embarrassed and uneasy in front of everyone. His protectors and brothers watched one another in an awkward moment.

"We had just found out ourselves, I couldn't believe it either. Who would have thought, eh?" Tommy asked giving a nervous titter in an attempt to lighten the mood.

"Council? What Council?" Benjamin snapped back, shocking both of his brothers at the table.

"Calm down," Tommy pleaded.

"Benjamin, Abasin has a board of members that make up our last government," Ariel began when Benjamin interrupted her.

"I don't care about your stupid government. Why wasn't I told about this? Did you know?" Benjamin demanded, eyeing the protectors around the table. "Of course you did. That's why you left George Johnston at the train station in London...and Jimmy Donald back at Gatesville. That's why you left us alone at Jacob's... to go and search for *him*," Benjamin yelled at Ariel as he pointed his accusing finger toward Sebastian. "And you knew all that time we were brothers...and you didn't think we had a right to know?"

"Benjamin, you're tired. You need rest," Ariel replied, awkwardly turning to her fellow protectors to help her pacify the distraught boy.

"Hey, don't look at me, *you're* the one that lied to the kid," Ban Pan said insensitively, raising his large claws into the air.

"He's right. You lied to us," Benjamin accused.

"She didn't lie," Cecil interrupted.

"She kept the truth from us and withheld information. Or should I say, *Peter* kept it from us?" Benjamin replied sharply.

"If you were told everything when you were still in your world, there's no way you would have followed her," Cecil explained.

"Darn right I wouldn't have," Benjamin said honestly through gritted teeth. He quickly wiped his eyes and left the table to follow Cassius into the grounds around the island.

"Maybe he's right. We should have been told the truth from the start. It sure would've made it easier for us to trust the lot of you if you had trusted us," Tommy said.

"You don't understand child, your world was without magic. Humans don't believe in magic, nor know it. Your hearts were different when you lived in the old world. You weren't open to the truth there. We needed to bring you here so that your perceptions could be changed...that way, you would believe the truth about your heritage when faced with the reality of this new world," Iris said gracefully. "You needed to know your true identity."

"And what *is* that?" Sebastian asked cheekily.

"That you're children of the King. Rulers of the future kingdom and defeaters of the False One," Cecil said, calmly and assuredly.

"It was vital that you knew who you were before you could come to know about magic, both the good and the bad," Iris added.

"There's a difference?" Tommy asked keenly.

"Of course. Magic is just like people," Iris added.

"Tea anyone?"

Trying to lift the sad and heavy atmosphere, Iris changed the subject and placed a supportive hand upon Ariel's shoulder.

"Me and my big mouth. Don't worry my dear... Benjamin will be just fine," Iris assured. "Come, let us talk more while we get these young men something sturdy to eat and a fresh bath before bedtime. There is a lot to explore in this large island, but that will be for another day." Iris clapped her hands three times for her plants to gather up the left-over mess of used cups.

Above the lake, Benjamin sat on the circular bridge, folding his arms upon the wooden divider while he dangled his legs over the edge.

"Don't be upset," Cassius advised, walking onto the bridge.

"I've wasted all these years alone without a family," Benjamin sobbed, wiping several tears from his cheeks.

"Well...you have them now. Seems like it was worth waiting for," Cassius said with a smile.

"I wanted a normal family, like everyone else. Not a family like..." Benjamin sniffled and trailed off.

"Like what?" Cassius asked curiously.

"Like fugitives," Benjamin mumbled, lowering his head to watch the ripples in the water below his feet.

"Oh, Benjamin." Cassius sighed, walking over to find a spot next to the boy. "You know, most people and creatures in the old world and the new world don't have normal families. I didn't. Many are out there as we speak, alone...like you were once – without anyone...some civilians even younger than you are now," Cassius continued.

"I don't care," Benjamin sulked, drying off his cheeks.

"Well then, let me ask you a question." Cassius smiled again as the tearful boy stared up at him. "If you could have it all, the normal family you've always wanted, but it would mean you wouldn't fulfil a greater call to change the lives of many boys and girls, who are alone like you were...what choice would you make?"

"Depends, I guess. How many?" Benjamin asked seriously.

"Look up...do you see all those stars?" Cassius asked while they both gazed upon the starry night sky together. "They're countless, right?"

"You mean as many as them?" Benjamin gasped.

"And more." Cassius sighed as he rose to his feet.

A flashback of Benjamin's youth suddenly hit him like a bolt of lightning. An act of kindness from the Minister at Woodson County raced through his fragile mind, revealing his earliest childhood memory. Without contemplation, the young boy stood up and called out to his protector.

"Cassius!" Benjamin called, smiling back as Cassius turned around to bow his head in respect.

"Good answer, Benjamin," he called back in the moonlight. Without having to hear it, Cassius felt the boy had made the right decision.

Benjamin shyly waited for his brothers to welcome him in when he lingered by the Pomperton's kitchen door. Tommy and Sebastian stood over a large basin sink, splashing suds everywhere and joking with one another. Both fell silent once they noticed their smaller brother enter the doorway behind them. Sebastian peered back at him through his foam-covered glasses, elbow deep in suds and covered in fluffy bubbles along his hair and face.

"Um...before we save the world and all that, I thought it would be best if I said, 'Hi,' first," Benjamin muttered awkwardly while he twiddled his thumbs in apprehension, awaiting their reply.

"Hi," Sebastian said eagerly without delay, nudging Tommy to greet his new brother.

Giving out a long sigh of defeat and a silent nod, Tommy greeted his brother with a typical order, hiding his sentimental side. "First dishes...then the world. Well? Are you gonna help us here or not, pip-squeak?" Tommy asked, showing a respectful smile after he threw his small brother a dry towel.

Taking the first wet plate handed to him, Benjamin stood in between the pair and began to help, unaware of the watchful amphibian eyes that snooped from afar.

31

A New Family

The Pomperton's cottage castle was so huge that it almost took each guest the first month to explore it. One warm night after a hard day's work of potion training taught by Senior Pomperton, Benjamin was woken from his disturbed sleep by a voice.

Rising out of his bed, he slowly made his way down the castle's stairwell to the living room area, led by a single fly that buzzed around his face. The housefly guided him past the flaming fireplace that ignited in his presence. The voice beckoned louder toward a huge bookshelf. Watching carefully, Benjamin observed the fly until it landed upon a peculiar rustic book.

He felt led to touch it when he noticed no title on its spine. It didn't even have a description on its front cover...just a familiar symbol. Benjamin's eyes lit up as his fingertips moved across the inner curves of the two-headed snake and crown emblem, embossed in the middle of the front cover in pure white gold.

The sporadic fly crawled inside the spine a split second before Benjamin pulled the book from the shelf. He felt a powerful urge to open the book and peer inside when he noticed a glowing from inside its pages. A magical beam of bright purple light shone out at his face and kept him from shutting the book. Benjamin started to read the spell on the first page when a hand tried to snatch it from his tight grip.

"What are you doing?" Iris snapped as the book slammed shut by itself and dropped to Benjamin's feet. "I mean...what are you doing up at this hour?" she added, tittering nervously.

"I couldn't sleep," Benjamin mumbled, kneeling gently to lift the spell book.

"Why don't you put it back, child, it's very late," Iris said calmly, giving him a half smile. But Benjamin's mind went blank, and without fibbing, he took a deep breath and bellowed, "*I don't want to!*"

An unsettling apprehension gripped Iris while she struggled to respond to the boy's sudden outburst. Benjamin felt ashamed and embarrassed at his disrespectful answer to his caretaker and felt obligated to explain. "I'm sorry. I can't remember where I found it," he mumbled.

"Perhaps it found you, my dear," she suggested with warning, holding out her hand to take the book from him.

Benjamin was slightly reluctant to hand the book back to her, which made the old lady keen to take it from him. Once the book had left his grip, Benjamin slowly stepped back from it.

"This is not a book for you...not now, anyway. In the meantime, we can just forget this ever happened." She smiled. "Don't let it trouble you. Go back to bed, dear," she whispered, motioning the boy back upstairs to his room.

Benjamin felt an instant cold rush trickle across the back of his neck when he walked out of the living room. It made him pause and look behind his shoulder.

To his horror, the fireplace hadn't been lit at all and the fly that buzzed around the book had vanished.

That night's introduction to magic wouldn't leave Benjamin's thoughts. The buzzing of the fly in his dreams grew louder and multiplied as time passed. Something or someone was trying to communicate with him, and Benjamin knew it as he patiently waited for the voice that spoke in his dreams to reveal itself.

The clear mornings upon the Pomperton Island greeted him with refreshing, bright blue skies. Every day in the new world seemed to wait for him as much as it depended on him. Benjamin's Brotherhood didn't know what struggles lay ahead, but the prophecy of their return to Abasin had finally given them a new sense of purpose.

Now that Sebastian and Tommy were reunited in his life, Benjamin was already halfway there...

...for, at last, he had a real family to call his own.

ACKNOWLEDGEMENTS

Special cheers to:

Liza Fleissig and Ginger Harris-Dontzin at Liza Royce Agency, I never thought it was possible to find my *Brian Epstein*. You put so much committed passion, faith, energy and love behind your authors. I am extremely privileged and proud to be part of the LRA family.

Jennifer Rees for working your magic. I am overwhelmed at the work and dedication you've shown to this book.

Clarissa Hutton, thank you for all your time and hard work.

Last but not least, to Georgia McBride and everyone at Month9Books and Tantrum – I am in awe of your love and fierce devotion to the art of storytelling. Thank you for the valor to believe in big visions.

MICHAEL GIBNEY

Born in Belfast, Ireland, in 1982, Michael Gibney is a writer whose interests in world politics, literature and the love of film encouraged him to do his studies at the early age of sixteen within the media and journalism field. Through his studies at college and the BBC, he developed an instant passion for creative writing that exceeded his love for media, art and music. Taking his influences from Irish writers W. B. Yeats and Belfast Born author C.S. Lewis, Gibney's somewhat emotionally-charged storytelling is derived from his personal heroes and experiences in his own childhood having grown up in Belfast during the country's dark history. Combining these influences with recent testing times of the world we live in today has helped create the world of Abasin that is introduced in *The Three Thorns*, his debut novel and first story in the epic The Brotherhood and the Shield Series.

He spends most of his time writing and painting within the United States and the United Kingdom.

Other MONTH9BOOKS and TANTRUM BOOKS titles you might like:

TRACY TAM: SANTA COMMAND

KING OF THE MUTANTS

CURSE OF THE GRANVILLE FORTUNE

DEAD JED

DAWN OF THE JED

LUCAS MACKENZIE AND THE LONDON MIDNIGHT
GHOST SHOW

GEORGIA MCBRIDE MEDIA GROUP

GEORGIAMCBRIDE.COM

CURSE OF THE
GRANVILLE
FORTUNE

KELLY HASHWAY

LUCAS MACKENZIE

AND THE

LONDON
· MIDNIGHT ·
GHOST SHOW

STEVE BRYANT

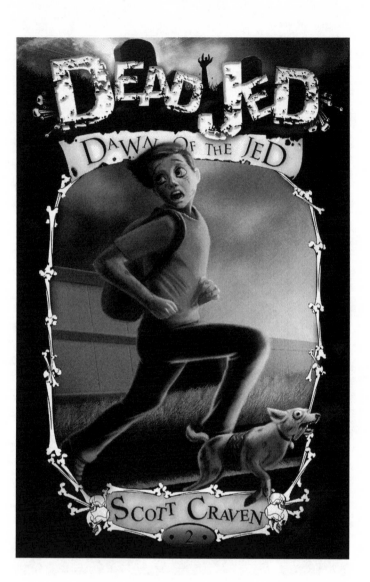

Find more awesome books at Month9Books.com

Connect with Tantrum Books online:

Blog: http://month9booksblog.com/tantrum-books/
Twitter: @TantrumBooks

Connect with Month9Books online:

Facebook: www.Facebook.com/Month9Books
Twitter: @Month9Books
You Tube: www.youtube.com/user/Month9Books
Blog: www.month9booksblog.com
Request review copies via publicity@month9books.com

DATE DUE

DEMCO 38-296